After the Death of Ellen Keldberg

Also published by Handheld Press

HANDHELD CLASSICS

1 *What Might Have Been: The Story of a Social War* by Ernest Bramah
2 *The Runagates Club* by John Buchan
3 *Desire* by Una L Silberrad
4 *Vocations* by Gerald O'Donovan

HANDHELD RESEARCH

1 *The Akeing Heart: Letters between Sylvia Townsend Warner, Valentine Ackland and Elizabeth Wade White* by Peter Haring Judd
2 *The Conscientious Objector's Wife: Letters between Frank and Lucy Sunderland, 1916–1919*, edited by Kate Macdonald

After the Death of Ellen Keldberg

Eddie Thomas Petersen

translated by Toby Bainton

Handheld Modern 1

First published in Denmark in 2013 by PeoplesPress as *Ønskebarnet*
This edition published in 2018 by Handheld Press Ltd.
72 Warminster Road, Bath BA2 6RU, United Kingdom
www.handheldpress.co.uk

ISBN 978-1-9999448-4-1

1 2 3 4 5 6 7 8 9

Series design by Nadja Guggi and typeset in Adobe Caslon Pro and Open Sans.

Printed and bound in Great Britain by TJ International, Padstow

Cover image:
'Bagatelle II tree circumambiency' by Anno Málie 2016,
used under a Creative Commons licence.

Translator's note: 'hip hip hurrah!' – and acknowledgements

Fiction lets us see a world from someone else's point of view – and one of the attractions of translated fiction is the unfamiliar, or even exotic, nature of the world we see. Unfamiliar territory can sometimes present a real conundrum for the translator. In this novel, for example, the author includes references to something which is general knowledge amongst his fellow Danes but not so well known in the English-speaking world. Luckily it concerns only one phrase and is quickly explained. On two or three occasions the protagonist Anne Sofie refers disparagingly to 'hip hip hurrah'.

Why is she so scornful? 'Hip hip hurra' is the title of a painting (1888) by Peder Severin Krøyer that portrays several artists of the Skagen school enjoying lunch in a garden. They're toasting someone in the traditional Danish way with a birthday cheer of 'Hip hip hurra'. For Anne Sofie, the painting embodies all the artistic traditions she feels she must escape, but which others still cling to.

A translator's note allows me to thank several people who have helped me. The enthusiastic support of both author and the publisher of this edition have of course been crucial. Thank you so much, Eddie Thomas Petersen and Kate Macdonald. I'm glad to record my thanks to my friend Roger Betts for explaining the technicalities of Mikkel's economics project, and to my daughter-in-law Elisabeth Jensen, to Lisbeth Møller-Madsen of the original publisher PeoplesPress, and to my friends Elizabeth Einberg and Annie Murray, who have all made very useful suggestions.

Toby Bainton

Bluish white, like skimmed milk, the mist seems so near that you could gather it up in your hands. The storm has blown itself out in the night and the wind has dropped, but you can still hear the waves breaking in a hollow roar out by the bar.

The boy holds his breath and listens. There's something out there, he thinks. There's a thin, fine sound like someone running their nail on a crystal glass. The sound of time. *It's the ship*, he decides.

A moment later it looms out of the mist in a cloud of spray, laden with gold and misery. The crew cling to the rigging, crippled by abscesses and ulcers. Someone shouts through the waves in terror, in a language he doesn't know, and he can hear the dry creak of the ship's masts and rigging. In a moment, the whole thing's going to shatter to splinters. In just a moment the keel will cut against the sand bar.

He can sense from the spray that it's close on shore now, and he holds his breath. Now he can make out the mainsail, shredded to tatters by countless tugs of the gale, and the bow, red with rust and heavy with seaweed and white shells. High in the mist, among the gulls, he catches a glimpse of a flapping black flag, which he knows means plague on board.

Further out towards the shoreline there's someone alive, someone in tears calling his name, and he starts to run.

*

The boys almost fall through the doorway, looking like inflatable fledglings in their thick quilted jackets.

'There's a man with no clothes on lying on the beach,' cries the elder brother.

'A what?' asks Zeppo.

'A man. A man with no clothes on', blurts out the younger brother with a troubled look. 'Down near the Sunset snack bar.'

'He's ... he's ... he's dead,' adds his brother, who has noticed a spectacular heap of eider duck on the table.

Zeppo adjusts the flame under his pan of fish stock. If it wasn't for the expression on the younger one's face, he'd send one of the girls down to look: but that boy seems really shaken.

'I don't know what the hell you're doing down on the beach in all this mist when there's nothing to see,' he mutters as he puts on his boots and fetches his jacket and hat from the store-room.

'What's happened?' asks Lis, the trainee chef, casting a sceptical glance at the younger boy. She knows he's got a lively imagination.

'He's dead,' he whispers, giving the ducks a wide berth.

*

Zeppo wades through the slippery snow with his hat pulled down over his ears. He clutches his mobile in his pocket. There's no point in ringing anyone before he's seen for himself. It could be just a porpoise or a piece of wreckage washed ashore. Anything might have got the boys' imagination going. He strides through a hedge of withered spruce, slithers down a snow-covered slope to the narrow foreshore, and struggles determinedly past the snack bar, shuttered for the winter.

Željko Popović you half-wit, what the hell are you doing here, he thinks despondently. Of all the places in Europe, you chose this godforsaken corner. You could have been conjuring things up in Le Petit Nice in Marseille, chez Gerald Passadat, or in the sunshine of Gran Canaria, where Mester takes great pleasure in bullying his apprentices these days. But you go and end up here.

Distracted by these irritating thoughts he finds he has to stand still to work out where he is in the mist. He can hear in his head the patter of countless guides with their groups of summer tourists. 'In centuries gone by, when the sky and the sea ran together in a snowstorm or in a mist like this, it only took a change in the wind for a ship in full sail to feel the sand under its keel. Then some of the crew, usually the young ones, would wash up on the shore, their lungs full of water and their life hanging by a thread.' That's how new blood reached this godforsaken backwater. Nowadays you only end up here if you're an idiot, he thinks.

Someone had seen him serving the wrong people in the café in Dubrovnik, and he'd only just managed to grab his passport, slide down the turf roof, and go running along by the stone wall and into the woods, while NATO F16s roared overhead.

You're paying the price now, you bloody fool, he whispers, as he carries blindly on through the slippery snow, knowing in his heart that his taste for fair skin and blonde hair was his real reason for avoiding warmer climes.

He stops and orientates himself. On the other side of the icy groyne he can make out a lump on the shoreline. The boys are right. Lying here is a naked human. A rather overweight naked human. A man.

He gets down on his haunches. He's seen plenty of dead people. Young and old. This is just another in a long line of scorching half-repressed flashbacks. With the corner of his jacket he brushes the snow off the face.

'God in heaven,' he whispers. It's Knud Harber. What on earth has happened? Why is he naked? One lip is split like a harelip, and the teeth give a grotesque smile. Thin black streaks of clotted blood run down over his face from small pricks on his head, like Christ on the cross. It's Knud Harber, who was chatting to him only the other day over a beer in the kitchen. Harber, who's ordered 'an unforgettable dinner' for nine this very evening.

Don't touch, he thinks, while he tries to work out what can have happened, and why Harber has washed up here stark naked. He's been beaten up, he decides. Beaten up thoroughly with a heavy implement. But what about those tiny wounds? A heavy implement with some kind of sharp point. He must ring the police.

The moment he gets up, he notices a quiver around Harber's split mouth. What was that? he asks himself, and squats down again and puts his ear close to Harber's mouth. It's impossible to make anything out against the roar of the sea. He hurriedly takes off his jacket and shapes a little dark hollow. Now he can feel his breath and hear a faint sound. He gives a start, and almost falls on his backside on the icy shingle under the snow.

'Jesus Christ,' he exclaims in shock. He's actually alive. Knud Harber is alive. He's breathing.

Impossible to move him. Harber's as heavy as a walrus. Instead he scrapes as much snow as he can from the fat, chill body, and lays his jacket over him. His fingers are frozen stiff, but with great concentration he manages to get at the keypad and dial the police.

1

A week earlier

Mikkel raises his head a couple of inches from the pillow and blinks. The broad slats of the dark wooden blinds are closed, but he can make out a strip of light at the bottom. His Nokia buzzes on his desk, like a fly trapped under a newspaper. That's what must have woken him.

He's just turned twenty-three. It's not a specially significant number, but it was feted in style the previous evening in the cafeteria at the Copenhagen Business School. Now it's Sunday. According to his diary, which he was looking at only yesterday, the sun rises at 8.32 and sets at 16.02. So at this time of year there are about seven and a half hours of daylight, and of those seven and a half hours there are now probably only about two left, or at the most three. The Business School reckons he's a good student, and he does have an innate ability with maths, but at the moment that's the best calculation he can manage.

Trying to turn on his side, he realises he's caught fast. It's Hanna that he can't free himself from. She's fast asleep with her breath in his ear and a warm thigh over his, as if she wants to make sure he isn't going anywhere.

His phone has gone quiet, and in the silence he can hear, over the sound of Hanna's breathing, the slam of a car door down in Nansensgade, an engine getting up to speed, and wild shouting from someone in the distance. But he can dwell on that drama only for a moment before his phone buzzes again and shakes itself towards the edge of the desk.

He twists himself free of Hanna's warm thigh, swings his legs out of bed, knocks over a beer-glass of tepid water and stumbles towards the band of light to grab his Nokia the very second it topples over the edge.

'Mikkel here,' he says hoarsely.

'Is that Mikkel Keldberg?' comes a half-shout, with another kind of engine running in the background. Not the thin sound he heard a minute ago from the street, but an engine with a deep, hollow piston thrust, like a team of horses at full gallop.

'What's this about?' he asks with a yawn.

'Am I speaking to the son of Bjørn Keldberg of Keldberg Ceramics?'

'That's me.'

'It's about your aunt.'

'My aunt?'

'I've been trying to get in touch with your parents. My name's Henry, Henry Olsen.'

'My parents are in Mexico. Unless they've moved on to Florida.'

'Ah,' comes from the mobile. The roar of the engine subsides and is replaced by a baby crying. Or perhaps gulls nearby.

'Has the caretaker spoken to you?'

'Who?'

'Ole Jørgensen.'

'I don't know anyone called Ole Jørgensen.'

'OK. But he'll ring you.'

'How did you get my number?'

'From the police.'

'What?' asks Mikkel, beginning to wake up.

'It's about your aunt, Ellen Kristine Keldberg. She's died. I've spoken to the police. They've been trying to get in touch with you.'

'I was at a party,' he apologises, rubbing a little sleep from his eyes. Now he comes to think about it, there is an aunt somewhere up in north Jutland, but he can't remember when he last saw her.

He listens, half-freezing, to Henry Olsen talking about the imminent funeral, while through the semi-darkness and strips of light from the blinds he observes Hanna very slowly pulling her pillow towards her, as if she's dreaming someone's about to steal it. He promises Henry he'll ring back when he's made contact with his parents, and thanks him for the call

He finds a pair of boxers and a crumpled T-shirt in the heap of clean washing. Thursday is the deadline for the project report he's writing with Jesper and Simon on 'The telecommunications industry: empirical economics and theoretical approaches'. Friday is Astrid's housewarming in the four-roomed flat she's inherited from her grandmother. And Saturday is the day they set off. His skis have been out of the cellar for quite a while, standing in the hall as a daily reminder that life, after all, has its advantages.

In the bed, Hanna is sound asleep, and on the floor, near the overturned beer glass, a lake has formed round some black silk tights and a used condom. From where he's standing it looks like a half-rotten whale, beached on a barren volcanic island.

Not a good omen.

2

Holger Strand steps into his daughter's bedroom. The door was ajar, and he'd felt in a strange, counterintuitive way that it would seem presumptuous to knock. He stands in his dressing-gown, a little damp after his morning shower, and gives an embarrassed smile, as if he's entered the wrong room.

Sharp winter sunshine falls on the bed, where Anne Sofie sits in a sleeveless vest filing her nails. She's moved the gauze bandage on her wrist, and ostentatiously fastened it with a large green safety pin. Her nails are varnished blue.

'We didn't hear you come in last night.'

'I didn't think you did,' she says, concentrating on her nail.

She hasn't been home for a week. They've been anxious, as always when she disappears without a word, but it's pointless getting into that argument.

'Are you pleased with your new camera?' he asks, in a tone which is a fraction too optimistic.

'Yes,' she says, giving him a short, cold glance before resuming her examination of her nails.

'You've had your hair cut,' he says.

'Yes.'

'It suits you.'

'Thank you.'

'I'm driving into Copenhagen in an hour,' he says.

She gets up from the bed and moves to the dormer window.

She's only just twenty, but when she stands there in her sleeveless vest, slender and long-legged, with shoulder-blades like the sprouting wings of an angel-child, he thinks she looks like a girl of fourteen.

'Did you speak to Knud Harber?' he asks hopefully.

'He's in Skagen,' she says.

'In Skagen?' he repeats, a shadow of unease crossing his face.

'Yes. He's setting up some kind of phoney gallery up there.'

'Knud Harber's in touch with what young artists are up to these days,' he says, hoping that she appreciates his description of her as an artist.

She turns towards him, and he wants to hold her. To embrace her and rock her to and fro, as he did when she was little, or take her by the hand as he did on her first day at school. But he simply stands there, his eyes slightly downcast.

'I met the professor the other day,' she says casually.

'Otto Bremer,' he says, brightening, with a nervous smile.

'I had to go to bed with him to get the meeting with Harber. That was the deal.'

He shakes his head in resignation and takes a deep breath.

'Otto recommended you because of your talent.'

'He had mirrors in his bedroom.'

'Spare me the stories,' he says and raises his hand while the furrows tighten at the corners of his eyes. She laughs.

'The worst thing was the stink of soap. He was scrubbed like a slaughtered pig.'

It isn't the first time she's aired her lewd fantasies, and he shouldn't be surprised. That Otto could have demanded anything of the kind for a meeting with Knud Harber is unthinkable. Why does she say that? None of the psychologists and psychiatrists they've consulted since she was twelve has been able to give a plausible explanation. Why does she try to disrupt his and Helene's friendship with Otto? Otto is a thoroughly nice fellow. A bit of a show off with a rather loud laugh, but a decent man. And anyway he's a homosexual, as she knows very well.

As she opens the window, the frosty-clear air makes the translucent curtains fly like banners into the room, and without meaning to he draws his dressing-gown more tightly about him.

In the garden, the new flat-screen television and colour printer from the house are frozen fast amongst the broken rushes at the edge of the pond. He'd managed to pile up on the lawn all the kitchen appliances, his new laptop, the video player, the telephones and the sodden books. They'd just got out of their taxi after a weekend in London, and it was like a scene from the theatre of the absurd as he rummaged in the frozen pond for his jazz records, while Helene, bent double in her red suit with her hands clenched over her stomach, screamed with anger.

He looks at the slender nape of her neck and downy shoulders, visible now that she's had her hair cut. Of the diagnoses, 'extreme pubertal defiance' was the most banal. But there had been as many explanations of the mysteries of her behaviour as there had been psychologists.

'I'm going up there,' she says.

'But you've only just been there.'

'Yes. And now I've got to go there again.'

He nods.

'I'll ask Mum to give Sigvardtsen a ring, so the house is warm when you arrive.'

She's concentrating on her nails again, and he wonders if he can find something to say to placate her. The slightest little thing. But he can't think of anything.

'As I said...' he says a little too loudly, as if he's closing a meeting at the Ministry, 'I'm setting off in an hour. If you'd like to come to town with me, you'll need to be ready.'

She screws up her eyes, which means that she's registered his offer, and scratches herself, leaving small white streaks on her shoulder blade.

*

Helene stands in the living-room and wrings her hands. Twenty-five years ago, the spontaneous happiness in her face, always ready for laughter, had led him to kneel before her. The joy has forsaken her now. She's colourless, and there's something neurotic about the movement of her hands, as if they're directed and corrected by decisions she's already taken. Now I shall reach for the coffee cup. Now I shall turn and look out of the window. She watches as her husband reaches the foot of the stairs.

'How did she get home?'

'I didn't ask.'

She shakes her head. Helene has been shaking her head for five years, he thinks, as he fills a pan with water and lights the gas. The coffee machine is still out in the snow with all the other kitchen equipment. While he's waiting for the water to boil, he automatically switches on the answerphone. A hoarse voice. A woman, pleading, 'Yes... now... go on... now.' And a man singing through his nose: 'Happy birthday to Mads.' (Pause) 'Yes...Yes' (encouragingly); then, in a whisper 'Happy birthday to Mads,' and then a shouted 'Happy birthday to you!' so loud that the speaker distorts it.

Mads is singing it himself, he realises. Because there's nobody else to sing it. Is that how he should interpret the call from the carer? Did Anne Sofie hear that? Is that why the answerphone wasn't thrown out into the pond?

'I'm going up there on Friday,' he says as the water in the pan begins to boil.

Helene turns from the window and comes into the kitchen. He opens his arms and draws her to him. They stay like that a long minute holding each other tightly.

'How long will she be here?'

'I imagine you'll be free of her sometime this morning.'

He regrets the choice of words the moment he's said them.

'Sorry,' he says and reaches for the jar of instant coffee. He carefully fills his cup with boiling water, which hisses over the edge of the pan.

They hadn't seen a sign of her since they came home from their weekend in London. That was a week ago. They supposed she was with that boy Thomas. She didn't warn them she was coming in last night, and they didn't notice she was back until first thing this morning.

'She's going up there again,' he says, and Helene sighs as if that was what she feared.

'There's nothing there, except darkness.'

'Knud Harber the art-dealer is apparently there, and Otto has kindly arranged for her to meet him.'

Helene pulls her arms across her body as if she were cold.

'That house is ours, Holger. We can forbid her to go there. What will she do up there in winter? It's a bad habit.'

He pours a dash of milk into his coffee and sits down at the kitchen table. It's late, but he'll just have to be late this morning. He's heard all Helene's arguments so often that he's begun to interpret the slight deviations in her monotony. This time she chose the words 'bad habit'.

He sips his coffee and looks out over the lawn, white with new-fallen snow. The space round the pond looks like a rubbish tip. A beautiful, white rubbish tip, with the snow lying like a blanket of reconciliation over everything. The whole of December has been the usual slush of rain and sleet and wind and grey within grey. And then it suddenly changed to hard frost and snow.

'Have you rung the insurance people?' she asks. He shakes his head slowly.

'I can only make a claim if I report our daughter to the police, and I'm not going to do that.'

Helene laughs.

'And now you're letting her go up there again. What will it be next time? Maybe she'll think it'd be interesting to set fire to the house. That would certainly make some good pictures.'

He won't be reprimanded.

'Helene,' he sighs. 'She's an adult. We can't force her into therapy. We can push her away from us, reject her, but we can't force her to do anything at all.'

She gets up from the table and moves away from him, as she's done so many times before.

They had everything and they had each other. And they got Mads, who was all defects. And then they got Anne Sofie in compensation. Since they came home from London and found the house emptied of its electrical equipment, he's been desperately wondering when Anne Sofie's downward slide began.

It took years to get a diagnosis for Mads, while Anne Sofie slowly grew accustomed to having a toy snatched from her hands, or to be pulled violently off the tricycle when she least expected it. In moments of peace he'd wished they'd had a Down's syndrome child with a smile. It would have been easier. Mads lacks the warmth and empathy of Down's syndrome. When he reached thirteen and had the strength of a sixteen-year-old, they couldn't manage him any longer, and gave up, in the hope of saving the rest of the family.

It was about then, that it began, he thinks, and glances at his wife, who stands at the window with her arms folded.

When he goes out to his Mercedes, he fancies he sees an angel sitting in the back of the car. A little dark angel with green eyes and an angry expression. He gets in without saying anything. He starts the car and backs out of the drive, as a spark of happiness begins to kindle.

'Are you leaving today?' he asks, as the heavy Mercedes sinks fractionally on its suspension and accelerates noiselessly from the snow-covered drive.

'Yes, but I've got something to do first. You can drop me near Kongens Nytorv,' she says, rummaging around in her shoulder-bag. The bag business means she's not going to talk, he knows, so he contents himself with giving a nod.

They drive through the smooth snowy lanes of north Zealand, past riding-schools and farms and out through the woods to the main road.

'Are you sure you haven't got time for some lunch before you get the train?' he says, as the sun breaks through the heavy coke-grey clouds and casts a biblical light over Copenhagen. 'We could meet wherever you like.'

She doesn't answer.

'And you'd be welcome to come with us to Holstebro on Friday, if you're back from Skagen,' he adds with a smile. 'We can stay at the Scandic. They've got a swimming pool. *Holstebro la nuit.*'

She rolls her eyes. That means the joke has met with approval. As a joke. No one can maintain that he doesn't communicate with his daughter. A subtle language of small signs and hints through single words. A tone. A sparkle in the eye or that rolling of the eyes that meant that he'd said something amusing.

They drive onto the urban motorway in a salty yellow slush. Her friend Thomas had photographed her in the pond, she said. It was something for the exhibition she's preparing, to get her into the academy. She'd bled herself of a dramatic quantity of blood and lain in the ice-cold water for three minutes, which was dangerous of course. But strangely enough she didn't even catch a cold.

When they reach Kongens Nytorv in the city centre Holger Strand pulls in at the Hotel d'Angleterre, and she gets out with her red wheelie-case.

He keeps the car stationary for a moment and watches her go down Ny Adelgade. She walks along the freshly salted pavement in her short coat with silver buttons, her bottle-green velvet flared trousers and snakeskin boots, trailing her red case, looking like any other young woman from a comfortable background. No nose-rings or lip-rings.

She's passed that stage, he observes. The young lady is vain, and that seems to him a healthy sign.

And she's an artist. A young, fragile artist. That's how he sees her. That's how he wants to see her.

3

Mikkel has been lost in his 'Telecommunications' for so long that the passengers around him look entirely different when he looks up from his laptop.

Back towards Copenhagen the carriage was half-full of commuters. Now four middle-aged women sit across the gangway playing cards. He's been roused not by their laughter and small-talk, but by their sudden silence. He realises that the train has stopped. He presses his forehead to the window and looks out over the winter-white fields.

It had taken three attempts to get in touch with his parents. Thereafter, everything had ensued exactly as he'd feared. He hadn't expected them to cut short their holiday on the other side of the world, but he can't comprehend why he, personally, should be required to go and take charge of everything. They've had nothing to do with this aunt Ellen for ten years, as he forcibly pointed out to his mother. But there was to be no discussion. There was something desperate about her insistence, and it irritated him that he was even going to be required to apologise for their absence.

'I've got no money,' he'd said in a last attempt at evasion, but naturally that eventuality was provided for. Under the blue box in the little bureau in the bedroom he would find a credit card, and inside the lid was the PIN in the form of the last four figures of something cunningly disguised as a telephone number. And by the way you can get a perfectly good room at the Seamen's Hostel. Basta.

As far as he knows, his mother has never slept in a Seamen's Hostel. As far as he knows, she's never been north of Århus. They'd always spent their holidays in the summer house on Bornholm, or, if not there, on the Costa del Sol or on Samos – with the occasional long weekend on Samsø, where aunt Lone has an apple orchard. Then they sold half the land round the factory, and now that they have serious money their travels are more exotic.

The fields slowly begin to slide past, and the train finds its rhythm again and gets up to speed. In a dizzy second, as the sun breaks through the grey clouds and shines a white light into the carriage, the coming week passes before him like the fluttering pages of a calendar in a black and white film. Organising a funeral must take more than two days – unless you're in Africa and there's some kind of risk of plague or cholera – so the last real teamwork on the group project with Jesper and Simon will have to be done over the internet, and Astrid's party and the ski trip to Val d'Isère will very likely go ahead without him. He has a sudden urge to pull the emergency alarm in panic.

'I'm on my way to Skagen,' he says quietly into his mobile, moving from his seat and out of the carriage. 'Yes, I have to bury my aunt. My parents are away travelling.' It's Astrid, whom he has abandoned without managing to leave a message. He'd promised to help her with her party. Now she's rather cross because she thinks all this stuff about his aunt is a feeble excuse. The conversation falters, until Astrid gets on with her preparations with a sigh.

On Monday he'd been tearing around trying to organise things. Simon had said he'd find someone who could take his place on the flight if necessary. Hanna would go to Tisvilde, and he would pack.

He'd promised his mother he'd water the flowers once a week. Not too much and not too little, she'd twittered. And remember to set the alarm when you leave. And don't forget to clear the post-box of junk mail. Each pot-plant had its little label on the kitchen table showing its exact measure of water, including notes in brackets in most cases. ('A little dry, please', or 'leave the soil spongy'.)

When at last he'd been through all the rooms and found the credit card in the bureau and written the PIN on his left forearm, he'd sat down on the floor by the bookcase and got the family photograph albums out.

Aunt Ellen had been at his confirmation, he remembered, and eventually he found the album from the time when he was about thirteen. There were the pictures of the confirmation, held fast by their little glued triangles. Faded photos of the whole family in their stiffest finery, faintly flushed with over-eating. Uncles, aunts, cousins, and friends and acquaintances of the Keldberg and Svendsen families. And there she was. To his surprise he was in the picture too, with his hair slicked down and wearing a white shirt and bow tie. She had her left arm behind his back and a hand on his shoulder. A small heart-shaped face with a sad smile and a critical eye on the camera. She's certainly beautiful, he'd thought, and for the first time, with the album in his lap, he realised she was a Greenlander. Or at any rate half-Greenlander. Something about a Danish tradesman and an unhappy ending. Adopted by the Keldberg Svendsen family. Later simply Keldberg. Not a real aunt at all.

After he's had a pee, he goes back to his seat and takes the rucksack down from the luggage rack. In the front pocket is his diary, and tucked inside it is the photograph. He sits and looks at the picture for quite a while.

*

The girl with the refreshments trolley smiles, and Mikkel smiles back, but he has no appetite for ham or chicken sandwiches. He buys a cola and a banana for no reason but charity.

Beyond the sliding door to the next carriage a problem has evidently arisen with one of the passengers. A confused woman in her early fifties with bleached bobbed hair and red cheeks stands shouting hysterically, while the ticket inspector patiently waits for her to calm down. A man with a crewcut, a silver cross dangling on his chest, comes out of the next carriage with a vacuous grin on his face. He orders a cola, expectantly, as if he's in a cinema.

'What's going on?' asks the stewardess wearily.

The man laughs.

'She hasn't got a ticket. She says it's been stolen.'

'Oh no, not one of those again,' she sighs.

Over in the other carriage Mikkel notices a girl with a short boyish haircut looking at the woman in surprise. The inspector turns to her and she produces her ticket.

The woman begins her shrill shouting again. It can be heard through the sliding door.

'Come here with my ticket. You should be ashamed of yourself!'

The girl stands up. She seems nervous about the woman's aggressive behaviour, and with a lost look she appeals to the inspector for help.

'You'll have to buy a ticket or get off the train at Hobro,' he says to the older woman.

The woman stares in disbelief at the inspector and the girl, whose wide fearful eyes show evident discomfort at the situation.

'Listen,' sighs the conductor, laying a soothing hand on the woman's shoulder. 'You got on at Odense. The young lady's ticket is from Copenhagen. You're going to Ålborg. The young lady's ticket is to Frederikshavn.'

'She took it with her into the loo,' the shrill sound penetrates the sliding door. 'I was sitting talking to my sister. She interrupted me. She wanted to take my picture. She wanted me to hold my ticket out in front of me.'

The ticket inspector is tired.

'But why should the young lady steal your ticket? And why would she want to take your picture?'

Several passengers smile at this last remark. The girl looks downcast and shakes her head in resignation, and the inspector raises a comforting hand to her.

'She took it away into the loo.'

The woman points in the direction of Mikkel and the two others following the drama through the glass door. The inspector and the woman move towards the toilet. Mikkel's companions stand aside so that the inspector can get in. He stands a moment looking round and gestures with his arms.

'There's no ticket in here,' he says, in a tone of resignation clearly indicating that he hadn't expected to find one.

'She's flushed it away then. She's flushed it down the loo.'

The inspector comes out.

'Excuse me,' he says. 'Has anyone any information about this lady's ticket?'

'Maybe she never bought one,' says one of the seated passengers, while the woman in question looks around desperately for help. It's as if she realises for the first time that she herself is the problem. She gives a short glare at the inspector and looks towards the girl, who has picked up her fashion magazine again.

'The little bitch,' she hisses and moves determinedly through the carriage. The inspector takes her by the arm but she is well-built and not to be held like that. Two students come to help him, and then all four of them tumble in the gangway, whereupon the woman has a fit of dizziness and sits gasping on the floor. She gives a loud groan.

The train slows, rumbling and swaying over some points, and a red-haired soldier arrives with a bottle of water. The water evidently has an effect on the woman, who points like an ill-tempered child at the girl.

'I know her type. Those eyes. There's something wrong with her. I've worked with girls like her. She's dangerous.'

The woman must be unwell, thinks Mikkel, as he returns to his seat in the forward carriage.

When the train pulls into the station, he sees two policemen and a railway official on the platform. People get out and wince at the cold. The woman emerges in the company of the ticket inspector who carries her suitcase. She looks apathetic. One of the policemen speaks to her. She produces some ID from her handbag. They go over to the waiting room as the platform begins to slide by.

Mikkel closes his eyes and sighs. There just aren't enough psychiatric beds.

The first thing that strikes him about the tourist information website is that it's always summer in this town. Blue sky. Yellow houses with red roofs. Narrow streets. Lilacs in flower. The harbour. Dried fish hanging out on lines. The fish-packing sheds and the yachts and the beach, the sea, the dunes and the sun. And the museum with the famous painters, Michael Ancher's fishermen in sou'westers with pipes in their mouths and Krøyer's women in the dusk. And the hotels, the motels, the bed and breakfasts and the time-share opportunities.

Skagen is a holiday town, he reads, becoming thoughtful. The wind rasps at the window, scratching like sandpaper over the pane. He closes his laptop and sets off through the train in search of the catering trolley. He's decided to buy one of the ghastly chicken sandwiches, knowing perfectly well how soggy it will be.

He sees her just briefly as she comes out of the loo. She casts her eyes down. From a distance, as she sat looking miserable in the carriage listening to the woman's accusations, he guessed she was sixteen or seventeen, but here, in the moment she slips by, he can see that she's older. He thinks he's seen her before. Maybe one of the new ones at the Business School. A little too conscious of her middle-class background, feminine in her movements and with a hint of something exotic about her eyes.

In the local train on the last leg of the journey he simply sits looking out into the twilight. Little remote houses, fields and smallholdings drift by. After a couple of stops at stations he's never heard of, where solitary schoolchildren leave the train, their bags battered and their coats half off, the houses are succeeded by low stunted spruce. It's begun to snow again in earnest, with hard flakes pelting against the window.

The train runs on into the darkness, and when the last daylight has vanished, the wall of dunes surrounding the heath in the distance becomes nothing more than a gentle contour against a blue-black background. The train rumbles between low houses and snow-filled back gardens, with stacks of firewood and tumbledown greenhouses, and suddenly he's arrived.

In the dark, he stands on the station forecourt in surprise. Where's the red carpet? Where's the brass band and the limousine, which at his parents' considerate request will take him somewhere friendly and warm? Where are the ample-bosomed dancing girls in their lacquer and tulle, and the frosted champagne glasses with sugared rims and light red straws? Where is everybody?

The girl who was humiliated is crossing the square purposefully with her red suitcase trailing through the snow, her march perfectly timed to catch a taxi. The taxi door gives a hollow thud, the light from the headlamps blinds him for a second, and she's gone, leaving him alone in the whistling wind.

The name of the man he's supposed to get in touch with is Henry Olsen. Henry Olsen can wait, he thinks. First he's got to find a hotel, and he's already made a decision about that. It won't be the Seamen's Hostel recommended by his mother, which he supposes must be near the harbour. He'll stay at Brøndums, the traditional meeting-place of the illustrious Skagen painters. Whatever the cost.

The fast-food place at the crossroads smells of vegetable oil and soap. In the corner sits a man in his late thirties with his two small children. They're absorbed in the burger menu. The man seems slow in his movements. His face is expressionless while he distributes bottles, drinking straws and ketchup.

The waitress must be about his own age and evidently mops the floors and wipes the tables too. She has mauve hair, wide, frightened eyes, bad skin and a sweet smile.

'Just carry on over there,' she explains, scratching her scalp. 'When you get to the sign for the museum, you can't miss it.'

He thanks her, pulling his hood well over his head. 'Over there', she'd said. What does 'over there' mean? Over where?

As he trudges 'over there', half-blinded by the prickly snow, he longs for the lights of town at home, and the warm cafés, and Hanna's soft thighs, angry that his aunt has died at this particular moment. Of all times it couldn't be more inconvenient.

In the end it may work out OK, he thinks. The order of factors. Like at Frederikshavn station, where the intercity train arrived late, but just late enough to connect with the local train.

*

The receptionist's name is Vigga Petersen, according to the little badge on her dark green waistcoat. She's tall, blonde, in her early forties, and preoccupied with something that must have happened just before he arrived. From the long corridor towards the kitchen he can hear someone laughing.

Vigga looks at his frozen appearance with a sympathetic smile.

'Welcome!'

He explains as distinctly as he can, through a face anaesthetised by the cold, that he is here for his aunt's funeral, at a time yet to be determined, but hopes to be back in Copenhagen on Friday. The last part is wishful thinking.

'Room 29,' she smiles, handing him the key. 'The bathroom's at the end of the corridor.'

He thanks her and picks up his rucksack. The lighting on the stairs is subdued and the thick carpets absorb any sound. It's warm, and the banisters have the wear of history upon them. Everything is precisely as he'd imagined it.

He puts his rucksack on the end of the bed and opens the heavy curtains. Through the darkness and the fine snowflakes, swirling in the light of the street-lamps, he can make out the great red museum on the other side of the road. It looms like a rock over the low houses. One day he'll go in there, he decides, hanging his wet jacket on the hook on the door.

As he unpacks his deep-frozen laptop, he realises something's wrong. What is this? A hotel room without a bloody television? He searches for sockets and jackpoints. No television and no internet connection to civilisation! Something tells him that the Seamen's Hostel would have had both.

He sits on the edge of the bed, rubbing his cold fingers, while he considers whether to move there straight away or wait until morning. He decides to ring Henry Olsen and arrange a meeting, and finds the number in his diary. Beneath the clear plastic sits the little faded photograph. He takes it out and studies the odd pair, as he's done many times before, both yesterday and today, on the last stage of the train journey. Each time he looks at it, his aunt seems more beautiful.

4

Passing from window to window, Anne Sofie draws the thin linen curtains. She's smiling. It's so easy to work out which people are in their fixed routine, and which only visiting the town. You notice it in everything. Their clothes, their attitude, even the way they're sitting in the train. Full of expectation about their arrival or indifferent to it. She puts a hand on the radiator: it's hot. The gardener's evidently been in. While the kettle boils, she opens her suitcase and takes out the portfolio with all her material. She lights the lamp, lays her glossy black and white pictures gently on the table and slightly rearranges their order.

Thomas is a master at photography, and she's entirely satisfied. In a mauve envelope are the trial prints on tissue-paper, and the grainy enlargements from Reprotryk in Rødovre were waiting in the hall when she came through the front door.

She'll emphasise the shadows in the pictures once they're transferred to tissue-paper. And when she shows them to Knud Harber, the versions touched up with orange and blue-black oil paint will be saved until last. Like that he'll have a carefully thought-out sequence to consider.

He'd told her he had quite a lot to attend to, and to her disappointment he's arranged to see her in the old factory by the herring-salting plant, while he's there for a meeting with a local architect.

Pouring the boiling water slowly onto her tea, she soon becomes lost in thought while it brews. She sits in silence, feeling gradually warmer as she drinks, studying her pictures. Later she'll go down to the Italian place, Firenze, and have a pizza, and she'll take her camera. With all the reflection off the snow she'll be able to use her fastest film. Especially if the cloud breaks and the moon comes out. It's waxing and nearly full.

She hears a car stop at the gate, and she draws the curtain a fraction to the side. She can see the white steam from the exhaust, and the light from the headlamps setting the snow-covered briars on fire. Who can it be? No one lives round here in January. At this time of year the only person who ever turns up is Gahm, whose house is just down the track to the beach. It had suddenly struck her one afternoon that

Gahm – who monopolises the street scene in summer, with his wife and his children, his mistress, his au pair and his chauffeur – always comes alone for a few weeks in winter. One day when she sees him on the beach she'll speak to him and ask him what the attraction is.

There's a knock at the door. She switches on the outside light and recognises the cap through the small frosted panes. It's Sigvardtsen, the gardener who keeps an eye on the house. She opens the door and looks at him as if he's a salesman hawking something very expensive.

'So, you've got here all right?' he says, instinctively touching his cap.

'Yes.'

'And the house is warm?'

'Yes, everything's fine.'

'There's something wrong with the thermostat on the tank in the bathroom. I could come back tomorrow.'

'Thank you,' she says, 'but it doesn't bother me. It can wait.'

'Of course. But at least now you know about it.'

'Yes,' she says.

Sigvardtsen touches his cap again, and she shuts the door before he's had time to turn round, and stands waiting in the hall until she hears the click of the gate.

She goes into the kitchen and up the narrow staircase to her room in the attic. Up there, unchanging in the silence and the dust, are all the years from as long ago as she can remember, preserved in the form of hats and dresses and dolls and bath toys and tricycles and drawers full of letters. Hanging next to the sea-captain's jacket with the rabbit-fur collar is the Russian fur hat, which she only uses up here, when it's cold like it is now: and there are her lace-up boots, and in the wardrobe are her leggings. While she gets changed she's beset with both anxiety and happy expectation about tomorrow's meeting with Harber.

Howling and gusting, quite a wind has got up, and the snow begins to build up in drifts along the street. She takes a deep breath and shuts the gate behind her, enchanted by the light from the moon sailing at full speed across the breaks in the cloud. She runs with the wind at her back, does a quick sprint and then slides down to the main road and walks briskly along beside the whitened fences. By the time she's got to Brøndums Hotel she feels hot and breathless. The lights are on in the dining-room, and she sees a lonely party of guests behind the thin curtains.

She goes on, behind the museum and past the red brick villas towards Kappelborg, and takes another run, sliding along the road in the fresh snow, as yet undisturbed by the gritters. She can think only of her movement and balance, swivelling round on herself and snatching snow from the hedges, though it's too dry for anything but sprinkling around. Thomas will be so happy when she rings and tells him that Harber thinks she's a genius, and they'll celebrate together, and she'll have an exhibition in Copenhagen in the spring, and next year they'll do something bigger and even wilder. She stops and looks up at the moon, which moves enfolded in shiny silver ornaments. As she stands like a little soldier with her face upturned, a middle-aged couple go by, arm in arm and bent against the wind. The woman's in mink and the man's wearing a long wool overcoat. She hears their low voices.

'Thomas!' she calls up to the moon, and the woman casts a brief glance over her shoulder and whispers something to her husband.

She'd got out of the ice-cold, blood-filled garden pool and let him bandage her wrist with shaking hands. He was white and afraid.

Now she stretches out her arms again and runs with the wind, leaving her thoughts behind her, gathering speed and sliding again through the snow. Lovely, she thinks, and walks for a while before coming to the lights of the harbour road and the Firenze pizza house.

She goes into the warm. In here it smells of holidays, of safety, of freshly-baked bread and oregano. She chooses a table in the little L-shaped snug, where she's on her own. Disentangling herself from her jacket, scarf and hat, she realises she's perspiring.

'Good evening, miss,' says Marius the waiter, once she's sorted herself out.

'I'll have a pepperoni and a glass of water with ice, please,' she says, letting her fingers run through her short black hair.

While she's waiting she takes her camera out of its leather case to let the steamed-up lens demist. She'll take some photographs this evening. Just dawdle a bit round the harbour and find some routine subjects. The snow reflected in the light of the street-lamps like a swarm of fireflies. A drunk making his way back from the pub on his rusty bicycle: or even better, a drunk who's fallen off his rusty bicycle and lies scrabbling around in the snow.

There's a queue just inside the front door. Firenze stays open all year round, and people keep arriving in their four-by-fours to pick up their evening meal. The staff are sweating by the oven and shouting orders in the kitchen. Everyone wants a take-away. The only seated guests apart from herself are three men in their forties at a table at the front. They're sitting in their work-clothes talking in a language that she guesses must be Polish.

Suddenly shouts and loud laughter come from the entrance. Two younger men in quilted jackets come into view. One of them is Frode. He notices the camera on her table and comes purposefully into the snug and over to where she's sitting. His cheeks are red as tomatoes and he's smiling as if he's just won the lottery.

'Miss Soffi,' he says, snatching off his hat and posturing like a low-grade film star. 'Take my picture.'

She looks at him without even blinking. He doubles up with laughter, pulls out a chair, and sits down opposite her.

'How goes it?' he says.

'How goes what?'

Frode hides his head in his hands.

'Why won't you take my picture?'

'Because you look a complete idiot when you're high, and your boozy breath would get on the film and take off the emulsion so I'd get black holes in the negative.'

'Black holes?'

It dawns on him rather late that she's sitting there giving him a lot of nonsense, and he smiles and lays his icy hands over hers.

'Weren't you going to Århus to make yourself an expert in something?' she asks, withdrawing her hands.

'Århus,' he says, coming suddenly back to reality, and drumming his fingers on the table. 'Now what's so fantastic about Århus? Tell me, Soffi. I've forgotten.'

She picks up her camera anyway and focuses on his left eye. A drop of almost-melted snow shivers on his eyebrow. She quickly takes three pictures one after the other, while he blinks and a drop runs down his cheek as he looks down at the table.

'Are you on your own?'

'No,' she says, putting the camera down. 'You're sitting here with me, Frode.'

Frode puts on his happy high-on-hash face again, slaps a hand down on the table and screws up his eyes. For a moment he looks completely normal, and his cheeks begin to regain the colour people's cheeks usually have in their early twenties. He fidgets with his fingers on the table as if there's something he wants to say to her, some thought that's just escaped him.

'Have you been to Copenhagen?'

'Yes.'

'And you've come back.'

'So it would seem.'

He smiles again, his fingers drumming on the table.

'Will you come with us out to Bodil? We're going to watch some videos.'

She slowly shakes her head.

When Marius appears with her pizza, he gets up with a quick 'See you' and disappears to join his friend again.

'You be careful of him,' says Marius in his strong accent, putting the pizza and a jug of water on the table.

She considers taking a picture of Marius, but realises that all over Europe, even the smallest one-eyed town has a Marius, showing off his pizza-concept and his double-sided catholic morals. Of Frode, on the other hand, there is only one, and she's taken a good picture of his left eye.

She's known Frode since she began coming here in the summer as a toddler with her parents. Three summers ago Frode had a holiday job washing dishes at Brøndums Hotel, and they went skinny-dipping at night on Sønderstrand beach, and after the chef had gone to bed they would have goose pâté and champagne in the hotel kitchens with the waitresses.

But how would Marius know anything about that?

5

The taxi-driver is short and thick-set. It's almost as if he hasn't got a neck, and has his head sitting directly on his torso. He's chatting merrily about the weather, and about a fare he's just taken down to the Old Town, and how he can't understand people just sitting at home staring at their televisions, and how he'd give a million to know why a young man staying at Brøndums Hotel would want to go out to an address in Mosegården.

'Did you say number 26?' he asks. 'Isn't that where Henry Olsen lives?'

Mikkel pays his fare and gets out in front of a small block of flats built of red stone. Some of the balconies are decorated with Christmas lights. A tired-looking Christmas tree stands outside.

This is obviously where the real locals live, he decides, seeing the bicycles and buggies cluttering the hallways. Further along the street some children are trying to make a snowman, but the project is doomed to failure because the snow is as dry as flour. There's no entryphone, so he walks up the echoing stone stairway to the first floor. 'Henry Olsen, Dorte, Kasper and Svupper' is typed on a sheet of A4 fastened to the door. Near the letterbox a more official notice in small Letraset characters says simply 'Henry Olsen'.

The moment he rings the bell, the door opens. A young woman of about his own age, in faded jogging clothes and lightly-gelled blonde hair, flashes him a tired smile.

'Hi, my name's Mikkel,' he says.

'I'm Dorte,' she says, as her hand moves to her hair, 'and sorry about the mess.'

He's hit by a sour odour of wet clothes mixed with the smell of cooking from the kitchen.

Behind her two small boys push forward. They're totally alike, except that one has a bump the size of a pigeon's egg in the middle of his forehead. Behind the boys peers a rough-haired retriever, lashing his stiff tail.

'Just leave your coat on the chair,' she says, seeing that the coat-rack is bristling with overload.

He takes off his coat, and the boys begin pulling at him. There's something they want him to see.

'Leave Mikkel alone,' she shouts.

Quite a bit of shouting goes on here, he observes, as a man in his early fifties emerges from the living room. He's wearing a washed-out vest; blue-green tattoos cover his sinewy arms. He has a sprinkling of grey in his black hair, a neat, short beard and dark eyes. They measure Mikkel up.

'Can't you just leave him alone now?' The question is directed somewhat threateningly at the twins.

'Would you like a beer?' asks Henry, and Mikkel accepts it though he has no real desire for one.

Henry goes out to the kitchen, and Mikkel hears Dorte complaining about something: 'don't let him get started on that'.

He settles down on a worn green sofa to wait. The room is sparsely furnished. The most notable thing is a row of antlers on the wall over the sofa.

What has Henry got to do with all this? It was the caretaker he was supposed to talk to. The caretaker had rung him too but hadn't answered when he rang back. If Henry asks anything about his family, he'll explain just how things are. That his parents have had nothing to do with his aunt for the past ten years, and that right now they're sunning themselves on a beach somewhere in Mexico.

'Yes, it's sad about Krille,' mumbles Henry, half to himself, while to judge from the noise they're making, the twins are having a fight in the kitchen. There's another shout from Dorte, and a saucepan-lid crashes to the floor.

Henry calls her Krille. Ellen Kristine Keldberg was her name. Maybe she called herself Kristine.

Indifferent to the drama in the kitchen, Henry opens the beers and brings them to the coffee-table.

'What did my aunt die of?'

'She froze to death.'

'How?' asks Mikkel in surprise.

Henry scratches at his beard.

'She'd been sitting in the pub with Poul, and then she left.'

'Poul?' asks Mikkel, confused.

'Yes, Poul: 'the Crab', they call him. He used to go to her house a lot. When he left the pub he found her sitting in the square by the church in just her dress. No one knows where she'd left her coat. He tried to wake her up, but couldn't. He was worried and carried her home. When he laid her on the bed, he realised she was dead.'

'That sounds pretty weird.'

Henry smiles.

'Not if you knew your aunt or Poul.'

Dorte comes into the living-room. She looks upset.

'Why would she have taken her coat off?' she asks, holding her clenched hands to her sides.

'Relax, can't you?' says Henry, with an embarrassed glance at the young man, who's now looking confused.

'You heard what Poul said,' she says. 'Krille was in a good mood. She was wearing her best dress. She'd just come into some money.'

'How the blazes do you know?'

'I know what I've heard from Poul. Who the hell would go around without a coat when it's eleven degrees below freezing?'

'I think I know the dress you mean,' says Mikkel. 'I've got a picture ... from my confirmation. Perhaps it's the same dress.'

Dorte looks at Mikkel in surprise. She rolls her eyes as if it's the most idiotic remark she's ever heard.

Now the twins have started fighting again, and she spins round on her heels.

'Will you bloody behave yourselves. We've got a guest here,' she shouts, while the twin with the lump on his forehead comes flying in wildly behind Henry's chair, setting the standard lamp swaying ominously from side to side. The other twin appears through the doorway with a sly smile on his face. He's had an idea which trumps his brother's strategic positioning behind Henry.

'Come and see the birds,' he says sweetly, taking Mikkel's hand.

Henry smiles.

'You'd better go or we'll never get any peace.'

Mikkel allows himself to be led into the kitchen, where there's a door out to a balcony. Dorte has to move a little to let them go past, and the boy opens the door.

'Look,' he says, pointing. 'Grandad shot them.'

'Yes,' says Dorte drily, energetically turning some meatballs in a pan. 'And it's way out of the hunting season.' She shouts through to the living room: 'I don't understand how Zeppo can touch those birds.'

With a certain distaste, Mikkel looks at the birds, lying in a heap on a table covered with a thin layer of snow. This is a massacre, he thinks, and guesses that there must be ten birds with shrivelled eyes and spatters of blood on their white breasts. An acrid smell settles in his nostrils. The boy takes hold of the head of one of the birds and attempts to open its beak. Mikkel takes a step backwards and nods appreciatively.

'So Henry's a huntsman?'

'Grandad's a fisherman, but he gets money for these.'

'That's right,' laughs Henry from the kitchen, as he opens another beer. 'Eider duck usually stay so far out to sea that you never see them, but they've come further in now it's got so cold.'

Mikkel has seen enough and absently wipes his hands on his trousers, glancing at Dorte who is trying to find space to get the meal.

'Would you please get out of the kitchen,' she shouts again.

'What'll happen to this lot?'

Henry looks at him with a bemused expression, then laughs.

'Well, the idea is to pluck them and eat them. The chef out at Ruth's Hotel is going to have them. Some kind of fancy dinner he's got booked.'

The meal, of meatballs with steamed potatoes, cauliflower and white sauce with nutmeg, passes off peacefully. Everyone's hungry. Dorte has placed the twins, their hair combed and hands newly washed, on opposite sides of the table.

Mikkel breaks the silence and talks a little about his journey here: the delays to the trains – which are becoming quite normal – people's impatience, and a woman who insisted that her ticket had been stolen.

Dorte seems rather reserved and her smile is strained. He senses that they were having a row just before he arrived. What was it the boy said? Grandad. Dorte is Henry's daughter.

'I've spoken to the caretaker,' says Henry. 'If you go to the flat tomorrow at ten, he'll let you in.'

'Did you know my aunt well?'

He notices that Henry's on his third beer, moving imperceptibly from one to the next. Henry shrugs his shoulders, and Dorte reacts.

'My father got together with Krille when she was young and beautiful.'

It's the first time he's seen her really smile.

'OK,' he says. 'It was something like that.'

'Yes,' she says, spearing a meatball with her fork. 'My mother was pretty hacked off.'

Henry looks at his daughter in surprise and smiles affectionately.

'Let's say love comes in complicated sizes.'

Now it's Dorte who concentrates on her food.

When everyone has eaten well, Henry gets up, reaches for his tobacco and rolls a cigarette.

'She'd just take off once in a while,' he says. 'For several days at a time. Life goes its own sweet way.'

'And you go your own sweet way,' returns Dorte, who has started to clear the table.

'Steady now,' he snaps.

We're about the same age, thinks Mikkel, and she's really rather beautiful. There's a certain distance in her smile, and at the same time a curiosity in her blue eyes, and he suddenly realises that Henry hasn't left her a minute to do anything with herself, before the guest arrived on the doorstep.

'He thinks it's his fault she's dead,' she says, holding out her arms in despair. 'That's why he's drinking again. Even yesterday, when he shot the eider duck, he'd had a skinful. Staggering round half-cut with a loaded rifle. In a snowstorm out on the north shore.'

Henry smiles, indicating to Mikkel that he shouldn't read too much into that remark.

'Dorte's going to get her flat back on Monday. It's almost back to normal. Her boyfriend set fire to it. But only after she set fire to him.'

This brings Dorte back into the living-room, her cheeks red.

'Now you shut up.'

Mikkel is confused.

'My daughter has it in her to set young men on fire.' smiles Henry.

'He could have burnt the whole building down,' she says, going out with the dirty dishes. He can hear her throwing everything into the dishwasher.

Henry shrugs his shoulders. 'If you'd just behave yourself, madam superwoman, things would be a lot less complicated.'

All's quiet in the kitchen now. Mikkel concentrates on the label of the beer-bottle in front of him.

'You're a fisherman?' he asks.

Henry nods.

'At the moment I'm a stand-in, which is fine by me. The skipper's in Thailand with his family. And what does a Copenhagener like you do for a living?'

'I'm a student at the CBS. It's a business school.'

Mikkel straightens himself up on the sofa. He'd hoped that Henry would talk about aunt Ellen, but his thoughts seem to be elsewhere. Instead of telling him anything, he asks: 'So Krille was adopted by your father's family?'

Mikkel nods.

'And now your parents have gone off to Mexico? Is that how it is?'

Mikkel nods again.

'OK. Cheers to that.'

'Yes,' says Mikkel. 'Cheers and thanks for the dinner.'

Henry leans over the table and rolls himself another cigarette. That's what he does when he needs to think, notices Mikkel. Gets his Rizla paper, puts it between his fingers, teases out the tobacco and neatly makes himself a smoke.

'The Crab reckons someone was sitting with her, on the bench, when he came out of the pub,' says Henry. 'Someone who buggered off when he saw him coming.'

'And she didn't have a coat on?'

'That's what he says.'

'And it was cold?'

'It was minus eleven on Saturday night. That's the coldest it's been here for five years.'

'What do you make of it?' asks Mikkel.

Henry lights his cigarette, and a little flame curls up from the end, while tiny sparks drop to the table.

'Poul's paranoid. He carried her home and only realised afterwards she was dead. Now he's afraid the police will say it was his fault. That's why I'm glad to talk to you. Poul can't stop talking about it and he paints a picture of the situation that only makes things worse for himself.'

'It could be that he's right.'

Henry shakes his head.

'There's no one who'd wish her any harm. Poul can't have been thinking straight. If he saw someone beside her, it must have been someone trying to wake her. There isn't a bench in this town where she hasn't slept off the booze. There isn't anyone who hasn't tried to get some life into her at some time or other.'

'What about her coat?'

Henry sits and stares ahead.

'Well, there is that. They do that,' he says quietly. 'She wasn't well.'

'What do they do?'

Henry takes a swig from his bottle and sets it carefully on the table.

'Take their coats off.'

6

Željko Popović feels a touch giddy with wine as he goes out into the biting cold, and his lungs fill with icy air as he crosses the car park. Down at the foot of the beach the sea is rumbling like distant thunder. He puts the bouquet and the bag with the two bottles of white wine on the floor in front of the passenger seat. He slams the door and walks round the car. He's very happy.

For the past few days he's been distracted at work: he hasn't really cared about anything, in fact, despite having a group of guests to look after almost all week. He'd left them to Lis, and told her bluntly they'd have to have catch of the day from the harbour for three days out of the four. But the Swiss guests were quite happy with that. Cod with mustard sauce, liver, roe, beetroot and cider-vinegar casserole: they'd almost made themselves ill with over-eating. He'd made clear to Lis and the kitchen staff that it didn't have to be expensive or elaborate. And indeed both the cod and the big buttered plaice had enchanted them.

Countless ways can be found to cook fish. The point of most recipes is to disguise the fact that the fish isn't fresh, but that's not a problem around here. That was the first thing he noticed when he arrived in this town. Up here the world's richest fishing grounds are at your very door.

While Lis has been sweating away in the kitchen, he's been using the time to plan the dinner Knud Harber has ordered for his artist friends. Now at last he's had the expected call from Fru Vibeke. Just back from her extended Christmas holiday in the Italian Alps, she has indeed done as he'd asked when he managed to get her on the phone a few days ago. She'd driven into the square in Lecco and bought everything he'd specified: goat's cheese, Parma ham and bresaola. At these primitive latitudes such delicacies exist only in sorry industrialised versions. In fact most people haven't the faintest idea what they are, so they're not in a position to judge them, let alone miss them. And he'd promised Knud Harber an unforgettable dinner.

Naturally little Fru Vibeke must receive her reward, so he's had a good shower and cut his toe-nails, and purloined a squirt of Aqua di Gio from the young professor in room 12 while the group have been out for one of their windy walks on the beach.

The voltage in the battery wobbles a little and the engine takes a while to start, but it eventually judders into life. He turns the heater up to maximum and switches on the fan. Five minutes with the engine running while he scrapes the ice from the windscreen. The chances of meeting the police on a cold Tuesday evening in January are about the same as being struck by lightning on a balmy summer day, and he whistles a little tune as he holds the heavy car to the middle of the road.

Fru Gross has invited some friends round while her husband's abroad. There'll be Fru Gross and her friend from Viborg – Helle, the alderman's wife – as well as Fru Vibeke. The alderman has been pensioned off now, of course, though that doesn't seem to have affected Helle's spirits. And Fru Vibeke's husband is in a care home and no longer recognises his wife, who's twenty years younger. If the old skinflint pops his clogs, he might consider putting out feelers himself. Fru Vibeke is attractive, and definitely too sharp not to observe a Serb's hidden agenda. But he'd settle for less. Fru Vibeke values his gastronomic skills, his hairy chest and his 'circus accent', as she calls his hard-learnt Danish.

A party of artists will be coming on Sunday, Harber had told him. Five Scandinavian painters and one of Harber's personal friends. Fru Gross and Fru Vibeke would grace the occasion with their presence: Fru Gross would entertain at the piano, and Fru Vibeke, with her comely appearance and perpetual happiness, would oblige the vanity of these individuals in her own inimitable manner.

Harber had told him that a great deal would stand or fall by that dinner. Serve what you like, Željko Popović, but it's got to be unforgettable. Do you understand that word? And of course he understood. Maybe better than Harber realises. But to make it unforgettable you have to have the right ingredients, and when Henry had stood half-sloshed in the harbour tavern, gibbering about a flock of eider he'd shot down beyond the Højen light, he took it as a sign from God.

He'd promised Henry a free dinner and a couple of good bottles of wine from Ruth's cellar if he could let him have ten of the birds. Now they're on Henry's balcony getting nicely tender under a fine coating of snow. He'd been round that morning to check them, and there was good flesh on their breasts.

Henry had kept his promise, and it is going to be unforgettable. And this evening with Fru Vibeke will be unforgettable. At least for Fru Vibeke, he's decided.

He can sense ice under the car, and he slows down as he goes into the gentle bend where the lane comes up to the main road. Suddenly it's there. Right in the middle of Fru Vibeke's seductive smile. It leaps into the light, and he feels he has eye-contact for a fraction of a second before it hits the radiator with dull thud. He puts his foot on the brakes: a mistake, because the car sets off like a toboggan at the bend and lands in the ditch.

He cuts the engine and struggles out on all fours. The car's half overturned. What about the deer? He looks around in the dark. Where the hell's it got to?

He walks back a few paces and sees it in the ditch. It's still alive. It's lying writhing with terror in its eyes, just like the humans he's had to witness writhing in ditches. It's trying to drag itself up on its fore-legs.

Shit, he whispers, as he gets out his phone. He must ring Lis. She's sober. Lis will have to call the recovery truck. And he must put the deer out of its misery, before it turns to him with the look in its eyes he knows only too well.

Now he can hear it bleating, as if it would like to get it over with, and he blunders in amongst the spruces and throws up.

7

Despite the late hour, the lights are on in the museum. The paintings from the P S Krøyer retrospective in Bergen have come back, and as always when their paintings have been on a journey, the staff feel slightly elated. And Hanne, the director, has a significant birthday today, so a little table in the large exhibition room is decked with flowers and bottles of good wine from her colleagues.

For the last three days everyone has been working virtually around the clock. But now everything is organised and under control: some items have been checked back into the store, and over the next few days the others will be hung according to a scheme that's been discussed and revised ever since the collection left for Bergen in November. While everything in the Krøyer collection is down off the walls or out of the store, and the archive's been disturbed anyway, they decide to fetch the sketches that Hanne has promised for Knud Harber.

Tine stands by a table spread with birthday presents, her feet aching and her cheeks glowing, listening as Hanne enthusiastically explains how she's been fortunate enough to persuade Knud Harber to give a lecture in the spring. Harber will outline a theme connecting the ruthless love between Marie Krøyer and the Swedish composer Hugo Alfvén – and how it affected P S Krøyer's paintings – to the destructive forces he sees in contemporary young fatalists.

A kind of panic grips the staff when they can't lay hands on the little still life by Marie Krøyer. To everyone's relief, after a long hour of searching, it turns up in a packing case full of frames.

'Well, we won't mention that to anyone', laughs Hanne, opening a bottle of wine from the table.

That's something Tine likes about working in the museum. The wild waves of happiness, and the pride of the staff in their collection. In the spring Anna Ancher's paintings will be going to Stockholm, and Hanne has promised that she can go over with them.

Her boyfriend had rung to find out where she was. She moved in with Bjørn last summer. He rings again now because she's half an hour late. She'll have to go, even though the party has hardly begun.

*

Caught in a sudden blast of wind, the fine snow smashes against the fence around the museum, then moves in circles, like a swirling translucent bridal veil, in the light spilling from the dining room of Brøndums Hotel.

Tine unlocks her bike and places the bouquet of roses Hanne has given her in the basket. She ties an extra knot in her scarf and looks quickly over her shoulder. Bjørn has begun to spy on her. Last time was when she went to handball, and the game had gone on longer than planned because they were enjoying themselves. He could well be doing it again, she thinks.

The going is good through the snow past St Laurence's. With the wind at her back she hardly has to push the pedals. She can't remember the last time she saw the high street completely white. It looks like a fairytale. The little yellow lamps shine out beneath a sky dark with heavy scurrying clouds, and the moon peeps out from time to time, changing the light on the snow.

But she's unhappy. She feels awkward that Bjørn rang her. The others acted as if nothing had happened, but Bjørn kept expressing surprise that she was still there, and in the end it was embarrassing and she had to leave the room to explain. They've been together for eighteen months, but he's begun to say hurtful things. He laughed about her new job as a museum attendant. 'Tine doesn't know the difference between a Kandinsky and Friedlænder's *Weeping child*,' he'd said, and their friends laughed and talked about children and nappies and politics, but instead of being angry she'd felt sorry for him. Bjørn really wants to have a child, to be a father like his friends. For six months they'd tried, but nothing had happened. Only once had he ever hit her: last week, when she made the mistake of saying perhaps he was the one with the problem.

When she reaches the viaduct she gets off her bike and wheels it along by the wall of the churchyard. How's she going to explain to him that they were looking for a particular picture, and it got so late that it's nearly midnight now? And what about these roses?

She leans the bike against the churchyard gate and picks up the bouquet. The roses will only make difficulties, she decides. It was sweet of Hanne, and she's fond of her: she couldn't really refuse them. She certainly can't bring herself just to throw them in a bin or into a garden.

She opens the iron gate and enters a strange white landscape of statuary and crosses distorted by snow shining in moonlight. The stars seem to prick her cheeks, and the frost is hard enough to crunch at every step she takes along the path.

She'll lay the bouquet on the memorial inscribed THOSE WHO DID NOT RETURN. Her father was the last to have his name engraved on the marble plinth.

It's a mistake to think that little children can't hear what's being said, and she'd been listening in the living-room, not understanding what it means when a fishing-boat 'ices up'. But later she realised, and could visualise such a thing for herself. Millimetre by millimetre the ice had crept over every piece of rigging and the mast, and gradually and mercilessly the centre of gravity had shifted while the fishermen fought for their lives, until in a few seconds the vessel had rolled over like a toy boat in a bathtub.

Bouquet in hand, Tine walks down the last stretch of the path between the graves. There's nothing to be afraid of here, she thinks, hesitating, all her senses alert.

When she nears the memorial, she glimpses a flash of light. She stops still, frightened. It was a flash that she can't relate to anything around her. She remains absolutely still in the whiteness and listens, clutching the bouquet, while her heart begins to pound. There's a sound of dry crunching footsteps in the snow down by the chapel, and the squeak of the rusty hinges of the gate and a metallic click.

If it's Bjørn, I'll scream, she thinks and catches sight of a shadow behind a cross. She stiffens. A girl is standing in the darkness behind the cross. A girl in a knee-length coat and a fur hat. Now she recognises her, and her fear subsides, turning into irritation and relief at the same time. It's Soffi.

'What are you doing here?' she asks, and notices the camera.

'What are you doing here yourself?' comes the reply through the darkness.

Tine shakes her head.

'You're nuts,' she says, moving quickly to the memorial stone, and in the instant she lays down the bouquet, her father's name is lit up by a flash.

She's angry now. Angry because she was frightened, and angry because that shitty little Copenhagener has chosen this very evening to be hanging around the graves.

'CARL ÅGE TVEDE,' reads Anne Sofie over the bouquet. 'Is that your father?'

'No, it's Father Christmas.'

'I'm sorry if I scared you.'

Tine softens a little. She knows that Soffi is the daughter of the Permanent Secretary, who's one of the museum's trustees and owns the long white house in Østerby. When they were children she'd often see her in the summer, with her straw hat and her nose in the air, sitting in the back of her father's big black Mercedes. The worst of it is that her slow-witted half-brother Sonny was in love with Soffi then, and probably still is.

'Have you just got here?' she asks.

'Yes.'

Tine doesn't know what else she can say. It's a bit cold to stand around, and she's uneasy with Soffi, who seems to see right through her with her cat-like eyes peering out from under her fur hat.

Suddenly Anne Sofie's face lights up with a smile.

'I saw a ghost just before you got here. I took a picture. I want to see how he comes out on the film. People say they never come out. Isn't it weird? What the eye can see, and how the film reacts chemically, are obviously different. What do you think?'

Tine resorts to smiling.

'It's true,' says Anne Sofie. 'He came sneaking down towards me from the chapel, as if he'd just opened the lid of his coffin.'

'Have you got any other good stories?' asks Tine, though at the same time a doubt nags at her. She herself had caught sight of something in the darkness, and heard the click of the gate. In fact she's surprised she's still standing here. The snotty little Copenhagener has something repellent and at the same time attractive about her.

'Have you seen your brother lately?'

Tine shakes her head.

'If you see him, say hello from me.'

'I'm not going to do that. Bye.'

Tine turns on her heels and goes straight towards the gate.

'Maybe it wasn't a ghost I saw,' calls Anne Sofie from the darkness. 'Maybe it was only some idiot who'd gone mad in here. Or just someone who was feeling ill, or maybe someone who wanted to see what you were doing in here. Maybe someone you know.'

Tine half turns and looks towards Soffi. Really she doesn't need to be afraid of her, but she has those burning eyes, and she says things you never expect, and worst of all she hangs out with her half-brother Sonny, who's nuts too.

She's sat down on the sheltered side of the monument, and she's opening her camera-case.

Tine goes back.

'Are you sure?' she asks.

Anne Sofie shrugs her shoulders. She deftly changes the film in her camera.

'Well, you could take a look round and see if one of the graves has opened. If not, I've got him here,' she says, and pats her camera-case.

Even Tine has to smile at this. She kicks the snow a little, as if she has something on her mind.

'Someone came here on the train this afternoon,' she says. 'He goes round in a huge black parka jacket. He's staying at Brøndums Hotel.'

'Who is he?' says Anne Sofie, getting up.

'He got here this evening. You know Iben, who works in the fast-food place. Erik goes around with her. She spoke to him. He wanted to know the way to Brøndums Hotel.'

Tine stands absently for a while, and Anne Sofie shakes her head, as if she hasn't understood at all.

'What are you trying to say?'

'Iben said he was really nice.'

'Nice,' says Anne Sofie. She takes Tine's arm and turns her just a little, so the moonlight catches her face. Then she takes a step backwards, lifts her camera, and takes a picture without flash. Just the dry mechanical sound: ker-lick.

Tine accepts this treatment and looks in front of her.

'Nice,' repeats Anne Sofie, and brushing a lock of hair from Tine's forehead, she places a gentle hand under her chin to lift her head a fraction towards the moon. She takes three quick pictures one after the other.

'Nice,' she says again, this time so quietly that it's almost inaudible, and Tine smiles dreamily.

'And your boyfriend. Is he nice too?'

Tine looks up in alarm.

'If I were you, I'd give him rat poison,' whispers Anne Sofie. 'You can get it anywhere. Or a quick slash through the throat. Problem over.'

Tine looks in horror into her eyes. She's shaken by the seductive tone of her voice. Quickly she turns and goes straight back towards the gate. As soon as she reaches the grille she turns, out of breath, and shouts:

'You're a pervert. That's what you are. Even if you're so shitty posh. Everyone knows who you are.'

Once Tine is wheeling her bike by the viaduct, she regrets what she's said. It wasn't necessary to say 'everyone knows'. It isn't like her to make that sort of remark, and now she's nearly in tears. In fact they'd been talking about Soffi at the museum that evening, because Steen had seen her in Firenze, when he went in to order a pizza, and Hanne had laughed at all the talk about her, and had declared that she was an artist.

She starts to cry. What will Bjørn say if he sees she's been crying? She stops, burrows in her handbag for a tissue, and dries her cheeks and eyes.

Anne Sofie walks towards the chapel, where the ghost came from, and follows the tracks to the gate. At the traffic lights a car slides by in the salted slush, and the driver gives her a wave, though she doesn't recognise him in the dark.

She carries on past St Laurence's church and stops at the entrance to the yard of the pub. A single car is parked there, and a few cycles are heaped against the fence.

Through the fuggy windows facing the yard she can see people playing billiards. The usual for a deadly Tuesday evening. Middle-aged men, every one of them old enough to be her father. They're absorbed in the intricacies of the game and in each other's idiosyncrasies, fuddled to the blissful point where everything seems to betoken a deeper meaning that they can't quite grasp. Banished are the humiliations of the working day, the hangovers, the bellyaches, the interrogations at the job centre or the factory.

But that's Henry in there. And Poul and the fellow who was on the train. Mr Nice. Tine's dream-guy. There he is, smiling awkwardly, as Henry explains about the different corners of the billiard table. He's listening and nodding, and she has the feeling that he'd rather be somewhere else.

She goes on towards the high street, which has an impoverished air in the light from the shop windows with their yellow 'sale' posters.

Tine really couldn't control herself, she thinks, but she only wanted to wake her up. Wake her from the Sleeping Beauty slumber she's fallen into. The rose of Skagen, as the secretly enamoured Frode likes to call her. And the rose was quite willing when she photographed her – as if Tine knew about the beauty she keeps hidden in her sulky face. And now she's living with that middle-aged idiot from Ålborg who can play a few things on his guitar. She'd met him at the festival two summers ago, and now he's bought a house, and since then her smile has completely vanished. Anne Sofie knows all about Tine. Frode has told her everything.

As Anne Sofie puts her hand on the gate, she glimpses a figure further down the road, by the driveway of Gahm's villa. She notices him by chance, because her eyes were caught by a plastic bag blown with the drifting snow across the street.

He's drawn himself into the darkness against the hedge. She too remains perfectly still. Can it be an optical illusion? The outline of a person shaped by the hedge? If not, he'll make a movement. There's nothing there. Only the wind and the snow blowing like a veil down the road.

It is a person. She's almost sure of it. A tall man. He's standing quite still and looking towards her. She holds her breath. If it isn't her imagination, he must eventually make a movement. Lift an arm, or shift his weight from one foot to another. To be certain she must keep frozen-still without blinking. Now she sees him move. Very slowly the shadow turns and disappears behind the hedge.

She opens the gate and scampers to the door. Where's the key? She rummages frantically in her pockets until she finds it.

She locks the door behind her and stops in the middle of the living room with her heart pounding. Under the streetlight she can see the gate and the roadway. She doesn't remember ever being frightened before when she's been alone in the house. But something isn't quite as usual. For nearly half an hour she stands staring out at the gate and the snow-covered rose-bushes, before her anxiety gradually subsides and she draws the thin linen curtains, and switches on the light over the table.

8

Mikkel's been dreaming of eider. Soft warm eider duck, falling limply from the ceiling and lying over him like a heavy duvet. In his dream he's had to crawl on his hands and knees to the door, which was locked. He found a tiny gap under the door, and shouted as loud as he could, but no one could hear him – feathers and down got into his mouth and caused the choking sensation which must have woken him. He lets himself fall back on the pillow with a sigh, relieved to be alive.

It got rather late yesterday. He went to the pub with Henry, while Dorte's sharp reproaches were still hanging in the air. Henry had his sleeping-bag with him: Mikkel gathered that he'd be sleeping aboard his boat.

They couldn't find much to talk about, and simply walked side by side in the dark, hunched in silence against the driving snow. When they reached the steps into the pub, Henry put a hand on his shoulder saying that he shouldn't pay too much attention to all that about his aunt falling asleep on a bench. Up here things could quickly get exaggerated.

The heavy brown curtains are drawn back, and the sunshine sits in sharp squares on the walls. He closes his eyes again and notices the faint sound of something going on in the corridor. Someone's whispering. The wind has dropped. It's nearly nine. In Mexico it's two o'clock in the morning. They're asleep. It's Wednesday.

What have I got to do today? he asks himself. Meet the caretaker at his aunt's flat. Henry had the impression that she didn't owe anyone anything, except for a few little debts here and there that people would probably write off. Later he would have to call in at the parish office, and see the undertaker and the priest.

With a bit of logistics he ought to be able to get everything fixed up today, and perhaps, just perhaps, there was a chance he could persuade Henry to take charge of the funeral. Slightly ashamed of the calculation, he takes a guess at what he might pay Henry to take responsibility on his family's behalf. A suitable round figure withdrawn on his parents' credit card and handed over in a brown envelope. Then he could be sitting on the train again in the evening, be up for the party at Astrid's on Friday, and ready at the airport on Saturday morning.

All his prejudices about provincial life had been confirmed yesterday evening when he'd gone into the town with Henry to say hello to Poul. Not a soul was about, and the Old Town was so dark it looked as if it was in the grip of a power cut. Two drunks and the barmaid at the bar, and two Poles, still in their overalls, at the billiard table. Just as Henry had predicted, Poul was sitting pushing coins into a fruit-machine when they came in and Henry introduced him.

Around closing-time one more customer turned up. A man in his late thirties with dark curly hair, a foreign accent, and a plaster on his forehead. It was Zeppo, the man Henry had mentioned earlier that evening: the Zeppo who'd spoken up for the eider duck. Zeppo was with them for the last game of billiards, while the barmaid was ostentatiously putting the chairs up on the tables. At about two in the morning he'd struggled back to the hotel, freezing cold and giddy with beer and shorts, his fingers totally dead without his gloves, which he'd left in the muddle in Henry's house.

No one's expecting me to give an address at the funeral, he thinks. I didn't know her. Or hardly knew her.

Under the lime-caked shower, the feeling of choking subsides at last. For a long while he lets the needles of water prick against his scalp while he considers how much a funeral might cost, and what he might get done today. Flowers. He mustn't forget flowers. A notice in a newspaper. And what about the funeral address, if the priest finds out that she possibly took her own life? And then there's the coffin and the urn, and when it's all going to take place, and who her friends are, and what about the reception Henry has in mind, and where should that be held: and would that would be at his parents' expense as well? And why was it so important to his mother that he should come here, when his aunt had been more or less airbrushed from family history?

'Henry,' he says out loud, so his voice echoes round the bathroom. 'I fear I have to return home. I have an extremely important assignment that I'm obliged to prepare. Here's 3000 for your trouble. The coffin and headstone are charged to my account with the undertaker.'

Mikkel rehearses the speech in a less forthright version until his face becomes a blur behind the steam gathering on the mirror.

*

Out of nothing, the picture slowly emerges on the paper, as Anne Sofie carefully tips the tray so the liquid glides evenly over the surface. The high forehead, the prominent eyebrows and that sulky set of the mouth. Tine. Her face is slightly lifted, and the moonlight falls softly on her cheeks.

That's a good one, she thinks, and takes it gently from the fluid and hangs it on a clip over the table.

Then she comes back to the picture of the ghost, who had stood near the chapel, rigid and hunched like the devil himself. He's too far away, but she glimpses a scarf caught in the wind.

She gets out more developing paper and focuses, so that she has only the face on the paper. Four seconds and quickly into the bath, and now the hand appears with the right side of the face and the single eye, grainy and underexposed. The lower part of the face is hidden by the scarf, and it's impossible to see who he is. She stares at the head and at the hollow round the single eye. They darken to a kind of death-mask before they completely blacken, eclipsed in the remorseless reaction of the chemicals.

Is it maybe the same figure who stood in the darkness down by Gahm's driveway, when she came home last night?

With a certain unease she develops the other pictures from the churchyard and dries them gently with a small hair-dryer. She's annoyed that the picture of the ghost didn't come out. It happened too quickly. He came out of nowhere, and she had the wrong lens. The focus is on a white marble cross in the foreground.

As a photograph it's interesting in itself. As she'd joked to Tine, you could decide that here's a good old-fashioned ghost, except that he's quite definitely caught on the film, even if trying to identify him is useless.

She thought about Tine last night and couldn't get to sleep. Later she'd dreamt of the shadow by the hedge, and was woken by the sound of the gate shutting. She went down and sat for nearly two hours with a blanket around her and her ear straining towards the door, convinced that he was prowling round outside the house. When she awoke in the morning she went straight out to look for tracks in the snow. But no one had been in the garden.

9

'E K Keldberg,' it says on the door in small white plastic lettering. The door itself is rather battered, and below the letterbox is a small hole made by some sharp object. Across the doorway to the living-room hangs a bead curtain through which he can see a stocky, dark-haired man wearing blue canvas trousers shuffling through some papers.

'I'm Mikkel,' he says, holding out his hand.

'I'm Ole. I'm the caretaker.'

Mikkel looks round the living-room. He's not sure what he'd imagined. Certainly not an elegant black Hornung & Møller piano against the wall. Above a low coffee table hangs a lamp with a red shade, overlooked by a black and white poster of Janis Joplin. The dining-table is by the window, and on the window-sill some colourful carnival masks are tastefully arranged between two candlesticks.

He realises that he's the only person entitled to open drawers and cupboards. He's the family. He's the next of kin. That's why he's there.

'What happens to all her stuff?' he says.

'When you've been through everything we'll have a talk about that. Whatever your parents aren't interested in can go out for recycling. I should think that piano will cover the cost of the funeral.'

'Where did she get it from?'

'From a friend who worked at the factory. She died afterwards of cirrhosis.'

The caretaker goes to the piano and sits down.

'Nothing wrong with this,' he says, and plays a few notes, as if Mikkel hasn't appreciated the quality of the instrument. Then he settles a little more comfortably on the stool, tries a few crisp chords and begins to play. Cautiously at first, as if the piano might collapse under his hands, but from the gentle beginning the music suddenly develops into something lovely and familiar, while his thick fingers dance over the keys as if he's done nothing else all his life.

Mikkel takes a seat in a sunbeam by the dining table, and the music fills him with a sad feeling of being alone.

So it's here that she held her alcohol-fuelled parties, he thinks. Lived her life. Burnt her candle at both ends like Janis above the sofa. Here amongst the cigarette burns on this table she'd sat and written to his father about a loan, here she'd laughed and wept, smoked her joints and drunk an impressive quantity of beer.

He can remember the day of his confirmation now as if it were yesterday. The day, and the church, the host lying dry on his tongue, and a hand heavy on his head. Snatches of the obligatory speeches at the dinner. His father's insistence on a sense of responsibility and the duties one must perform before one can enjoy oneself.

Sometime after the dessert the guests took the chance of stretching their legs before coffee. Smoke a little. He'd felt that the party was about everything except him.

Aunt Ellen, who had been placed right at the end of the long table amongst the older children, where she was least conspicuous, had got up and gone over to him. She had sat in his father's place and held on to him; she had looked at him and kissed him on the cheek with the insistent affection of the Greenlanders, and had said that he had lovely eyes. That was the moment when someone had taken the photograph.

Here in the winter sunbeam, with the indescribable delicate sound of the piano, the confirmation dinner shines clearly in his mind, and he remembers that day as one of the worst in his entire childhood.

After a few moments the room falls silent. The caretaker gets up from the piano with a blissful smile on his face.

'He could certainly turn the stuff out.'

'Who?'

'Mozart. Would you like to take a look at your aunt?'

'Take a look at my aunt?'

The caretaker nods towards the door to the bedroom.

'She's lying in there.'

'Get away,' says Mikkel, looking for the glint in the caretaker's eye that might indicate a bad joke.

'The police were here yesterday. They dug out all her documentation. The autopsy will be in Ålborg, but there's apparently a bit of a queue this week. They won't come for her until tomorrow at the earliest.'

'Why an autopsy?'

'It's quite usual when people die alone. To be sure there was no foul play.'

Now he understands why Poul's so worried, why the caretaker has left all the windows open, and why it feels like a cold-store in here.

The caretaker opens the bedroom door.

'There's nothing to be afraid of,' he says. 'She looks quite nice.'

He's never seen a dead body before. Except of course in films and in photographs, but never like now. She's lying on the bed in a stylish dark blue silk dress, with her arms crossed over her chest. She's as small as a schoolgirl, and her face is waxen white and peaceful.

'Yes, she fell asleep on a bench down by the church,' says the caretaker. 'That's really not advisable, when it's ten or twelve below zero.'

'Do the police know that?'

The caretaker pauses while he considers the question.

'Not unless someone tells them.'

Mikkel sighs. He has a pain in his stomach. He doesn't really know what he expected to find when he arrived up here. He'd maybe meet a few people who knew his aunt. Listen to a few reminiscences. Sit in church and sing a couple of hymns. People would ask who he was, and what he did. He would be a breath of air from the big city. Something like that. But not this.

With downcast eyes he goes back to the dining-room table.

'OK, what now?' he asks.

The caretaker notices his discomfort.

'How old would you be?'

'I was twenty-three on Friday.'

'It does seem a bit much that you've got to organise it all.'

Mikkel takes a deep breath and the caretaker thumps a friendly hand on his shoulder.

'Just decide what you're going to keep, and we'll take it from there. I'll help you with the rest. My number's on the table there.'

'Thanks,' he says.

It's so cold here, and with his dead aunt in the bedroom he'd rather make a quiet getaway when the caretaker leaves. But he needs to go through her cupboards and drawers for papers and valuables. That's what he's here for. It's about checking for bequests and debts, his mother had said.

He's been left on his own. Just the caretaker's faint whistling as his footsteps recede down the stairs. He surveys the room in resignation.

There's a close atmosphere of a life lived entirely separately from his. He doubts whether aunt Ellen had anything of value apart from the piano.

He opens the top drawer of a chest of drawers and takes out a sketchbook from amongst the tobacco and candles and odds and ends. It's full of portraits of people she knew, drawn in pencil and charcoal. 'Poul' is written under a smiling oaf with a cigarette hanging from his mouth, and there's one of Henry, portrayed so true to life his picture deserves a place in the museum. There are other portraits too. Her friends, one supposes. He muses at a picture of a young girl with long dark hair. She's sitting at a table laden with bottles and glasses, her head slightly turned, beauty touching her long eyelashes and soft round cheeks.

On the table lies his aunt's social security card. A bank statement. The lease on her flat. A passport, a slip of paper with his father's name and phone number, and a leather purse. The statement shows a balance of forty-two kroner. Not quite skint then, when she died, he thinks wistfully. Why does he know nothing? Why didn't they prepare him for the fact that she had a life like anyone else? Friends and acquaintances. Why didn't they tell him that she could draw? Maybe she was musical too. Perhaps that was why her friend gave her the piano.

From deep within the space where one's first experiences are recorded, and where every subsequent event is hidden and forgotten, he remembers her as she laid her hand on his shoulder. Grief presses through his diaphragm and unfolds like a feeling that he's lost something, and he simply wants to weep.

10

Anne Sofie has her material laid out on the long table. The black and white self-portraits are arranged in the order she'll show them to Knud Harber in the afternoon. She puts back in her portfolio the colour proofs on tissue paper, with their blue-black and orange colouring in thin strokes of oil-paint. She'll show him those only if he asks to see them. She mustn't seem too keen.

She holds up the portrait of the ghost in the churchyard and studies it for the umpteenth time. All she can see amongst the crosses is a dark silhouette. Frode had said that Tine's bloke was a jealous type, that he followed her when she was in town, and that he hit her.

She spends a long time gazing at the hunched figure. What she finds disturbing is the absolute certainty that this is not Tine's boyfriend. It looks as if he's wearing a sort of one-piece track-suit or boiler-suit. Perhaps the kind of Helly Hansen that all the fishermen go out in when it's cold. Tine's boyfriend never wears a Helly Hansen.

'Soffi,' calls someone from the road. She puts down the picture and draws the curtain aside. It's Sonny. How did he know that she was back? Hardly from Tine, his half-sister: she's ashamed of him.

He's leaning against his red Toyota, screwing up his eyes against the sun. Ears sticking out, crew-cut hair, and a trail of tattoos leading from one ear down his neck and under the collar of his half-open crimson bomber jacket. It's the same Sonny she used to boss around in the garden when they were children. Sonny, who used to live just down the road with his uncle, the butcher. Sonny, who was so strong for his age that he used to carry her on his back over the dunes to Sønderstrand beach because the lyme grass caught at her tender legs. She would pull at his right ear and he would turn right, his left ear and he'd turn left. Sonny used to go to the special needs class at the Kappelborg school, and she tried to teach him to read when she was playing at being a strict schoolteacher.

She puts on her boots and grabs her coat.

He stands fidgeting impatiently like a child who can't wait to say something important.

'Krille's dead, Soffi.'

The temperature's so low that his breath steams white as he talks. She takes hold of the zip of his jacket and zips it up.

It's a catastrophe: she can see that. It was Krille's house he always went to when no one else would let him in. When he'd gone too far. When he'd lost control of himself. At Krille's there was always some kind of party going on, if one could call it a party, when more than three people got intoxicated together.

'I know,' she says, 'Henry told me.'

Sonny screws up his eyes and takes a deep breath. She looks at him. It's as if he doesn't know how he's going to cope with the gap in his feelings. It isn't anyone's fault. There's no one he can hold responsible. No one he can beat up for it.

She gets into his rusty Toyota, knowing full well that they won't be going anywhere. They'll drive around for half an hour just because she's come back. Although he's never been in a position to take his driving test, he demonstrates his car-handling skills with a U-turn in the road, which is so icy that the car spins round completely before the wheels get a grip on the surface. With the few of his teeth that haven't yet been knocked out, he gives a grin.

They do their usual drive out of town to Højen, where Sonny parks by the Sunset snack bar. The clouds are patchy, and the sunlight sharp and white. They sit in the warm while Sonny has a cigarette, and survey the swollen grey sea with the surf breaking on the icy-smooth fringe of the beach. At every break of the foam on the shore the black gravel is sucked back into the grey seawater. Further out, beyond the mist from the spray, lie the ships seemingly strung together, not making any noticeable movement, though if you look away for a couple of seconds they've advanced a little further, like the minute-hand of a clock – north towards Grenen Point, or west towards the ocean.

Sonny smells of salt and fish. This must be his lunch-break.

'Look,' he says, pointing, and she bends forward towards the windscreen, as they watch two wild geese, their wings outstretched and their feet forwards, come in to land on the beach. The geese are taken by surprise by the ice and slide along on their rumps before they quickly regain their balance, like children on skates, only to run into some snow and roll over like two shuttlecocks.

Sonny thumps the steering-wheel in gleeful hysterics and she laughs too, because he foresaw the hilarious outcome before their antics unfolded.

They sit for half an hour listening to the pulsing rhythm of music while he talks about the harbour and his work at the factory, his friends, who has done what with whom since she was last here, who he's afraid of, and who he has a score to settle with. As she listens she knows that it's only with her that he's able to talk in long fluent sentences without a stammer, because unlike everyone else she never gives people advice.

*

They drive back into town and down to the harbour, past the shipyard and right out to the lighthouse point and back along Østerbyvej. She lets herself be taken around. It's so simple. It's what he wants, just to go for a drive with her. She sits, small and cool by his side, picking up his slang, her accent changing imperceptibly from the refined tones of north Zealand to the slightly slow local speech. Everyone they go past is an idiot. That fat one on the moped with the box on the back is the biggest idiot of them all, and Sonny gives him a blast of his horn.

'See you,' she says, getting out.

The long low house is half hidden behind a luxuriant snow-covered hedge of wild rosebushes. In the snow-decked lyme grass in front of the house stands a dilapidated rusty swing. The moment she opens the gate she sees Sigvardtsen in the garden. She stiffens.

Sigvardtsen peers with curiosity over her shoulders as Sonny speeds away throwing up a cascade of salted snow behind him. It irritates her that Sigvardtsen has seen her with Sonny. What Sigvardtsen knows, Helene knows.

She goes briskly to the door and opens it.

'I've put a fresh rubbish-bag in the bin,' he says, approaching and touching his cap.

'Thank you,' she says drily, stamping the snow from her boots.

'Is the water heater OK?'

She turns in the doorway, looking at him briefly as last night's nightmare returns. She has an inner struggle to prevent herself from expressing the fear she had then.

'I got Frode to fix it this morning.'

Before Sigvardtsen manages to answer she shuts the door. The gardener unnerves her. She's seen him with Helene when they were alone: when Holger was away travelling. The intimacy. Sigvardtsen will ruin everything if she's not careful, she's convinced of it. She can see it in his water-blue eyes.

Get yourself into a better mood, she thinks, as her heart begins to thump in her chest. Music: she must play some music. Play it loud. She kneels in front of the bookcase and chooses a record at random. Her hands are shaking as the lowers the needle onto the disc. The music is powerful and pompous, with drums and strings moving quickly upwards in excited staccato towards a climax.

Now for Knud Harber and the meeting at the factory, she thinks. She dances around on the spot until she's giddy, while the music, out of its usual context, has the same effect as a bucket of icy water over her head. It puts an end to stupid thoughts.

Sigvardtsen's playing with fire, she whispers breathlessly as she spins round and round. He's playing with fire.

11

A rusty beam falls from the ceiling. It smashes down on the concrete floor with a metallic yowl before bouncing several feet into the air and crash-landing flat. Dust rises in the room.

Knud Harber looks up at the two builders. When everything's finished by the end of June, this place will be the equal of galleries he's seen in London and New York, but nowhere else.

But his feelings about his project are ambivalent. He loves pictures. The unfathomable miracle in the effect of a line. The inexplicable authority of a single colour sweeping aside all doubt. When he was younger and sixty kilos lighter, he'd walked the shoes off his feet in Chelsea and Williamsburg and from 10th Street to 26th Street. He'd met the patrons – property developers usually – who could see the profit in letting places cheap to artists as a way of gentrifying an area. He'd supped with the philanthropists, the wealthy widows and the speculators trying to foresee the future. He'd sat late into the night at Rose's on 12th Street and seen Dylan come round the corner with a girl on each arm. He'd drunk himself senseless with artists who could hardly afford to eat, yet who five years later were exhibiting in the world's most prestigious museums. Armed with the knowledge and insight he'd brought back from those years, he's hardly ever been wrong in valuing a work.

Art is absolute, even if some people maintain the opposite. But times are changing. There's suddenly a shameless demand in the market, an unhealthy competition. It's partly due to spiralling valuations around certain well-established but burnt-out names; and partly to the new generation of dealers in pin-striped suits who've been aggressively promoting certain younger painters whose talent he fails – with the best will in the world – to see.

First he was disappointed at the lack of respect for the substance of art, and then he was offended, and then he got drawn into the debate, only to be sidelined as a misanthrope. Harber the misanthrope. Of the possible explanations for that epithet, the best was that it was character-assassination by a rival; the worst was that it was ignorance.

In an art-world that was becoming ever more dubious, the strategy was banal but effective. If someone will give fifty thousand for Jannik Sørensen's *Utopia*, then Jannik Sørensen is an artist. He didn't buy that theory, and he'd let that be known in a newspaper article which had nearly cost him a libel suit: he'd suggested that the price of paintings was being driven up by a veritable circus of dealers using onward sale guarantees until in the end the pictures were dumped on the dull-witted cultural committee of some local council in Jutland at a price that could only be described as farcical. In protest he'd looked across the Atlantic to the young Black painters, mortgaged his little paradise in the Old Town in Skagen and mounted an exhibition in Copenhagen's Bredgade which was rubbished by the critics, and in the middle of that perfect storm he'd lost a court case about the rent.

The idea of the gallery here, where two seas meet, took shape one evening in August as he stood beside the Sunset snack bar in the Old Town. He had hidden himself away in his house behind the dunes, and in his plight of near-ruin he had licked his wounds and mulled over his future. Then and there, as the red sun settled on the horizon, he'd suddenly realised that the days of honest enthusiasms were finally over. This was the last dance. Skagen had entered its mercenary phase, from which there would be no going back. The thought came to him that the sky, and the red blush of the sun in the silver-blue sea, and the sand and the wind, would of course endure for ever. But the rest would change dramatically, both in spirit and in the imagination. The generation of young nouveau riche event-promoters, property developers, financial speculators and advertising executives who've moved into the little fishermen's cottages south-west of the town have already been everywhere. They've done their Christmas shopping on Fifth Avenue, they've seen the sun rise over Angkor Wat, and every experience the world has offered them has simply confirmed to them that they belong here. This place is theirs, just as the Côte d'Azur belongs to the French.

And he suddenly understood how simple it was. What they hunger after, what they'll pay anything for, is what they cannot buy with their money. They want to smell the paint, to hold the brush. They want to party with the artists like the patrons in the old days. Some might say it's for the love of it, but he judged that what they're really looking for is something more like an osmosis. They want to get into the artist's soul and feel what the artists feel.

Encouraged, he had climbed back over the dunes and down to his house, where he set down his thoughts in writing, terrified that he might forget them. As the weeks went by the idea of the gallery came into being. He would replicate the golden age. The new patrons would have someone to see themselves reflected in. Someone to drink a toast with.

He had chosen the painters with care. Hans August Joensen from the Faroes, Harald Eskelund and Tobias Dalmann from Norway, and Janick Söderholm and Sabrine Holm from Sweden. The Danes would come unbidden, he foresaw. His five artists shared certain qualities: their youth, their self-confessed poverty, and their partiality to burgundy.

He had sought each of them out and assembled them in the dramatic setting of Torshavn last winter, and told them straight off how he saw the world going nowadays. 'Hip hip hurrah,' said Sabrine Holm, just before she keeled over. Grey sand and cubist houses in tasteful contrast with the sea; colours and optimism, everything tastefully dreamlike: just add their innate talent, plus parties and fireworks. Those were the conditions, and they would be rich: and if anyone could stamp the mark of approval on these young opportunists and turn back the clock, it was him. And if he didn't do it, someone else would be ready to.

When springtime arrived he'd promoted these young Scandinavians as powerfully and urgently as a new antibiotic. He'd written countless articles and got others to do the same. He'd used his connections to persuade a distinguished producer to do a whole series of television features, and he'd set rumours flying. He'd hinted at a suicide attempt and a personality disorder. And he succeeded in making the Young Scandinavians, as he consistently called them, interesting to a much wider circle, and any of their works already in circulation soon doubled in value.

Knud Harber looks at his watch. He's almost finished with the architect, but he does have one more appointment which irritates him. Holger Strand, from the top of the Ministry of Culture, has a daughter who's coming to show him some photographs. Otto Bremer had introduced the girl to him during a weak moment he'd had in Hviids, where he'd just revealed the programme for his exclusive summer gallery. He'd gathered that Otto was a good friend of Strand's, and although he was deeply disinclined, he chose not to show it. Otto Bremer's judgement of the Young Scandinavians when the exhibition opens in the summer will not be insignificant.

The architect appears from a room somewhere, with a roll of drawings under one arm and a cigar clenched in his mouth. Harber shakes his hand. They agree about most of the proposals. They agree about rather too much, thinks Harber, who would actually like to make a minor objection. But the man's reliable, and he keeps the local builders at it, and time is money.

12

In the undertaker's window is an artistic display of whimsical structures made of flotsam from the shore. Plastic bottles, lengths of string and pieces of wood sharpened by the sand have all been transformed into fantastic trolls, the kind every child dreams about. Beneath them, dried seaweed and mussel shells are scattered over sand from the beach.

Hanging from two thin wires is a portrait of the artist, a young man with a peaked cap, a red beard and an Icelandic sweater. The label says 'Paw Johansen'. On the opposite side of the window is a more colourful poster, a picture of two older people with a golden retriever sitting between them. The sky is blue and the field full of yellow flowers. The poster says: 'Keep memories alive in simple beauty'. On the sand under the poster is an urn surrounded by Paw Johansen's mussel shells.

Inside the parlour there's a smell of something like soap, or maybe insecticide, he thinks. The undertaker introduces himself as Jantzen. He's in his mid-thirties, rather younger than Mikkel had expected an undertaker to be. Tall and pale, with his hair combed back and gelled, he's wearing a coffee-coloured velvet suit with gold buttons. He extends a hand. It's soft. Mikkel introduces himself as Ellen Keldberg's nephew, and as he explains, briefly and fairly incoherently, the reason for his parents' absence, he realises it sounds like an apology.

The undertaker looks at him in slight surprise but listens and nods attentively. After a sigh and a deep intake of breath he asks who will be paying for the occasion. Mikkel reassures him with a wave of his parents' credit card, and Jantzen pulls out a chair in front of a highly-polished desk, inviting him to take a seat while he produces some brochures from a drawer.

Mikkel flicks through them. Colour photographs of coffins with various draperies and ornamentation and in different types of wood. Oak and fir, the 'statesman' model in mahogany and the 'traditional' in white-painted pine. He learns that there's a wide range of qualities for the lining too. Jantzen points out that they also have an environmentally friendly model which is becoming quite popular.

'How exactly is it environmentally friendly?' asks Mikkel, and Jantzen explains about the wood treated with raw linseed oil, the lining made of recycled paper, and the paint which is free of any additives not approved by EU regulations. He's tempted to enquire whether the other coffins don't comply with EU regulations, but he leaves the question unasked.

Mikkel leafs again through the brochure, noticing at random that there are coffins for children, and it strikes him that the undertaker must constantly be seeing the gravity of death in the faces of the living, and has therefore assumed an attitude of reserved composure.

'Nowadays people usually prefer to be cremated', explains Jantzen, as if he's discerned by intuition that this young man has little idea of funeral procedures. 'People can't bring themselves to think of being eaten by worms. Apart from the question of the groundwater.'

These matters haven't crossed Mikkel's mind, but he can see that a layer of bodies decomposing two metres underground must inevitably pollute the groundwater.

'Of course,' he says. 'Clearly. We must protect the groundwater.'

Jantzen becomes absorbed for a moment in a leather-bound notebook, where with a click of his ball-point pen he makes himself a note.

'When you've chosen the coffin, the urn and the flowers, and discussed with the priest or the churchwarden what hymns you're going to have, the rest more or less takes care of itself. And if you'd like a little reception afterwards there are several possibilities. I can arrange that for you. The Seamen's Hostel is the usual venue. Coffee and cake. But I shall need to know by tomorrow at the latest how many will be coming.'

Jantzen pauses briefly and looks at Mikkel to assure himself that he's grasped everything. He continues his explanation in a monotone. 'After the funeral the coffin will be taken to Frederikshavn where the cremation takes place. Then you receive the ashes in the urn you've chosen. A little ceremony in the churchyard is arranged a few weeks afterwards for close relatives and friends. The urn is buried then. Sometime in advance you need to order the memorial stone with the name and wording of your choice. We take care of that, too. Mind you, death brings certain constraints to freedom of speech. You mustn't choose an inscription that might cause offence.'

Mikkel can't help smiling.

'What sort inscription might cause offence?'

'Well, for instance, "Hell, it's hot down here". When you have a rule like that, it's a bit of a moot point as to what might be reasonable, but that's how things are. Or you can choose to keep the urn and bury it in your garden, or scatter the ashes somewhere the deceased has chosen. As long as that won't cause offence to the public. There are restrictions about that, too, but I think they're trying to relax them a bit.'

'What sort of place?'

'A lot of people scatter the ashes out at Grenen Point where the North Sea and the Baltic meet. That's very popular at the moment.'

'I'll have to think about it. I'll come back tomorrow morning.'

'What will you have to think about?' asks Jantzen, his voice suddenly less sorrowful.

'Everything,' says Mikkel. 'Everything.'

With this he gets up and marches resolutely through the door before he's finished putting on his jacket.

It was a little too much all at once. He still hasn't spoken to the priest, has no idea when aunt Ellen's funeral can take place, and as he sat and listened to the undertaker's long-winded spiel he suddenly had the feeling that the man had known he would show up at his parlour.

He takes a deep breath as he zips up his jacket, and walks briskly along the high street where, in a little square, an elderly teacher is making purchases at a cheese van, surrounded by a crowd of youngsters.

There's far more to decide than he'd anticipated. There are dozens of coffins in the catalogue at very different prices, there are different urns, the flowers have to be ordered, he needs to choose the hymns, and what about the priest and the address? While all that is spinning in his head, his mobile buzzes in his pocket. A text from Hanna. He has no wish to answer that now. He's uneasy. She froze to death, but no one seems to know what to do about that. Poul had carried her to her bed, and the police had come. What hymns are appropriate for a woman who sat down to die on a bench?

The entrance to the Co-op is evidently the meeting-place of choice for the women of the town. Their arms flail around their bicycles and pushchairs and prevent anyone from going in or out. He crosses the street to the hot-dog van in the square and asks for a frankfurter. In Brøndums Hotel the recommendation was halibut, he noticed when he left his key at reception, but there's nothing quite like a frankfurter first thing in the afternoon in seven degrees of frost.

A ruddy-complexioned man in the obligatory blue Helly Hansen is staring at him. He concentrates on his frankfurter while he considers setting out to see Henry's daughter: she's the only person

he knows here. He left his gloves there yesterday evening. But maybe not. Dorte has plenty on her plate already.

'Well, look who's here, it's the demon of the billiard table.'

It takes him a moment to realise that he's being spoken to.

'What?' he says, peering at the man's fleshy face.

'It was you playing billiards with Henry and the Crab last night.'

'It certainly was.'

'It was an expensive lesson,' chuckles the man to the hot-dog seller.

Mikkel shrugs.

'And you've come here to bury the Parrot.'

'I don't know what you're talking about,' he replies, pushing his frankfurter round in his ketchup.

'Krille.'

Mikkel gives no more than a nod.

'You were playing billiards with Henry and the Crab and that Serb.'

'So you've just said.'

The ruddy man seems satisfied with his reaction and smiles knowingly at the hot-dog vendor again.

'And she's your aunt?'

'Yes.'

'But I don't see much Greenlander about you.'

By now he's lost his appetite.

'No,' he says, 'I'm strictly the standard model.'

'Ha! Ha!' laughs ruddy-face. 'They say she left a painting in her will. I bet that was worth a penny or two.'

'People say a lot of things.'

'And they say she froze to death.'

Mikkel thrusts the remains of his frankfurter in the bin and hurriedly wipes his mouth with a paper napkin. This is a real idiot, he thinks, angry at the insistent attempts at intimacy. He remembers the fellow now. Flimmer, Henry had called him. He'd sat on his own at a table in the corner while they played. Came out with all manner of half-baked remarks, the kind people only make when they've given up hope of being taken seriously. Poul had been drunk and had been saying that someone or other had been sitting with Krille earlier the evening she died, and he remembers he'd told Zeppo himself about his parents' trip to Mexico and the skiing holiday he'd had to miss. Zeppo had danced around the billiard table with a broad grin on his face and a large sticking plaster on his forehead while he burbled on about Mexican food. The conversation had gone to and fro and the ruddy man had just sat there listening.

But what's all this stuff about a painting? She'd inherited a piano from a friend, he'd gathered. The caretaker hadn't said anything about a painting.

A train of container wagons rumbles across the high street towards the harbour with a shrill scream of steel against steel. When the last one has passed, a pub can be seen on the opposite side of the road. It's closed at the moment, but a notice in the window advertises music tomorrow.

So things do sometimes happen here, he thinks. His stride as he passes the library settles into the aimless rhythm of a walk with no particular destination. He stops at the museum to check the opening hours. He's promised himself that he'll go and see the famous paintings while he's here. That'll have to be tomorrow. While he was standing at the hot-dog van he'd had another text. This time from Jesper, who's messing around with his piece of project work. Jesper the weakest link. Jesper who was only asked to join their team because he's a nice guy. He can't be bothered to reply. What can he say? Hi, it's fantastic here. I've just been to look at a load of coffins.

A listlessness comes over him as he admits to himself that he doesn't know what to do for the rest of the day. Of course he could go and call on the priest, but he has no appetite for that after his interchange with Flimmer. Besides, you probably have to make an appointment.

He feels abandoned: betrayed by his parents, cheated by the undertaker, disregarded by Henry, who has put to sea, and stultified by the town, which looks like every other miserable, bog-standard provincial dump. Just look at the women crowding round the Co-op, and flabby-face at the hot-dog van in his blue romper-suit like an overgrown child. The only thing that idiot needed was a string through his sleeves to stop him losing his mittens.

Henry's right. Rumours are going round, Poul is paranoid, and shy little aunt Ellen is as well known in this town as the mayor. That's really all there is to it. Everything settles like a knot in his stomach. He misses his own city. His neighbourhood. The throbbing crowds of normal people in normal clothes: and for a second time he considers simply sneaking off home. It would be easy, and his parents would probably never find out. He could go back to the undertaker and get him to organise everything. Coffin, urn, flowers, newspaper announcements. Everything.

What did this drunken little aunt ever do for you? he asks himself. Nothing, except to sit down and die on a bench, the very week you should have gone to Val d'Isère. And of course to clasp you in a faded photograph from a decade ago.

He stops to assess his own sense of decency, while he peers at the opening times outside the museum. It clearly meant something to Henry that he's come here. He's certain about that. Likewise to Dorte. And yes, it even meant something to the caretaker who's been so reassuring to him. His presence has confirmed to them that Ellen has a family; that no one is completely alone.

What bullshit, he thinks. She didn't have a family, because her family turned their backs on her – and are sitting at this very moment under the palm trees on a beach, slathering themselves with sun-cream. And she wasn't alone, in any case. As far as he can see she had loads of friends. Even when she sat down to die she wasn't alone. Someone had sat down beside her.

He has a pain in his gut just now. Poul, or the Crab as Henry had called him, had suggested that someone had taken her coat while she sat on the bench and had killed her like that. In his drunken state yesterday evening he was definitely trying to say that. Somebody ought to do something about it. Someone ought to tell the police what happened. Suppose Poul was right?

An elderly couple comes out of the museum. The woman helps her husband zip up his jacket, just as, almost in the same movement, he drops a leaflet into her pocket.

Mikkel decides to fetch his laptop from his room and install himself in Café Jacobs. Vigga had said they've got wifi there. He'll just sit and have a little on-line chat with Simon and Hanna and maybe tweak something in the project work.

As he goes into the lobby he notices a birthday party going on in the dining room. One of the tables sports a solitary Norwegian flag on a silver stick, and a young girl is placed between a middle-aged couple in their smartest clothes. The girl is in a wheelchair, something that ought to make him value his own fitness and health, but instead the girl's arbitrary fate pulls his mood one final degree down to freezing-point.

The street lights make yellow patches in the snow all the way down to Anchersvej, and when he comes out on the road skirting the eastern shore he can see the chimneys of the fishmeal factory. The wind has dropped completely, and their white smoke is near-vertical in the sky.

He's been sitting for three hours in the café and nearly gone blind staring at the work project, making more changes than were called for, probably, before sending it back to Simon.

He walks past some smaller factories and the smoke-house, where people are still at work, before he reaches the harbour. The light is a matt yellow in the mist and the water a glossy black like marble. Out at the end of the pier lies a trawler shining in its own floodlights. He walks towards it. There are people on deck and someone behind the windows of the bridge.

The trawler is being emptied of its catch. It's lying with a slight list, and the mass of fish is apparently being sucked up out of the hold through a system of belts and tubes straight into the factory. Can it be Henry, back early into harbour? He'd said they'd be putting in just before evening: that's a pretty vague time-frame. But no, the trawler is Swedish. It's called *Fjordö*.

Two dockers in orange oilskins are on the deck pressure-washing the aluminium chutes leading down to the hold. He stays a while to watch the process. Everything is slimy smooth, and the work goes on in determined silence against the shrieks of the gulls wheeling widely around them.

The cold is creeping up slowly but surely from the soles of his feet, and he realises that he'll freeze to death himself if he doesn't move on. He decides to go back past the fish-market and down towards the shipyard in the hope of finding a burger bar and a newspaper.

By the first pier a team of fishermen is taking an empty trawler net ashore. The green nylon glitters in the harbour lights as they haul it over the quayside with the help of a truck and spread it out across an area half the size of a football pitch.

He pauses to think, trying to work out what goes where amongst the hard orange floats and the ropes and cables thick as his arm. Suddenly the wind gusts into his face and the snow comes out of the darkness.

It's as if the weather up here changes every three hours. In the morning the sun was keen, and the sky was lofty. Now here comes the wind and the biting cold. He thrusts his hands deep into his pockets, while the wind whistles in the spindly aerial above the bridge. In the middle of everything someone on the bridge turns up the volume of a song by Elvis, and the skipper on watch begins to do the twist on the spot. Laughter spills out over the quay.

13

She lies naked as God created her under the surface of the water. The perfect exposure of the picture is marred only by small dazzles of sunshine from the ice clinging to the edge of the pond. Her hair is dark and flowing, as if in a painting by Munch, and above her pale body a few goldfish are held frozen in the instant, like tiny zeppelins. From her wrist, blood pulses out like a thundercloud, growing larger from one picture to the next, until in the last of the five it entirely covers one side of her body. Around her in the pool lies a collection of electric domestic appliances of every kind imaginable.

Knud Harber is standing in the largest hall in the factory, beside a long sheet of chipboard on a trestle. He examines the black and white photographs by the light of a halogen lamp.

'Have your parents seen these pictures?' he asks, subconsciously putting a value on the scale of the damage.

'The sequence is important,' she says, indicating with her small hands how it should be understood. 'As... as a repetition, as a pattern, but also as a continuum.'

For a long minute Harber simply stands there, his lips pursed.

'The idea is to enlarge them to one metre by two, so you can see the grain,' she says. 'They're not digital. I've got a proof here.'

With a determined gesture she opens her black portfolio and lays the grainy enlargement on the table.

'And they can be broken up into separate pieces like a jigsaw puzzle,' she explains with nervous enthusiasm.

Harber regrets becoming involved in this meeting. The young woman has clearly built up considerable expectations of her journey here. He feels a twinge in his large intestine which releases a muted squeak from his stomach, simultaneously with the heartburn that always afflicts him when he forgets to take his bran in the morning.

This stuff is unsellable, he decides. But the way she has portrayed herself, naked like a sleeping mermaid, delicate and white under the surface, makes her a real pleasure to behold. To cut the vein in her wrist is an affected provocation, he thinks.

She watches him as he looks at her pictures.

'What did your parents think of the – er – concept?'

She shrugs her shoulders with a sigh.

'It's important that the pictures stay in a particular order,' she says. 'The last one's missing, actually. The last one's going to contain an answer, so it complements the first five. Or, if you like, it'll create a contrapuntal balance, if an expression needs to be found for that.'

'A balance,' mumbles Harber over the murmurings of his stomach.

'Yes,' she says, looking at him.

He clears his throat.

'What do you think your pictures express?'

'Contempt and release,' she says. 'But the release is reserved for the last picture.'

Harber gives an almost imperceptible nod and his lips tighten.

'Contempt?'

'One has to react.'

'Against what?'

'Against the liars. Against the falsehood.'

'Who has to react? The girl?'

'Everyone, of course.'

With a weary movement Harber lays the photographs down on the table.

'Your time is coming, Frøken Strand,' he says, expressing all the seriousness he can in the lines of his face.

Your time is coming, he thinks to himself, is both diplomatic and gentle as a rejection. He's used the turn of phrase before, to young painters with the desperation visible on their faces as they tried to read something different into what he's said. By contrast the burnt-out older artists who turned up uninvited at his gallery in Copenhagen usually received the formula that their pictures 'deserved a less conservative space than he was able to offer'.

He can feel the stomach acid right up in his throat now. He didn't manage to get to a chemist for his tablets this morning. A disturbing start to the day. The meeting at the airport had dragged on and on, and the printer in Frederikshavn had made a terrible error on the poster he'd ordered: and then an annoying call from Otto Bremer had reminded him about the appointment with Frøken Strand at the end of the afternoon.

Despite the groaning of his stomach he smiles disarmingly as he speaks of the international artists who, unbeknown to her, have inspired her: Andy Warhol, Man Ray, Caroline Coon, or for that matter the photographers Lorreta Lux and Mari Slaattelid. She's closest perhaps to Cindy Sherman, who, like her, took pictures of herself. But no one can be familiar with the entire field, and when it comes to photography, he's a novice. He's been lucky enough to gain a thorough overview through the study of certain magazines. *Fruits* is essential reading on transatlantic flights, and he and Otto Bremer have seen a few things in the little galleries of Greenwich Village.

He senses at this point that it would be advisable to adopt a cheerful tone, and he hopes the Permanent Secretary's lovely daughter isn't going to break down in a fit of hysterics. If she'd come on her own initiative, unexpectedly and without Otto's recommendation, he might have seen it all in a different light. Not that she doesn't have talent. The talent is obvious. But that reckless perseverance, and that blood, pumping unmistakably from her wrist in a great cloud, massing like an omen of Doomsday on the whole left side of the picture: it has a very unpleasant directness as a subject.

One thing he's clear about: these pictures are not only unmarketable – they'd have his chosen clientele running away screaming, never to return.

Here in Skagen he's going to sell a dream packaged with exquisite craftsmanship. In a few years' time, this entire fishing port and the picturesque old quarter of the town will be converted into a combination of heritage memorial and Scandinavian Las Vegas, encased in an enormous glass bubble, protected from wind and weather so that the season lasts twelve months of the year. That's the way it will go, one can predict it with absolute certainty, and he comforts himself with the knowledge that when that time comes, he himself will be nothing but a breath of wind through an arboretum. Meanwhile he'll make his money on the downward curve, when they simply can't have the genuine article. The desperation she demonstrates in her photographs is disturbing to his vision.

Stepping carefully over some cables which the workmen have left trailing over the concrete floor, he names, *en passant*, the young

Black Americans from Queens who, likewise, are attracted by the theme of death. He feels a certain satisfaction in the thought that they incidentally cost him a small fortune.

'Have you been to New York?' he asks.

'When I was a child, with my father.'

He was going to offer her something to drink, but he changes his mind as his hand reaches the large free-standing refrigerator. At this safe distance he can look at her, without being too obvious about it.

For the moment she's intact, and it strikes him how delicate she is there without her coat, which she took off and, since there was no rack, casually let fall to the floor. In her choice of clothes, timeless. In her movements, like a fallow deer. Her breasts two oranges beneath a chocolate-brown polo-neck mohair sweater. Slender and erect like a ballerina. Short black hair and remarkable eyelashes and – if you're experienced in reading a face – something faintly ethnic about her appearance.

He'd expected a reaction to his refusal, a tearful scene, but she simply regards him with an insistent look, like a cat that's caught sight of a bird, and when he suddenly finds himself at a loss for words a silence falls on the bare factory, bringing a clarity and immediacy to the screams of the gulls round the harbour.

'How old are you, actually?' he asks cautiously.

'Twenty.'

Harber strides back to the table. Her discreet lilac perfume sets thoughts going in his head that he tries to repress. He thinks he's seen her somewhere before. Less than a week ago. Or a month. No, many years ago, which can't be right. He weighs up the pros and cons as he examines the black and white photographs a second time.

She's so bloody young, he thinks. So young that it hurts. With a vulnerability, and a sweetness of breath, that can't be bought for money.

He forgets his rumbling stomach and his heartburn and the sweat which has settled on his neck. That scarcely noticeable smile in the corner of her mouth when he asked about her age made him blush. He can't remember the last time he blushed. The forbidden fruit is the sweetest, he well knows. 'Who dares wins.' He'll make her an offer.

Ostentatiously he holds one of her photographs up to the light, as if he's just noticed something interesting, and with a sigh he weighs the arguments for and against, one final time.

'Would you like to come round for dinner?' he asks, his eyes fixed on the shiny surface of the photograph.

'To dinner?' she says, in evident surprise, unconsciously taking a step backwards.

He puts the picture down and looks at her. He's actually said it now. He knows he's severely overweight and looks like a bulldog, with his wide cheek-bones and somewhat protruding lower jaw. He also perspires strongly in the slightest heat, and has a paunch which his doctor says has displaced his entire digestive system. But after thirty years in the art business he's developed certain instincts, such as the wisdom of pursuing one's luck when one catches sight of it. He's met Holger Strand only once, he calculates swiftly, and Otto Bremer has his own fish to fry. And this delicate orchid, this Venus, is definitely an adult over the age of consent, hard as it may be to believe. A little lightning-bolt of good fortune. With lips that are actually red, because she's young. A sweet, soft plum that he can't possibly reach for without picking.

He turns to her. He lays aside the paternal attitude he greeted her with, and regards her with sober, bloodshot eyes.

'Out at my place, let's say Saturday. We'll have a nice evening with some good food and wine. Then we can have a serious talk about it.'

14

As she walks through the factory gate the snow is falling out of the darkness hard as grit, and it spreads itself like a shroud over everything she has hoped for. In the light of a shop window at the street corner snow is blowing down the length of the street like white wood-smoke, only to change direction abruptly in a sudden gust. To the right shine the orange lights of the harbour, with the gulls like screaming white blotches in the sudden darkness. She's heard that the lights are orange for the sake of the ships: but why, exactly, isn't at all clear to her.

Orange and black, she thinks. Orange and black. Her pictures must be orange and black. That's what she's envisaged.

'What time on Saturday?' she'd asked. She shakes the fantasy away from her as she walks towards the harbour. Past the modern factory where people are still at work. This is where the herring are salted, and her thoughts are disturbed by the sharp, sour odour.

I must keep things separate, she thinks, clenching her hands in her pockets. The little story she told her father the other day about Otto Bremer annoys her. Nemesis, she grumbles, taking a kick at a lump of ice. Black and orange. Harber and Otto. A solitary gull, totally alone, swoops above her in the darkness. Without any reason, it gives a sudden cry like a new-born baby.

Crossing the road she passes a refrigerated truck ready to be loaded. The driver's a lean man in his early forties, wearing a thin suede jacket and clogs with no heels. He clambers down from his cab and walks into the factory office with some papers in his hand. She knows she can get a lift out of town if she turns on the charm. Where to next, mate? Milan, Madrid, Paris, Hamburg?

In other ways, things had started well. On Helene's instructions Sigvardtsen had turned on the heating and the house was warm when she arrived. Tine looked lovely in the pictures, and the ghost looked like death.

She'd been convinced Harber would understand her. She'd been well aware that the transfer technique on to thin tissue paper wasn't original: neither was the method she'd used to colour the black and white photos. No longer does art come into being solely between the idea and the material form. It's a secondary question whether it's created with a paintbrush or by computer graphics, or made to shock with a rusty bicycle wheel or a urinal. Obviously, other people have made collages and photographic prints like hers. Object art, as Harber had suggested. But this stuff is mine and only mine, she'd thought, and it's unique, because I myself am the work.

Why wouldn't Harber understand that?

She shivers in the cold. The only thing she still needs is a final picture. One that releases the first five. She's had some ideas about it.

Someone has put a red shipping container down on the quayside in exactly the place where she enjoys her favourite view over the harbour. The snow has spread to the very edge of the quay, and she eases herself carefully sideways in front of the container.

A small wooden sailing-boat is berthed at the quayside: the *Stella*. Reflected in the windows of the wheelhouse she can see the lights in the Kabyssen café, and she can make out two workmen from the shipyard coming out of its doorway. She hears them laugh.

The mirror effect is disturbing somehow, and she edges a little further on, to get away from the reflection. The surface of the water is black, streaked with thin dark green-and-lilac traces of oil, while against the harbour wall the first ash-grey soft ice of the winter is forming. A little off the bow of the sailing-boat, a dull green plastic drum marked with Cyrillic lettering sticks up through the ice, and further out the harbour lights are reflected in the black surface of the basin like orange stains.

She takes her camera from its case, focuses on the plastic drum and holds her breath, achieving a thoughtful inner peace as she takes a single picture and puts the camera back.

Far out on the other side of the old piers some tall thin chimneys decorated with a blue 'FF' logo stand like cigarettes in a larger and uncertain dimension, with their white smoke drifting in over the town now that the wind has veered to the east. On the opposite side of the basin a vast dark building rules over the blue night. During the summer days of relentless yellow sunshine, it's simply the cement-grey building where rust-red coasters are sandblasted before they're repainted. But here in the winter darkness, in the glow of the orange lights along the pier and in the falling snow, it's a cathedral, and the ship moored in front of it seems suspended on invisible threads.

For a long while she stands watching the gently rocking ship as she tries to make sense of the meeting with Harber. She really ought to go home on Thursday morning: home to Thomas who's going to help her with the pictures. But she also ought to have an exhibition in Harber's gallery in the spring. That's what they'd planned. What had Harber said? A dinner. Then we can have a serious talk about it.

The last word hasn't yet been spoken, she thinks. Harber has his weaknesses. He's sentimental. She could see that as he stood beside the fridge and talked about the Black artists from Queens. Harber can be persuaded.

She screws her eyes up. How exactly are things now? How does Harber remind her of the others?

The psychologist called Bent had asked if she'd like some tea. The psychologist called Gert had nodded in a friendly way. The psychologist called Marianne Schmidt had simply smiled.

I'm an only child. At any rate in the sense that my brother Mads is a psychopath and has been put in an institution. I love him, and I'm afraid of him.

'What do you feel you are?' the psychologist called Bent had asked.

I'm Anne Sofie. An angel. A sophisticated angel who can't bear to be contradicted.

She spoke clearly, there in the clinic, as if she were addressing a packed lecture-theatre, her hand describing a gentle curve, so alluring that Bent followed its movement.

If I'm contradicted, I break into pieces like porcelain. Yes (long pause), *like porcelain.* And the psychologists nodded and smiled or looked offended.

'Imagine that you're someone else, and look at yourself from the outside.'

Now she had to laugh. Here on the edge of the harbour she had to laugh. She knew that trick, which was provokingly stupid. Why on earth should she look at herself from the outside?

I see myself in the awkward and controlled manias of others. In my family's lack of courage, in my teachers' indignation that I was allowed to move up a class, and skived off two months before the last exam. They're the ones who ought to look at themselves from the outside.

It was obvious that the psychologist called Bent was in love with her. She sighs. Knud Harber is neither in love with her nor a psychologist.

She won't forget his bloodshot eyes for a while. Nothing was revealed in that look. Except when she'd just arrived, when she noticed some annoyance. But after that, once he'd collected himself and given her a partial refusal, which was actually the introduction to a proposal, his look was quite inscrutable. It was nothing to do with her pictures, she realised. It was all to do with Otto Bremer. Harber was simply taking his payment. A little dinner on Saturday evening, so we can talk about it. It's me who's going to be the dinner, she thinks, and manages a smile in the midst of a tragedy.

It's cold standing still, and she works her way carefully along the side of the container and crosses the quay to Kabyssen.

'Pork cutlets with vegetables' she reads on the menu. Vegetables, she whispers as she steps into a sweet smell of frying.

A few workmen from the yards are sitting eating. They read their newspapers without speaking. In the corridor towards the toilets some younger ones stand at the fruit machines.

She orders a cup of hot chocolate and takes a seat at the opposite end of the room. While she was standing in the dark on the other side of the container, looking at the dull green oil-drum, she had decided to accept Knud Harber's invitation.

15

As he comes into the café he brings in the icy air, looking about as frozen as she was ten minutes ago. She recognises him from his parka. He was on the train yesterday, and he must be the very same guy Tine was going on about, all starry-eyed, in the churchyard. Mr Nice-Guy.

From her vantage-point in the innermost corner she observes him as he pushes back his hood and unwinds his scarf. He's obviously in the polite category, giving a friendly nod to the shipyard workers in the corner.

He orders today's special and hangs his jacket over the back of his chair. He chooses *Jyllands-Posten* from the heap on the newspaper table and settles down, engrossed in the yellow business pages, until the waitress appears after a surprisingly short time with his food.

She gets up, goes to the newspaper table, choosing a fashion supplement at random, and carries on towards the counter, where she orders another hot chocolate and takes a cheese sandwich from the glass cabinet. She waits until she's been served: then, with the newspaper under her arm, the cup and saucer in her left hand and the plate with the sandwich in her right, she takes care not to spill anything until she's walking past his table, where she lets go of the cup. It smashes on the floor, splashing hot chocolate in a star shape several feet long. She stares at the floor, paralysed, until he puts a hand on her shoulder.

'I'm so sorry,' she says. 'I think there's blood on your trousers.'

Mikkel looks at her in surprise.

'You mean chocolate.'

'Yes, of course,' she says, shaking her head at the slip of her tongue.

'I've been out by the factories,' he laughs, pointing at his jacket, where a gull has left a white streak. 'A bit of chocolate won't make much difference.'

'What the gull leaves brings good luck,' she says. She moves slightly to make way for the waitress. Then the two of them stand like expectant children, devoid of initiative until she's mopped up the chocolate and dried the floor, sighing noisily.

'You were on the train yesterday,' he says, flashing her a broad grin. 'That mad old woman had a real go at you.'

She nods.

'Yes. Sometimes you just run into the wrong people.'

'I'm Mikkel. Have a seat,' he says, and she sits down.

'I'm Anne Sofie,' she says, taking a bite of the green pepper in her open sandwich. 'So you've been down by the factories.'

'Yes, I know a fisherman here, Henry Olsen. I went to see if he was back in harbour yet. They don't fish that far out,' he adds casually, as if he knows all about it.

'Is this your first time in Skagen?' she asks.

He shakes his head as he tackles his food.

'I came here once on a school trip. I've forgotten almost everything about it. We did ride on that funny little train out to Grenen to see where the two seas meet. That's the only thing I remember. How about you?'

She looks at him and considers whether this has been a waste of good chocolate. He doesn't have the touch of madness that Thomas has. He's a bit too nice, too boring. He'd be fine for Tine.

'My parents have a house up here. In Østerby.'

'Østerby,' he repeats thoughtfully, as the waitress sets a fresh cup of chocolate down on the table. 'I'm staying at Brøndums Hotel. I thought it would be the lap of luxury but it's really a crappy old place.' He laughs. 'No television and no internet.'

She lets him eat in peace while she concentrates on her hot chocolate, noticing that he's taking a discreet look at her as she examines a photograph of a silver-coloured dress.

'Are you interested in fashion?'

'A bit,' she says with a nod at his newspaper. 'And you're interested in economics.'

He shrugs his shoulders as he chews.

'Yes and no,' he says. 'I want to work in renewable energy if I can. Something meaningful. That's what I really want to do.'

'Renewable,' she says. 'Nothing's really renewable. Everything's always in a state of change and decay.'

'That's how you see it, is it?' he asks with a smile.

'And you've decided to save the world?'

'Well, in all modesty I think I can make a contribution. We've got to make it profitable to get the CO2 emissions down. By developing wind energy for instance.'

Mikkel wipes his mouth with his napkin and leans back in his chair.

'What about you?'

'I take photographs.'

'Do many artists come up here?' he asks.

'No,' she says, taking another bite of her pepper.

'I saw on the web about a colony for artists just outside the town. So there must be a few.'

'There's something like a litmus test,' she says, pushing her sandwich aside. 'If people come here, they're not artists, however wide the brims of their hats are.'

'OK. But if they're not artists, what are they?'

'A joke,' she answers.

'I really don't get all this,' he says, smiling indulgently. He glances up at a sudden burst of laughter from near the fruit machines. The one with blond curly hair has said something to make his two friends look over at them.

'I know what you mean, though,' she says, softening her tone. 'A load of well-known people come here in the summer. One or two of them aren't that bad, and the others just stink with money. But real artists here are about as rare as sea-lions.'

'What about you, then? Maybe you're "not that bad"?' he chuckles.

She shrugs her shoulders.

The door opens again and an elderly workman shakes the snow off his hat. He looks round and, catching sight of Anne Sofie, breaks into a toothless laugh.

'You're back again, are you?' he exclaims, with a shout that can be heard out in the kitchen. 'So that's why we've got this bloody awful weather!'

The group by the fruit machines laughs.

Anne Sofie frowns and settles down to her chocolate, while the wind howls through the cracks in the storm porch. On the wide windows overlooking the harbour the snow settles in great blobs, only to melt gradually and trickle down to the window-sills.

'If I was condemned to live here I'd go bonkers,' says Mikkel. The old man makes his way behind the counter and out into the kitchen.

'You probably would,' she says.

'I certainly would. I came here late yesterday and I've already started talking to myself.'

She smiles.

It's obvious that they're going into town together. He finds a rhythm which will keep them in step with each other. Bent against the wind and the sharp granules of snow, they walk along the quayside with their scarves wrapped over their faces. He half-shouts an explanation of why he's here, and how the aunt of his who's died was adopted as a child by his father's family. How his own parents have taken themselves off to Mexico. How Henry rang him up about his aunt's death, that he has a daughter called Dorte who has a pair of twins, and how a pile of eider duck on Henry's balcony gave him nightmares last night.

She laughs.

He's been missing someone to talk to so much that he tells her about Jantzen the undertaker with the Brylcreemed hair, and the caretaker who could play his aunt's piano like a concert soloist.

She listens to everything he says, and their walk warms them up again. It takes them the whole length of the eastern shore until they reach the lighthouse, which stands on the hill in black silhouette against the dark sky like a gigantic souvenir. Then they follow the road round and continue back towards Østerby while he describes with wild gestures the project report he has to hand in tomorrow and the trip to Val d'Isère he's missed.

He forbears to mention that his aunt froze to death. That's not relevant, he's decided. On the other hand he can say (because it was so bizarre) how strange it was to come into her flat that morning and find her lying there on her bed with her hands neatly folded together. He adds that she'll be taken away tomorrow morning at the earliest.

She suddenly stops and seizes the sleeve of his jacket.

'Can I see your aunt?' she asks, looking up at him because he's more than a head taller than her.

The only thing he can see of her between the fur hat and the scarf, which cover most of her face, is a pair of eyes.

'Well, I don't see why not,' he says. 'Have you never seen a dead body before?'

'I've seen someone die,' she says.

'Really?'

'Yes,' she says. 'There was blood everywhere. You could slither about in it.'

Mikkel isn't sure whether to be impressed or feel sorry for her.

'A road accident?'

'You could call it that.'

She lets go of his sleeve and starts walking again.

'What happened?' he asks, catching up with her.

'His legs twitched a bit and he dropped dead,' she says.

'How?'

'I don't want to go into it.'

The way she speaks of it so casually makes him uneasy. They continue down the road until he realises they've reached the place where she lives. She stands, hesitating slightly, her hand on the gate.

'I've only got tea.'

It's what he'd been hoping for. The alternative was his laptop in his hotel room without the internet. Added to which he finds her interesting, and so delicate that he wants to put his arms around her.

'Mind your head,' she warns as he steps into the hall. 'The ceilings are low.'

Mikkel blows some warmth into his hands while he looks around the room. Clearly the place is only used for holidays. Seashells and painted pebbles on the window-sills. Small sketches on the walls. In a corner next to some bookshelves under the little windows overlooking the harbour stands a lightweight armchair covered in a worn poppy-patterned fabric. On the shelves are four or five feet of vinyl disks and a Bang & Olufsen stereo system that would fetch good money as an antique. On the side of the room towards the road runs a long table with an old-fashioned bench. A chest of drawers beside the door leading to the kitchen is stacked with old magazines, mostly fashion and knitwear, long faded by the sun.

'Take your coat off,' she says, going into the kitchen.

He can hear her lighting the gas and putting the kettle on. Then she disappears from the kitchen up a narrow staircase and he can hear her footsteps on the floor above while he takes off his scarf and hangs his damp jacket in the hallway.

This feels good, he thinks: a hundred times better than his room at the hotel, where he's driven mad by the silence and the creaking of the floorboards in the thickly-carpeted corridors.

She comes down again, her cheeks ruddy from the walk up from the harbour.

'Would you like to see what I'm working on at the moment?' she asks with a smile. She hurriedly wipes the melting snow from her leather portfolio, unzips it and takes out a large envelope. Then she lays two glossy A4 photographs on the long table. He sits down on the bench, looks at the pictures and gives an embarrassed smile.

It's her all right. She lies naked in a pool that has ice clinging to its edges, though her smile seems to indicate her indifference to her situation. On the other hand he gets the impression that the sequence is important, because she quickly, and apologetically, rearranges the pictures.

'What's the difference between that picture and this one?' she asks.

He stares at the black and white photographs, trying to concentrate on every detail. Beneath the surface of the water around her lies a collection of electrical appliances, a flatscreen television, mobile phones and old gramophone records.

As far as he can see, the pictures are identical apart from a dark shadow in the water spreading from her wrist.

'Are you bleeding?' he asks in amazement.

'Yes.'

'Is it faked?'

She shakes her head.

'Couldn't you have cheated, I mean, put some kind of colouring in the water? It's pretty sick,' he says, with a look on his face as if he's tasted something bitter. She shrugs her shoulders as if he's mentioned something quite trivial.

'Come on, show me the difference between that picture and this one.'

It's a bit like a spot-the-difference puzzle, he thinks, staring at the laptop in the water under her left arm. It's a model he held longingly in his hands only last week. It cost a fortune and remains only a dream.

'That's the niftiest Dell on the market you've got there,' he says, forgetting all about the blood.

'You're not allowed to talk about the hardware,' she laughs.

'Differences,' he says, still shaken by the waste of the beautiful laptop. 'I'm not sure, but I think there's more blood in the water in this one.'

'It's the fish!' she laughs. 'Look! It's having a careful peep out from behind the mobile, and in this one it's got as far as my breasts.'

Hesitantly he asks, 'Is that art?'

Now she laughs, for the first time with warm, genuine laughter, holding her sides.

'No, the fish is definitely not art. It's just funny.'

Now it's his turn to laugh, relieved that he hasn't missed something deeply significant, and he begins to hope that the freezing weather will continue, that the entire rail network will break down and that they don't move his aunt until the summer.

'They're going to be enlarged, so the grain shows, and then they'll be printed on tissue paper and coloured with gloss oil paint: orange and blue-black,' she says, gently putting the pictures back in their envelope.

'They're certainly going to catch people's attention,' he says.

She puts the envelope away on the shelves.

'You can't separate me from my work,' she says quietly, almost as if to herself. 'If you do that, it gets to be a bit like the biscuit-tin art the Skagen painters produced. The paintings in the museum are a diary. That's what's unique about the collection there. But those idiots you asked about in Kabyssen – the ones who come here in the summer – they're a hundred years out of date.'

He detects a shadow clouding her face, and a child-like anger in her green eyes. It takes several long seconds before she regards him again with the look he likes so much. He'd noticed the same moments of blank disengagement in the café when she stood gazing at the broken cup.

'Don't you know anything about painting?' she asks, suddenly laughing. 'Or have you only got a load of numbers in your head?'

He has to smile.

'Just numbers really. But I like going to the cinema. When the national film festival was on I went to see a Czech film. It had won hundreds of prizes and it bored me absolutely rigid. At one point a fat loo cleaner sat and stared at the camera for well over a minute.'

She laughs.

'You'll never forget her.'

'Forget her? I dreamt about her for days, and now she follows me around every time I take a piss in a public lavatory. I'd rather have a few car-chases and a bit of popcorn. And I'd like to be allowed to have a piss in peace.'

She smiles.

'In the Third World there are painters who sit copying old masters so perfectly that you can't tell the difference,' she says, holding the kettle ready to pour. 'They're very talented craftspeople and they can make a living like that, but it's only repeating the same thing. It's the same with your car-chases.'

She puts the mugs down on the table and looks at him.

'Either it hurts, or it's meaningless,' she says.

'I'm not sure that I get what you mean,' he says, tasting the jasmine-scented tea.

When he thinks about it, he's felt bad all day about missing the ski trip to Val d'Isère. That morning at aunt Ellen's flat had felt bad in a different way. He sat staring at the burn marks on the table, almost in tears, without really understanding why.

She sits a while with a worried frown on her face, drinking her tea. Then she looks up at him.

'Just the thought of them sitting here in the old artists' colony with a glass of burgundy, shouting "hip hip hurrah", as if they were toasting the artist in that painting of Krøyer's – as if they were the next link in an unbroken chain – it's hilarious,' she says. 'But that's what makes them mediocre.'

'Who?'

'You don't know them.'

Mikkel smiles.

'But the scenery up here is unique. That's why they come, I should think.'

She shakes her head.

'I know only one person here who's an artist,' she says, and for a second he sees coldness in her green eyes again. 'He puts himself on exhibition. He's called Knud Harber.'

'I've never heard of him.'

'No,' she says, going into the kitchen and up the narrow stairs.

He's surprised at the direction the conversation has taken. He needed to talk to someone, and she clearly needed to too, but every so often she seems irritable, as if she's had a really bad day.

He can just hear that she's talking to someone else now. He gets up from the table and sits on the floor next to the bookshelves. To his surprise he finds a worn copy of *Das Kapital*. He opens it. The name 'Holger Strand' is written in fountain pen on the flyleaf.

When she comes down again, she's changed into a bottle-green jacket, and flared dark brown trousers with top-stitched little blue flowers on the pockets. He holds the book up so she can see it.

'This ought to be essential reading at the Copenhagen Business School,' he laughs.

'Hmm,' she says, looking around restlessly, as if there's something she can't lay hands on.

'Who's Holger Strand?'

'I'd rather not talk about him,' she says, passing through the living room and out into what must be a kind of scullery. A little door into a larder is open and she goes in, returning with a camera. On the bench lies a small camera case. Carefully she puts the camera in the case and lays it on the table.

Mikkel flips randomly through the pages of the book.

'Why not?' he asks.

She looks at him with a sigh.

'You don't have to tell me,' he says, as she fetches her boots from the hallway. He gathers that they're going out again. She looks determined.

'He's my stepfather,' she says, pulling on her boots. 'My father died when I was a child. He got his throat cut in a fight. Maybe you read about it. It was in all the papers.'

Mikkel shakes his head and puts the book back on the shelf as if it were hot.

'Holger Strand married my mother and destroyed her. When I was fifteen I ran away from home.'

'What did he do?' asks Mikkel.

She looks at him patiently.

'What do you think?'

'Why didn't you report him to the police?'

'He said that if I told anyone he'd kill me the way you kill a pigeon before you pluck it and eat it. Do you know how you kill a pigeon?' she asks, looking at him as if he were in an exam.

'You cut their heads off',' he says.

'Wrong,' she says.

'You don't have to talk about it,' he says, getting up off the floor. 'I really mean it. It was stupid of me to ask.'

'It was quite natural of you to ask,' she says. 'You squeeze them under their wings.'

'I don't want to hear about it,' he says, sitting down in the poppy armchair.

'You squeeze them under their wings with your thumb and forefinger,' she insists on explaining, holding up her hand to show how. 'You simply squeeze the air out of their lungs in a tight grip, and they die slowly and painfully.'

Mikkel thankfully can't remember if he's ever eaten pigeon.

'That's what he was going to do to me if I talked. He'd squeeze the air out of my lungs. He once held me tight to show me how easy it was, and pointed out that it didn't leave a trace.'

'You ought to report him. It's never too late.'

Anne Sofie bends to tie her bootlaces.

'He's had his punishment,' she says.

'How?'

'He knows that it's always a possibility.'

'The bastard,' says Mikkel, shaken by what she's confided.

'Yes,' she says, standing upright. 'Shall we go?'

'Where to?' he asks.

'You promised I could see your aunt.'

16

As she opens the gate she looks instinctively towards Gahm's driveway. Then, shaking off her unease, she starts to run with the wind behind her, sliding in the snow as she did yesterday and laughing back at him.

'I just love this town in winter,' she says, breathless, and he's beginning to feel the same about her. He feels like stopping to kiss her, though he's only known her for an hour and a half.

In Kappelborgvej the sparse lights in a few houses simply strengthen the impression of a town abandoned. They cross Havnevej, a minefield in summer of pubs, pizza parlours, ice-cream stalls and souvenir shops. A workman from the harbour dressed in a light blue boiler-suit and an enormous crash-helmet approaches on a spluttering moped, legs outstretched, with both feet reaching for the support of the snow.

'An astronaut,' she says with a giggle.

On the steps of a pub on the outskirts, three middle-aged men are talking in a cloud of smoke and the smell of hash drifts slowly down the street.

'What a bunch of jerks,' he whispers.

'It's not their fault the town's been bought up by half-wits. They live here. They do their work and they don't give a shit about all the tourist stuff.'

A sudden bitterness comes over her from time to time, he's noticed, and her choice of words surprises him: they're out of keeping with her refined appearance. One minute she's considering things thoughtfully and the next she suddenly breaks into an anger he wishes he understood.

'Do you know them?' he asks.

'I know them, and I know about them,' she says with a smile. 'The little one on the left is called Pisspeter. He comes from Hjørring, but it was too hectic for him there.'

He laughs.

They've come a rather roundabout way, he realises. It was as if she's been leading the way, and he hadn't thought about it before now. Down by the primary school at the end of the viaduct they have to turn right and go quite a way back along Skagavej with the wind against them and with the hard snowflakes sticking like little tacks in their faces, until they get near the red blocks of flats.

*

He gets out the keys the caretaker gave him and opens the door. Aunt Ellen's papers are lying on the table where he left them. She takes off her fur hat and mittens, casts a quick glance round, and opens the door to the bedroom.

He stays in the living-room. He saw his aunt in the morning, and that was enough. Besides he's not entirely comfortable about this arrangement. It's as if aunt Ellen is a curiosity that he can put on display in return for some kind of payment. But it was her insistent look as she caught hold of his jacket that softened him, and he had a desperate need for company.

She's such a long time in there that he becomes impatient and opens the door.

She's standing quite still at the foot of the bed.

'Come on out,' he whispers, as if he's afraid of waking the corpse.

She turns to him, her eyes deep and angry.

'Is something wrong?' he asks, going to the window as if something interesting is happening in the street.

'No, no,' she says.

'Come on out into the living-room,' he repeats.

'She's beautiful, your aunt.'

'Yes, she is. Now let's go,' he says.

'No,' she says. 'Have a look in the kitchen and see if there's some tea. I'd like to stay a bit longer.'

'Why?'

'I can help you. Shouldn't you be going through her things?'

She's quite right. Better to go through them now with Anne Sofie than tomorrow when he's on his own.

He boils the kettle and makes some tea, and together they go through the cupboards and drawers. They work systematically and in silence: carefully, without disturbing anything. There's nothing here of value to a stranger, by the looks of things. Anne Sofie holds a dress up before her with an embarrassed smile.

In the chest of drawers are papers, a few books, knick-knacks, and postcards from friends on holiday in the south. From under the sofa she brings out a black shoebox. It's full of pictures, unsorted and not yet in an album. He hadn't noticed it that morning. She takes out a picture at random and considers it.

'Well, look at that,' he says. 'She was good at drawing.'

She sits down on the sofa and flips through a sketchbook she's found, while he goes out to the kitchen, opening and shutting cupboards and drawers. Apart from a good few empty bottles of spirits in plastic sacks, the place is clean. When he returns, she's sitting with a little straw hat on her head, still absorbed in his aunt's sketches.

'Can I have this?' she asks, lifting up the sketchbook.

He'd just been thinking of giving it to Henry. His aunt had drawn such a lifelike portrait of him that it could have been a photograph.

'You can have anything you like, except the piano. The whole lot's going to the tip,' he says, sitting down beside her. They laugh at a portrait of the toothless Poul.

'They call him the Crab,' says Mikkel. 'I'd recognise him anywhere from this.'

'Yes. He hasn't changed,' she says.

'Do you know him?'

She smiles as she looks through the sketches.

'Everyone runs into Poul sooner or later.'

He wouldn't mind mentioning Poul's concerns to her, but Henry had warned that the story would only grow with the telling. Instead he confides how he'd felt a great sense of loss the day before, as the caretaker sat at the piano. He tells her about his parents' frantic travelling, which is the reason his trip to Val d'Isère came to nothing.

Sitting at the dining table again she takes her camera from its case, adjusts the lens and takes careful aim at a vase on the window-sill. He has the feeling that his words have fallen on deaf ears.

'Maybe you can help me,' she says suddenly, putting the camera down on the table. 'I'd like to take a photograph of your aunt.'

'I realised that,' he says. 'That's why you brought your camera.'

'We'll take it in the high street tomorrow, in the middle of the day when there are people about. If they haven't taken her away by then.

We could take her out and sit her nicely, as if she's still alive. I can get hold of a car. It would only take a few minutes. Straight out of the car and onto the bench by the hot-dog van.'

He gets up from the table.

'What the hell's the matter with you? You can just drink your tea and we'll get out of here.'

He hears the little staccato click of the shutter as he's in the act of saying 'we'll get out of here'.

She smiles.

'What are you afraid of?'

'You can forget all about using my aunt in your sick experiments.'

She laughs, fiddling with the lens.

'I thought you were cool when you came into Kabyssen.'

'Well, that was your opinion.'

'What opinion?' she says, looking at him, her mouth half-open, and for a moment she looks slightly stupid.

'My aunt's done quite enough sitting on benches in this town.'

'I'm sorry if I've hurt you,' she says in the silence that ensues.

He shakes his head, gathers the cups from the table and takes them out to the kitchen.

'You can photograph yourself, but I'm not having my aunt messed about with for any arty-farty stuff.'

'Other people are going to be messing about with her. You realise they're going to burn her up in that bloody coffin you're paying for?'

'Have you been on work experience in an undertaker's or something?'

She shrugs her shoulders, and her glance indicates quite clearly how very naïve she thinks him.

'What you don't know doesn't hurt you.'

Mikkel recalls Jantzen's irritation when he'd postponed the business that afternoon. What the hell.

She sighs, and takes another picture at random from the shoebox. She remains looking at it for a long time.

'I'd like to go home,' she says, putting it wearily back in the box.

'Yes,' he says, 'let's get out of here.'

Without speaking, and unsure of each other, they put on their coats ready for the walk into town.

*

'I left the sketchbook behind,' she says, just as they reach the pavement outside. 'Give me the keys and I'll go back for it.'

'You give me your camera, and then you can have the keys,' he says irritably.

They make the exchange, and she goes back up, with a shake of her head. He looks up at the balcony. She's turning on the light in the living-room. What a stupid argument. It annoys him. But she started it.

A bit further down the road some children are playing under a street lamp. Faint happy shouts hang in the air. He can hear a girl counting, ten, twenty, thirty, forty, and it occurs to him that no toys in the world are as good as fresh snow and the magical light from a street lamp.

He hears the door shutting, and she comes over to him with the sketchbook under her jacket.

They carry on into town with the biting wind against them, concentrating on surviving this polar expedition without permanent frostbite. Neither of them feels the need to say anything. She knows the shortest way back behind the station through a little alleyway, and he follows. The snow gathers on their clothing and they bend forwards, needing to wipe it from their eyes every so often so that at least they can see something.

When they get near Brøndums Hotel she asks at last when his aunt's funeral will be, and he explains about the post-mortem in Ålborg, which is apparently still on hold.

Then they stand in the light from the hotel dining room, frozen and hesitant, neither of them quite able to relax. He asks if she'd like to come in, but she wants to go home to her pictures, and he watches her march off like a little soldier past the hotel in her jacket with her fur hat pulled down over her ears: she half turns and gives a wave just before disappearing round the corner in a gust of fine snow, and he waves back.

He hangs up his jacket and dries his face on a towel. His cheeks are numb with cold.

She'd tried to hide her disappointment at something or other, because she too had felt a need to talk. She'd brightened up and laughed while she was showing him her pictures, but from time to time she had a distant look, as if he wasn't there. He'd been allowed to look at the first two pictures, though she'd said there were five in all, and in the second one, where the goldfish had peeped over her breast, the water had already gone dark on her left side. If the loss of blood from her wrist had carried on at the same rate in the next pictures, she would have nearly bled to death.

He takes his laptop down to the lounge with the open fire, and sits by the fireplace. The waitress this evening is called Eva. He orders a cola. At the table in the corner sits the girl in the wheelchair with her parents. They're eating cakes. The mother is laughing at something her daughter has said. For a split second he has eye contact with the girl, and she looks down, as if apologising for the company she keeps.

It's far better sitting here by the fire than up in his room, where the invasive silence takes control between every creak of the corridor floorboards, and the wind thrashes against the window frame – and somehow gets through it.

He should have asked someone to come here with him. No matter who, really. He hates being alone. He hasn't noticed it before, but settled by the fire and hearing the subdued talk from the other end of the room, he realises that he's never normally alone. He's either on Facebook while he watches a rubbish film, or he's with Simon or Jesper, or Astrid or Hanna – often with all four of them. Someone is always at his side so he can share his thoughts. The lunch with his parents, a duty he performs every other Sunday, is a pain, and the nearest he comes to solitude. An endless waste of time spent in conversation which is pointless because the only things they ever find to say to each other are worries or complaints.

Eva brings his cola. As he thanks her he can barely stop himself from asking if she'll sit down with him, but obviously she's at work. The family in the corner call her over to their table, and when they've settled their bill she passes through the lounge past reception and into the kitchen, where the chef, the chambermaid, the kitchen-hand and the receptionist called Birger sit chatting. He could hear laughter coming from there when he came in from the street, and he had to go and knock on the door before Birger came out with an artificial smile on her face to give him his key.

He reads:

'The theory of economics stipulates that a business governed by market forces will adjust itself to demand, thereby regulating the need for supply.'

Tomorrow he needs to talk to the priest and the undertaker, in that order. The caretaker had said that the piano would cover the funeral costs. But no, that's just too bloody convenient. He can't be bothered to run around here negotiating on behalf of his parents. He'll give it to Henry's daughter. She'll be back in her flat on Monday. Maybe the twins are musical.

'An attempt was made to adjust the turnover in the telecommunications industry for deflation, but it proved impossible to find a net price index which covered the whole of the period in question.'

He sits for an hour over the report but he can't concentrate. In the end he gives up and stares at the embers and the sparks jumping in the grate. When he thinks about it now, it was as if she was looking for something in the flat. Calmly and systematically she'd been opening and closing all the cupboards and drawers while he sat moaning about the skiing holiday he'd missed and his parents' ego-trip.

He gets up and almost runs up the stairs to his room, with a strange feeling that something's wrong. He fumbles frantically in his jacket pocket until he finds the key to the flat: an ordinary Yale-type key. He puts it in the palm of his hand and examines it. Who can ever remember the pattern of the serrations? She'd suddenly wanted to go home, and couldn't get there fast enough. Something tells him that he needs to go back to his aunt's flat. Not tomorrow, but right now.

17

There's no shelter from the weather in this town, he's decided. The houses are too low, and the wind comes howling straight off the sea with nothing in its path.

Standing in the snow behind a low red fence is a sign announcing opening hours, and he learns that the house and garden once belonged to the artists Michael and Anna Ancher.

He fancies he can glimpse someone at the window, and stops. He takes a step sideways and realises it's a reflection of himself, back-lit by the moon which is hanging low, like a white egg. As he considers this curiosity, his mobile rings in his pocket.

'Hi, Simon', he says, trying to position himself so the reflection has the same effect again. There it is. It's as if a female figure is passing the window inside the house.

'There's something here I don't understand,' says Simon, against a background noise of clinking bottles and laughter.

'What?'

'You've got a positive current value of 1.2 million. I get a negative.'

'You need to use the average of the weighted interest rates, not the interest on the capital,' he answers patiently, adjusting his position a little.

'Hmm,' is the response. Mikkel can hear a calculation being done. 'The average?'

'Yes, the bank borrowing is 60% of the debt, as far as I remember. Don't forget they're only paying 5% on their bonds.'

There's a silence.

'Are you still there?' asks Simon.

'Yes.'

'What are you doing?'

He really wants to talk about Anne Sofie and her very bizarre idea. Yet despite the thought that Simon would probably find her interesting, he's reticent: maybe because he finds her unpredictability attractive, or maybe it's because the magic would disappear in the telling.

'I'm standing looking at Michael Ancher's house.'

'Michael who?'

'The one who painted fishermen. You know: white beard, pipe, sou'wester.'

'Oh, him. Is he at home?'

'His wife is, apparently. I think I caught sight of her at the window.'

'Aren't they dead?'

'Of course they are.'

'Stop bullshitting!'

He can hear someone laugh in the background and he guesses that they're still at the Business School. Was that Hanna? Perhaps it was. He won't ask.

When he moves slightly on the pavement, the moonlight catches on the curtain behind the window, and Anna Ancher seems to walk by inside again.

'Speak to you later. My fingers are freezing off.'

*

The children who were playing under the street lamp have vanished. All's quiet in the street. But to his surprise there's a light on in the flat. Did she forget to switch it off?

The steel banister clangs as he goes up the stairs. A child is crying behind the door on the first floor, and on the second there's the sound of a television and a woman complaining about something. He goes on up to the third floor and gets out his key.

It doesn't fit. He tries again, turning it different ways round, but it's no use. Then he tries the handle, and it opens.

A bright light comes from the living-room, shining in stripes through the bead curtain. He hears a door closing, and he carefully pulls the curtain aside. Dazzled by the light of a lamp, he can make out his aunt as a dark silhouette against the window, wearing her blue silk dress. He catches his breath. She turns and walks towards him, and in the split second she passes in front of the lamp he feels the glance of her dark eyes. He trips over a pair of boots that someone has left in the middle of the hall, goes over on his ankle and falls backwards, still clutching the bead curtain, and a cry of pain comes from deep in his throat.

She bends down over him and then he recognises her.

'I trusted you,' he gasps, getting to his feet but still entangled in the curtain like a fish in a net. 'What the hell are you doing in my aunt's dress?'

Without answering she goes back into the living-room, while he extricates himself from the curtain.

'What's going on here?' he demands, staring in disbelief at the sight of her camera and photographic lights mounted on stands. Lying on the table is a cardboard box from the Firenze pizza-house, surrounded by crumbs.

'You shouldn't have come,' she says.

He goes into the bedroom where to his relief aunt Ellen is still lying in bed in a white petticoat.

'I'm taking some pictures, as you can see.'

He sits down at the table and tries to control his heart-rate.

'I trusted you,' he whispers, his heart hammering in his breast.

'I'd like you to leave now.'

'You would, would you?' he says, as the anxiety slowly subsides and turns to indignation. 'Listen to me, you little shit. It's my aunt lying in there. She's dead, in case you'd forgotten, and I decide when I go, and when you go. Why does it stink of hash in here, by the way? What the hell are you up to?'

From the direction of the toilet comes the sound of the flush. He looks enquiringly at her and into the hall, where a lanky boy emerges with several buttons of his red shirt undone. His eyes are heavy, his mouth broad and gaping like a fledgling's. On the left side of his head, from the ear down to the neck, is a tattoo representing a kind of seam, which lower down turns into something like a cross on his chest. He holds a beer can in his hand.

Mikkel looks from one to the other in confusion.

'This is Sonny,' she says.

Sonny finishes his beer and gives a belch.

'This is my aunt's flat,' says Mikkel. 'I've come to look through her things.'

'It'll be better if you come back tomorrow,' says Sonny, ostentatiously crushing his beer can.

'I'm not so sure about that,' he manages to say.

Sonny sighs and glances at Anne Sofie.

'You can go down the stairs, or over the balcony. It's up to you. But you're not staying.'

He's just talking big, he thinks, looking over at Anne Sofie. But no help is forthcoming. She gives Sonny a knowing look and goes into the bedroom, shutting the door behind her.

He briefly considers whether to protest, or threaten to call the police, but Sonny's leaning in the doorway, ready for a fight, looking both unintelligent and completely heartless.

Mikkel goes past him through the door without looking him in the eye.

The wind hits him like a slap in the face as he comes out of the flats, bewildered at her calm departure from the living-room. She'd granted him only an inquisitorial glance and a shrug of her shoulders as she left him alone with that half-wit. His cheeks burning with humiliation, he walks towards Skagavej with tears welling in his eyes. He feels as if he's passing between two grandstands, one on each side of the road, and as if everyone he knows or has ever met is sitting looking down at him, each waving a white handkerchief and booing him for his cowardly flight down the stairs.

She'd put his aunt's silk dress on. For those few seconds when she walked towards him, was it death that he saw? And who exactly is Sonny? Where can she have got to know him?

He stops a short distance into the roadway, stretches out his hand to a lamp-post, and bends over. He wants to throw up but he can't. Instead he takes a deep breath and gives a desperate shout into the grandstands with all the air in his lungs.

In the silence that follows he notices someone in the car park. Deep in the darkness a figure stands looking towards him. He has the feeling that this night-wanderer doesn't necessarily wish him well. He gives him the finger and sets off, half-frozen, into town.

A middle-aged couple are sitting in the hotel lounge by the fireplace. On a table before them lie various brochures and a few books. They're sharing a bottle of wine, and the man speaks enthusiastically in low tones while the woman listens and laughs.

Journalists, he guesses. Two colleagues following the same story, which to judge from the books and brochures must have something to do with the museum. He decides to sit for a while gathering his thoughts by the fading fire. Right here with normal people for company. Where people speak quietly and discreetly. Here where he's not alone.

Taking off his coat he lays it on a sofa. An indefinable anxiety takes hold of him. He's beginning to feel cold here even in the warmth: he wonders if he's going to be ill. He ought to ring that caretaker. But what can he say? After all, he invited her up to the flat himself.

He doesn't understand it. He doesn't understand anything at the moment. Or at least, he understands that this Sonny character has sufficient intelligence to press the shutter once she's chosen the subject and adjusted the focus: and that's clearly what she's using him for. Is she using him for anything else? He feels embarrassed as the thought vanishes to nothing.

The woman at the other table looks across at him and smiles, and he realises that he must have been talking out loud. For the sake of appearances he snatches up a newspaper from the table and hides behind it. Thick black letters. Words. Words you can move around. The body count in Iraq rises dramatically. The same with house-prices in Denmark, and the same, therefore, with the flat in Nansensgade which belongs to his father, and whose rent he pays jointly with his flat-mate.

Just about everywhere, things are going wrong. With the body count, with his father's juicy equity, and with her.

Anne Sofie is awoken by the noise of something hitting the window with a dry smack. It's four in the morning. It's still night. It's three hours since Sonny drove her home. The wind has dropped, and now there's silence.

She swings her legs out of bed and looks towards the window with a shiver. Another snowball hits the window. Screwing her eyes up, she switches on the bedside lamp. Then she gets to her feet and looks down at the garden.

He's standing in the darkness with the white snow around him. She simply lifts her hand, gets her clothes together and goes into the attic to the chest of drawers. She rummages around, feeling for a thick sweater. Then she drags herself half asleep downstairs to the kitchen. The light from the fridge is so bright that she half shuts her eyes. She drinks some milk straight from the carton and goes into the living-room where she gets dressed, still stiff-limbed, in the comfort of darkness.

By the time she's locking the front door behind her, he's already standing out in the road. He's in a bloody hurry, she thinks, fumbling with the latch on the gate.

18

As he takes a final deep breath, before he lets go of sleep and wakes up properly, he tries to keep hold of his dream, which seems to co-exist with his senses of smell and taste and the sounds coming from the street. Suddenly he realises he's too late for his on-line meeting with Simon and Jesper.

He's wide awake now, and recognises the flower-patterned wallpaper. He gropes for his mobile, which is what woke him. The caretaker's sent a text saying his aunt will be taken to Ålborg for the post mortem in the afternoon.

He gives his face a quick wash at the handbasin and looks at himself in the mirror. He could do with a shave. His hair is blown about like a haystack. He needs a pee. He considers the handbasin but pulls on his trousers and hobbles down the corridor to the bathroom with his toothbrush and shaving gear.

Snow is falling in fine freeze-dried flakes and lying like a thin carpet over the road. He should have asked for a wake-up call. The sea-air makes you tired. It's like the first few days in the thin air of the ski slopes.

He goes down past the museum to the high street. After breakfast he'll go over to the flat to see if they've cleared up after themselves. And he must discuss with the priest the best time for the funeral, and order a coffin from the undertaker: and in the evening, when Henry's back in harbour, they need to have a talk about the reception that Henry says his aunt deserves. As for Anne Sofie, it's all finished with her.

It's nearly eleven when he goes into Café Jacobs to get at a life-giving internet connection. The blonde waitress with blue eyes considerately puts his breakfast tray on the little round table adjacent to his, so he doesn't need to move his laptop. Hot milk, coffee in a flask, juice, marmalade, salami and a little basket of warm bread.

There's an email from Simon and Jesper. It looks as if they sent it at 02.52. And another from Astrid, who would like to know if he'll be home for her party after all. Don't rub salt in the wound, Astrid. And there's an email from his parents.

'Dear chap. Hope you're managing everything. We're crossing our fingers for you. We were out in the hills the other day. Unbelievable how much happiness there is in the world. In spite of all the poverty, there's an optimism here which is a lesson to us all. PS, remember to water the plants when you get back, and remember to set the alarm when you leave. PPS, Dad has sprained his foot. Love from Mum.'

Out in the street leading to the harbour, a large bundle of clothing wearing a crash-helmet is riding past on a moped, leaving a black trail in the new-fallen snow. At the bank on the far corner a woman is about to withdraw some cash from a machine. Otherwise the street is deserted.

*

It's not until he's standing at his aunt's battered front door that he remembers he has the wrong key. How can he explain that to the caretaker? Maybe he could say he's locked himself out, and perhaps the caretaker would come back and let him in: but then what might he see?

He won't worry about it: it wasn't him messing around in there last night. But why should the caretaker believe that? No. He's got to get in. He's got to get in right now. He turns from the door and takes a quick look down the stairwell. People must be at work. Stepping back a pace he gives the door a well-placed kick just below the handle. The doorframe gives way near the lock, and the door springs open with a resounding crash. He steps into the hall with all his senses alert. Something scrunches underfoot: he's standing on the bead curtain that he wrenched down last night.

For a long minute he doesn't breathe. She's sitting in her petticoat with her legs tucked under her, in the pose of the Little Mermaid in Copenhagen harbour. Her head leans on a cushion. Her skin is yellowish and dry, her hair sparkling black. The table is cluttered with pizza boxes, empty beer-cans, charred silver foil and scraps of tobacco.

So she did take her pictures, he thinks, as indignation overcomes the nervous excitement he'd felt all the way here. He looks in the wardrobe which stands, huge and menacing, beside the bed. He has a momentary dread that Sonny's going to make a heart-stopping appearance by jumping out of it.

Why did they leave her there on the chair? He knows perfectly well why: because they knew he'd come back. A kind of sick humour. A complete lack of respect. She can't stay sitting there like that, when they're coming to fetch her for the post mortem.

There's only one thing to do. Aunt Ellen has to go back to bed. That's where people belong when they're dead. He holds his breath and lets one arm slide behind her back, and with the other under her thigh he braces himself and lifts her. Her head falls against his face as he carries her the few paces across the living-room, and he has to turn his body to get through the door to the bedroom. He's aware of a sweetish smell from her mouth which turns his stomach over, and he lets her fall the last couple of feet onto the mattress.

When he's got the nausea under control he turns and looks at her. She's lying in the wrong position, and her petticoat has ridden up. He seizes her by her thin ankles and straightens her, pulling the petticoat down so that she lies neatly on her back with her head on the pillow. Her hair is untidy so he finds a hairbrush, sits on the edge of the bed and combs it.

'Excuse me,' says the caretaker.

Mikkel gives a start. The caretaker smiles.

'Did I startle you?'

He nods.

'Have you taken her dress off?'

'Yes,' he says, getting up.

He's can't explain. Last night he wouldn't have cared if everyone on earth knew what was going on in here. But now he's made this admission, he feels everything's his fault.

'Well, she's fine like that too,' says the caretaker, walking back into the hall to examine the door, which hangs askew in its frame.

'And was it you who kicked this in?'

Mikkel shuts the bedroom door.

'Yes. I've lost my key.'

'We can replace the door easily enough. The frame'll be a bit more difficult,' says the caretaker, glancing at the dining-room table.

Mikkel screws his eyes up against the sun, which is shining relentlessly, sharp and white, onto the table. He has no wish to comment on Sonny's blackened silver foil, tobacco and beer-cans.

'Looks as if you've had visitors,' says the caretaker.

'Yes. Last night. I didn't want to be here on my own.'

The caretaker stands considering this answer.

'Did you ever meet your aunt?'

'She came to my confirmation. Henry told me she hasn't been well. I met someone yesterday afternoon at the hot-dog van in town who said she owned a painting. One that was worth quite a bit.'

'People say all kinds of crap,' says the caretaker.

It suddenly strikes Mikkel that this painting might be the very reason why his mother insisted he took the train here to fly the flag for the family.

'But does it sound possible?' he asks.

The caretaker's deep in thought again looking at the mess on the table, as if he can't work it out at all. He shrugs his shoulders.

'In the early sixties, when they installed the district heating system and started insulating these old houses, quite a few paintings turned up in people's lofts and attics. It was a bit like winning the lottery. The story I've heard is that your aunt was given a painting by the friend she worked with down at the factory. The one who had the piano too.'

'And now it's gone?' asks Mikkel.

The caretaker shrugs.

'She must have sold it sometime, unless it was just one of the usual rumours,' he says, going out into the hall to look at the door-frame.

'I'd better get hold of a carpenter,' he says with a sigh.

Mikkel hasn't the slightest desire to remain in the flat.

'I'll go downstairs with you.'

He stands on the pavement until the caretaker has driven off. Then he walks towards the town. He can't make sense of any of it. Nothing has turned out as he expected when he caught the train the other day. And right now he has a pain in his gut.

Aunt Ellen probably had a painting at some point. A painting she inherited from a friend who got cirrhosis. A painting people talked about in the town. A painting that was worth something.

'Hope you're managing everything' his mother had written. Managing what? The painting?

And what about that horrible little rich-kid who's been taking the piss out of him ever since he met her in Kabyssen. Could she have taken it? No. That wasn't why she swapped the keys. She just wanted a picture of someone dead. And luckily for her, a dead person was something he was able to provide.

19

The priest he's been referred to lives near the stadium, on the other side of the 'Hospital Wood', as the woman in the parish office called it. A tricycle stands in the snow by the gate, and in the garden a small motorboat has been covered with a tarpaulin for the winter.

She's in her late thirties, and with her short fair hair and pointed nose she reminds him of a bird. Like Jantzen the undertaker, she's clearly surprised at his youth. She smiles as they sit in her study among books and pot-plants. A toy train sits on a track running under her desk from the door. Mikkel briefly explains how he'd had a call from Henry Olsen, who for obvious reasons couldn't get in touch with his parents, and how it fell to him to take charge of his aunt's funeral. She nods and smiles, and they agree on the time of the funeral: Saturday at two o'clock, which is the earliest opportunity.

'People are dying like flies at this time of year,' she says with a laugh, and describes the kind of service and the hymns she has in mind. 'Is there anything in particular you'd like me to mention in my address?'

Mikkel shakes his head.

'I didn't know her,' he says with an embarrassed smile. 'But she came to my confirmation. I found a photograph of her in my parents' house. I gather my aunt's mother moved to Denmark with a tradesman, who left her when she got pregnant. Her daughter – that's to say my aunt – was adopted by my grandparents. They lived in Viborg. They couldn't manage her. My father, who was ten years older than her, tells me that she turned my grandparents' hair grey. She exploited them, he says.'

The priest smiles.

'She never made it into the middle classes of Viborg?'

'No, you could certainly say that. My parents tell me she was a drug addict. She rang them up one evening. I think she wanted to borrow some money, and the police were involved somehow. Apparently she was drunk. My father hung up on her.'

'It can't have been easy for your father,' says the priest.

Mikkel searches for the right words.

'I got a very clear idea that she was a nasty piece of work. Ruthless.

That she was out to ruin my family. I can remember my mother always stood up when my father was on the phone to her. It made her uneasy. When they talked about her, it was always in kind of short, coded sentences, or whispers, as if they wanted to protect me. I got the impression they were afraid of her.'

Mikkel sits up in his chair and smiles suddenly.

'But then she showed up at my confirmation. Uninvited. My mother was outraged, of course. It was weird. I didn't recognise the picture my parents had painted of her.'

He looks at the priest. He wishes he had the courage to tell her what's been going on in his aunt's flat, but he can't bring himself to say anything. Just as he'd felt with the caretaker. There are too many reasons not to talk about it, like the fact that he'd actually invited Anne Sofie in. Now he's at a loss for words, and he simply sits looking down into space in front of him, while the events of the last twenty-four hours pass him by, like fractional glimpses of faces, all talking around him.

The priest gives a gentle nod as she watches him. She stands up and smiles.

'It looks as if you could do with a cup of coffee and something to eat,' she says.

Gratefully he follows her through the house to the kitchen.

'I think I know who your aunt was,' she says, putting some bread and ham on the table. 'And I think she had a good life, even though your parents broke off relations. She had her friends. She had her flat. As I remember her, she was always happy. Sometimes a little loud and provocative, when she made fun of the respectable ladies of the town, but it was in a nice way.'

While he eats she begins to tidy up in the kitchen and put things in the dishwasher. She has a couple of drinks of cold water, and as she's putting the glass down the second time she drops it. It smashes on the floor and she utters a curse, quickly giving him an apologetic look. Anne Sofie had dropped her cup of chocolate and had a complete mental block, and he'd wanted to put his arms round her. As he sits watching the priest, quickly sweeping up the pieces, her husband comes in from the utility room with their youngest child in his arms.

'This is Mikkel,' says the priest with a twinkle in her eye. 'Mikkel's in Skagen to arrange his aunt Ellen's funeral.'

The husband looks younger than his wife. A lean man, clumsy in his movements, and thin on top when he takes off his hat.

'And that's just about the only reason to come here at this time of year,' he chuckles.

Bendt introduces himself. He takes a paper towel to dry his glasses, which have steamed up in the warmth. When he's got his sight back he beams at Mikkel.

'You need the best television deal you can get, if you're going to survive the winter here without getting irreversible problems,' he grins. 'Everything closes in on you, at every level.'

'Oh, it isn't that bad,' says the priest apologetically, giving her husband a look to indicate that that sort of thing can be thought, but not said, in a priest's family.

Bendt pulls his daughter out of her snow-suit using a kind of animal-skinning technique and smiles at his wife's reprimand. Mikkel lifts the child up on his knee. She's clearly used to strangers and just stares at him intently. It's very nice here, he thinks, jingling his key-ring which the little girl immediately tries to grab. Bendt asks what he does for a living and listens with interest as Mikkel describes his course at the Copenhagen Business School and their latest group project. Mikkel would like to stay, but gets up from the table when he's finished his coffee. With his thanks he offers his apologies for leaving, but he has to go to the undertaker's.

While he's walking past the wood, slightly bent against the wind, he's suddenly struck by what Anne Sofie had said about the business culture amongst undertakers. As his mobile starts buzzing in his pocket, he resolves to order the most basic coffin and the most basic urn.

Simon sounds wildly enthusiastic because he's just sent off his application for a place at USC.

'Do you know what a five-year-old BMW with a sunroof costs at the current exchange rate?'

Mikkel laughs out loud despite the terrible cold. They've spent countless evenings combing the internet for BMWs, fantasising about the trips they'll make along Highway 1 when they've managed to get on to a course at the University of Southern California.

'I've just been to talk to a priest,' he says, 'and now I'm on my way to buy a coffin.'

Simon laughs.

'Tough luck. You're not going to make it home for the ski trip?'

'No. My aunt's going to be buried on Saturday.'

There's a short silence as Simon considers what this means for the trip.

'We'll get Marlene to take your place.'

'Thanks.'

'Nothing else going on up there?'

'No.'

'No buxom farm wenches?'

'I'm not out in the country, you half-wit. This is a fishing village. A little, filthy, bloody cold and bloody windy, deep-frozen fishing village. At night, the wind howls in from the harbour, and the sky's black as coal, and when the wind's in the east, like it is now, a delicious stink comes in all over the town from the fishmeal factories.'

Simon erupts in laughter. They talk about the project again. Mikkel confesses his nervousness, and they reassure each other that everything's been taken care of. They're definitely the best team in the year-group. Simon reminds him that he must get his visa application in early. Everything they say has been said a hundred times before. Simon's found out where you can get a student discount on burgers, and they dream of blue waves and surfing and wide beaches. He tells Mikkel one more time that it's only seven hours' drive from a fantastic ski resort, and for a few happy minutes Mikkel forgets the problems of CO2 emissions, and where he is, and why he's there.

When he goes into the undertaker's he's prepared for both the odour of the place and for Jantzen's limp handshake. If people are dying like flies at present, as the priest had said with her wry smile, Jantzen ought to pull himself together and at least show a glimmer of good humour. But no: it's the same solemn demeanour as before. To Mikkel's surprise the office smells faintly of hash, and just as that thought occurs to him, he hears the rattle of a door-handle from the private accommodation behind the parlour, and catches a glimpse of a slim woman in a black nightdress hurrying across the passageway and disappearing through a door.

'Now where did we get to?' asks Jantzen, while the spin of a toilet-roll holder can quite distinctly be heard.

'What did you say?' asks Mikkel, slightly disorientated, turning from the passageway door to face the undertaker, who's wearing a slightly dazed expression. If he's not mistaken, Jantzen is high on something. There's something rubbery about his face. Something odd about his pupils, which look strangely enlarged, as if he's just emerged from a dark cellar.

'Where did we get to?' repeats Jantzen.

The door to the toilet is shut again, and music can be heard as someone turns the volume up.

'Ah yes,' he says, squinting at the passageway. 'It's going to be Saturday. The funeral's on Saturday at two o'clock.'

'Excuse me a moment,' says Jantzen, shutting the door to the private area. The volume of the music is only slightly diminished. He returns to his desk and gets out a black book.

'Saturday at two,' he repeats, recording the information in the book.

Mikkel nods and outlines what he's decided – he wants the coffin to be the cheapest available.

'Ah. The bog standard option,' says Jantzen quietly, as if the choice were something to be ashamed of.

'Yes,' says Mikkel. 'I suppose we could call it that.'

Jantzen leans back in his chair and shuts his eyes as he scratches himself through his shirt. Upright once more, he opens his eyes.

'Everything else will follow the same concept, I assume.'

'What concept?'

'Bog standard.'

'Exactly,' says Mikkel.

Jantzen leans over his black book and again writes slowly and neatly. Mikkel peers from where he's sitting and sees that Jantzen is producing extraordinarily fine handwriting, given the state he's in.

'The flowers as well?'

Mikkel nods.

'We'll arrange the coffee and cakes ourselves,' says Mikkel.

Jantzen stands up with a calm finality.

'I'll send the invoice to your parents. If you can be at the chapel twenty minutes beforehand, that's all we need,' he says, holding the door open. The meeting is over.

He's surprised to see people still in the street at this hour. Young people and old, evidently with things to do before darkness sends the town into lock-down. Teenagers from the secondary schools hanging around the clothes shops, young mothers with buggies, and old, gnarled, hunchbacked men with ears too big for them and wrinkled copper-tanned faces, all wearing the sailor's cap that seems to be an unbreakable convention.

Everything is more or less organised now. If it weren't for this ghastly weather, which has stiffened and numbed the muscles of his face, he'd be tempted to whistle a tune. Only the reception after the funeral remains to be seen to. He needs to talk to Henry about that, and he won't be back in harbour before evening.

From the tower of St Laurence's church the bells ring out a familiar melody, though he can't remember what it's called. He's relieved that his confirmation took place before his father withdrew the whole family from the church – reducing him by that very gesture to the status of infiltrator in the school choir. Needless to say, every Christmas the old man carried on turning up to the carol service, and sat complacently with the other parents wearing his pious smile.

Then something surges up in him, like an acid reflux, in the middle of his happiness. He knows it isn't normal – and for that reason he's never mentioned it to anyone – but he doesn't care about his parents at all. He's aware that this makes him different from everyone he knows. It was one of the things he would have liked to talk about with the priest, but then Bendt came home, and the opportunity was lost.

Where must they be now? Somewhere in the Gulf of Mexico, paddling in a blue lagoon. The thought occurs to him that he really wouldn't mind if their plane exploded somewhere over the Atlantic, and the two of them were scattered over the water in the form of fine white powder.

People would sympathise with him: no brothers or sisters, only an aunt in far-away Samsø.

Now that would make a really interesting funeral, because none of Jantzen's coffins would be required. After a memorial service in Sorgenfri he would sit in their big house with Anne Sofie and go through the photograph albums and clothes, and Anne Sofie would be disappointed not to find a single dress in the wardrobe to fit her. They'd go through all the share certificates and enjoy working out how big a pile his parents had made for themselves, and he could even leave the house to pick up a couple of pizzas, safe in the knowledge that his parents wouldn't need him to get something else while he was out at the shops.

The smell of the hot-dog van in the square reaches him. That smell really is in unfair competition with the fishmeal factory. Dusk is falling though it's only just gone three. Heartened by the negotiation at the undertaker's, he decides to pay Anne Sofie a visit. He'd sworn that he'd never see her again, but now he thinks that was an over-reaction. So he'll forget what happened yesterday and see if she'll come to the harbour in the evening when Henry puts in. A good excuse for going to see her, he decides, fully aware that he's totally lacking in principle at the moment. But he doesn't know anyone else in this town, and the blue cold is setting in. He's curious about her, and the curiosity won't go away. It's as if she's calling for help when that faraway look comes into her eyes, only for her to make some really vicious remark all of a sudden, in language fit for a docker. But the moment she laughs – like in the living-room when she was enjoying the picture of the fish swimming over her breasts – she becomes warm-hearted. She can fold herself inwards like a dandelion in the night, or open herself up to him with a burning spark in her eyes; and rather like the weather in these parts, she can change from storm to calm in an instant. Of all the girls he knows, he's never met one like her. She's quite unlike Astrid, with her voracious appetite for organising things. Or Hanna, who basks in the peaceful respect that naturally gathers round anyone at a business school whose father is the CEO of a pension fund. But Hanna could just as easily have done architecture, and Astrid has arranged her life so she can go off skiing twice a year for several weeks at a time, and still get top marks in the exams.

With Anne Sofie it's different. She comes and goes between two worlds, and he'd dearly like to take a little walk with her round the second one, if only she'd hold his hand and promise that he'd come back unscathed. That's the nearest he can get to the feelings he has for her. And that's what hurt yesterday evening. He couldn't go with her. Or didn't dare.

He'd like to talk to her about it. And he'd like to know what she thinks about the painting his aunt had, or perhaps didn't have. He quickens his pace and strides resolutely past the library. Someone seems to have knocked over all the parked bicycles so they lie in a tangle on the pavement. He half-runs past the museum back to Brøndums Hotel.

The whole business yesterday was a misunderstanding. If only he hadn't been such a bloody coward. If only he'd taken things a bit more calmly instead of being offended. It was really his fault, in a way, that things happened the way they did.

20

You can tell just by looking at a house that it's empty. He hasn't thought about it before. Maybe because he's never wished quite so desperately to see a light on in the living-room, and to glimpse her behind the curtains. But this house is dead. Behind the windows the linen curtains hang limp and pale in the darkness, and a thin dusting of virgin snow covers the path to the door.

Although it's a futile gesture, he unlatches the gate, walks to the door and knocks. If she'd left the house that morning there would be footprints in the snow just like the ones he's just made. Either she got up bloody early or ... he can't be bothered to continue that line of thought. He walks back to the gate. Is this really how things have to be?

He thinks back to the key to the flat. She swapped his for hers. He thrusts his hand into his jacket pocket for his bunch of keys. He goes back to the door. The key fits perfectly and turns. He opens the door and doesn't move for a moment. She actually gave him her key. That's just what she did, he thinks, stamping his boots free of snow. Then he walks in, shutting and locking the door behind him. He stands still in semi-darkness as he accustoms himself to the meagre light filtering through the curtains.

He's relieved to see her tripod and lamp standing by the old bench: so she has been home. She's come back and gone out again. A milk carton is on the table. She got up early, or got home late, drank some milk and went. Taking off his jacket he hangs it on a hook in the hall. He'll wait for her. Do a little reciprocal trespassing.

His eyes have gradually adjusted to the faint light and he looks round the living-room. On a chair his aunt's silk dress lies neatly folded. Even now the sight of it makes him uneasy. The dress fitted as if it had been tailored for her. There's actually nothing wrong in her bringing it home. After all, he'd said that she could take anything she wanted except the piano.

At the very moment he decides to switch on the light, he hears the click of the gate. He peers out from behind the curtain. It's a man on his way to the front door. He can hear him rattling some keys. Quick as a flash he dives into the kitchen and up the stairs. He has trouble orientating himself in the dark, and bangs his knee against a rack of clothes which, miraculously, he manages to catch before it falls. Then he stands completely still in what little light falls from a skylight.

At the furthest point, a half-open door leads to an attic bedroom. He's at the stairhead, leaning against a chimney, and behind the chimney is an area of open roof-space where he can make out a few packing-cases and a child's bicycle in the gloom. A window in the gable lets blue moonlight into a half-obscured bedroom: all he can see is the corner of a bed and a few clothes lying on the floor. That's obviously Anne Sofie's room. Remembering how he could hear her footfall upstairs the other day, he shifts his weight from one foot to the other with care. A light goes on in the living-room, spreading into the kitchen and up the stairs.

The footsteps come creaking nearer on the floor below. He has no idea what he'll say or do if this man puts his head up here. A tap is turned on, and runs for a long minute before being turned off again. Footsteps back to the living-room and out to the scullery. He hears a door being rattled: the door of the little larder, which is evidently locked. Then the man returns to the living-room. Sound of telephone receiver being picked up and tiny clicks from dial-buttons.

Carefully Mikkel lies down on his stomach and peers down from the top of the stairs. He can make out where the man is, with his back to him but just visible.

'Are you alone?'

Mikkel stretches further over the edge.

(...)

'She was out there yesterday.'

(...)

'Yes.'

(...)

'Yes, he was there too.'

(...)

'Yes. OK, I get you.'

(...)

Mikkel has to take hold of the further edge of the opening and put most of his weight on one arm, to get himself where he can just see through the half-open kitchen doorway.

'It's locked.'

(...)

'Yes.'

Mikkel can make out a lined face with a stubble of grey beard, and the typical seaman's cap. But he gets pins-and-needles in his arms, and has to withdraw once more into the loft.

'On Saturday.'

(...)

'OK, fine.'

(...)

'Yes.'

The receiver is replaced, and he holds his breath once more. The living-room floorboards are creaking again. Now the man's standing in the kitchen. He can see his distorted shadow lying on the staircase, his head extended on account of the cap. Now the shadow changes shape: it gets longer. Aghast, he realises the man is making towards the stairs.

He pulls himself on to his haunches and sits as tense as an archer's bow. At the very moment when the shadow puts his foot, with a creak, on the bottom step, he himself takes a step backwards into the darkness, and at the next creaking step he swings in against the chimney, letting himself slide downwards. As soon as he's done so he feels a terrible pain in his back. Feeling along the limewashed chimney he comes across a nail protruding from a joint in the mortar. He stops breathing while the man pulls himself through the stairhead and gropes slowly towards the bedroom.

A sharp bump and a quiet oath. He didn't see the clothes-rack either. He pushes it aside in irritation before putting himself right across the doorway. He switches on a light which floods the whole roof-space. Mikkel hurriedly reassesses his awkward position. Getting onto his knees he crawls to the far side of the chimney.

He can hear him opening and closing a wardrobe. Now he's fumbling around with something. An envelope. There's silence for a couple of minutes. Then he casts a dark shadow through the roof-space until he switches off the light and can be heard returning the way he came. Next there is careful, searching footfall as he feels for the narrow steps of the stairs.

Mikkel breathes again. The light goes off, footsteps pass through the living-room, and the front door is opened and closed.

Now that the worst of his fears have subsided, he registers once more the thin sharp pain down his back. Hanging next to the kitchen sink is a small oval mirror. He switches on the light, and taking off his jacket and T-shirt bends round to see a narrow scratch from his shoulder blades to the base of his spine, marked with little points of blood.

He gets dressed again and puts on his coat, relieved not to be trying to explain why he was behind the chimney in someone else's house. He doesn't want to stay there a moment longer.

As he walks back to the hotel, he ponders what that short, cryptic conversation was all about. His back hurts like the blazes. He needs to ask at reception for some kind of antiseptic.

Throwing himself on the bed, Mikkel logs into his laptop and shuts his eyes as it hums on his stomach. Then with a light tap of his index finger on the keyboard, the homepage of the group project appears against a sky-blue background.

Empirical finance: a theoretical approach
Module 1
Supervisor: Per Vestergaard
The telecommunications industry, with special reference to the development of telecommunications before and after the end of the Tele Danmark monopoly

He runs through the project, aware of a sneaking anxiety that the whole thing has become too ambitious. Why this sudden doubt? It was finished off last week.

Market share of landline subscribers
Quarters 1 and 2, 2004
Table 4.2
Landline sales 1996–2003

He lies there looking at the graphs: the green and blue lines. The curves, the years, the columns, the use of colours for the sake of clarity, the percentage rates, the distributions, the references to sources. He lets the text flicker over the screen, knowing quite well that he's lost his concentration, or rather that his concentration isn't going to materialise. He had imagined that while he was here, surrounded by beautiful views under lofty skies, he'd have every chance to fine-tune the whole thing. But the reality here is as uncomfortable as the abrasion he's just suffered on his back. He's restless, and the whole project, with its calculations and curves, its distributions and little humourous touches, suddenly looks irrelevant.

So does the little epigraph:

'Everything that can be invented has been invented, H Duell, Head of the US Patent and Trademark Office, 1899.'

The future belongs to those of enquiring mind, his professor had said. But not to those who go off on ski trips, he had thought to himself. It had been so obvious, when they'd taken the ski-lift up last winter. A silence had fallen when one of them pointed out that five years ago this particular place had been one of the best descents. They were there to have some fun, and yes, it was fun if you went up just a little higher: but the sight of those grey clumps of snow clinging to the withered grass hung like a thin grey film over the afternoon's happiness. The thaw was so depressingly early.

He dials Hanna's number. He can tell from the sound of her breathing that she's out in town.

'Any news?' he asks, and Hanna laughs. She tells him about Astrid and a new guy, and some new ski-boots she's seen for sale at a bargain price. He lies there and listens to her voice and the noise of the traffic around her, and then the sudden echo which makes him guess that she's gone down into the Metro.

'What about you?' she asks suddenly.

'They've messed up the world for us. Had their consumerist orgy,' he says.

Hanna falls silent. Then she laughs.

'Well, you've been part of it. What have they done to you up there?'

He asks about the party tomorrow, and mentions Astrid's incredible good luck about her flat. He just feels like lying on the bed listening to the city and to her voice. Hanna's quite capable of talking for half an hour: he simply has to insert a grunt now and then between her laughs and her abrupt changes of subject. He can hear a loudspeaker announcement and guesses that she's on her way to the Business School.

*

After his chat with Hanna he nods off for a second, and comes to with a start. It's pitch dark outside. Fumbling for the switch of the bedside lamp, he turns it on and stands up.

He gets dressed and stumbles drowsily down to reception.

'Any messages?' he asks sleepily.

Birger, the receptionist with the downy moustache and the knowing smile, shakes her head, and Mikkel realises that it was a stupid question. Messages? Who from? From her? That really is wishful thinking.

When he steps out into the darkness he has to orientate himself. Anchersvej, then the road to the eastern shore. He decides to go past Anne Sofie's house anyway even though it's a bit of a detour and it's beginning to get colder.

The pale linen curtains are drawn like last time, and in the window by the door they have the same fold he noticed in the afternoon. At the gate the only footprints are his own and those of the fellow who let himself in. He takes a narrow alleyway and comes out on the coast road with the snow-covered dunes to his left. Then he finds the little path through the wild rose-bushes and crosses first the dunes and then the railway track towards the harbour with its shipping offices and factories. He heads towards the chimney of the fishmeal factory.

There's quite a wind blowing out of the dark and the temperature has fallen again to well below zero. The stink from the factory is acrid, settling itself in his nostrils, and the gulls' screams are unbearably loud as they circle over a truck being washed down with a pressure hose. Fishmeal sludge and water from the back of the truck form a cloud in the air, and a foul brown gruel spills in a broad trickle across the quay.

Dorte said that they'd dock about eight o'clock, so he might as well go and wait in the dockers' café. There's no reason to stand out in the cold being shat on by the gulls. Giving the truck a wide berth he walks over to the café, feeling the spray from the pressure hose settle on his face in a thin film.

The conversation he'd overheard that afternoon had been more than usually private, and although he'd decided to forget everything about his visit there, he couldn't get the words 'Are you alone?' out of his head. Why begin a telephone call like that? Unless you were ringing your mistress.

With the freshening wind, the cold creeps slowly but surely into him if he stands still, and he decides to take Dorte at her word, but at the very moment that he turns to go, he sees a boat passing through the harbour mouth. He goes to the edge of the quay as it slides out of the darkness like a shining insect under a swarm of shrieking gulls.

The trawler is as big as a medium-sized ferry and it's lying strangely in the water as if it's about to sink. The bridge at the stern is as tall as a three-storey house, whilst the bow is so low that its gunwales are only just above the waves. It's almost sinking. Sinking under the weight of its load. A faint rumble from inside the hull and it turns round almost soundlessly by ninety degrees.

As it lies there in the harbour with its belly full, it looks like a living thing, he thinks. It breathes and sighs and snorts in the sudden silence, and then again there's a gentle rumble. Something white like a foaming river cascades along beside its hull, making it sway a little, then lie completely still, before gliding slowly and obediently up to the quayside, stern first.

Then the unloading team emerge in their orange oilskins, slipping and sliding out of the café with their shovels and forks. A docker takes the cable from the fisherman at the stern and drops a loop over a bollard. Moving ever so gently, the cable, thick as an arm, tightens almost to breaking-point, singing in a vivid demonstration of kinetic energy as the trawler comes to its berth precisely where the hatch to the hold lies beneath the suction pump hanging over the boat like an elephant's trunk.

Just as the unloading team clamber over the side, he catches sight of a figure on the bridge itself. A little creature in an Icelandic sweater with short black sticking-up hair, looking down to the deck. Mikkel takes a step backwards. It's her. It's definitely Anne Sofie in a worn Icelandic sweater. Henry suddenly appears behind her with a command to the fisherman aft.

What's she doing up there? How's she got there? He's dumbfounded. She stands unassumingly with her arms resting on the edge of the bridge, as if it were her boat, watching the fisherman slowly slacken the line. Henry stands behind her in his shirtsleeves. The moment he shouts 'That's it!' down to the fisherman, he lays his hand on her shoulder for a few seconds with obvious familiarity. She glances quickly down at him before disappearing beneath Henry's arm into the warm.

*

He's allowed to come on board, of course, but he has to wipe his boots thoroughly before he steps into the mess, which reminds him more than anything of a modern living-kitchen, with a flat-screen television almost the size of the large dining-table. Confused, he looks around. Where's she got to?

Henry beckons him through the passageway past the doors to the crew's cabins and up the stairway to the bridge. There the radar screen throws a green light into the semi-darkness, and little red and yellow LEDs wink from the ceiling and from the control panels as if they were in the cockpit of a jumbo-jet. In the middle of the room stands a well-lit chart-table.

Henry points at a red line on the chart in the form of a Z.

'That's where we were fishing today,' he says, and Mikkel works out that it must be the Norwegian coast at the top of the chart, and Grenen Point at the bottom. 'We usually fish out in the Baltic at this time of year, but right now there's a bloody great shoal of herring just there. Everything's gone bananas,' he laughs.

Slightly giddy, he goes down the stairway behind Henry, who invites him into the mess again for a mug of coffee. One by one the crew appear, dressed and ready to go ashore, and Mikkel observes that in every workplace there's a hierarchy. Emptying the boat is left to the landlubbers. Finally, after twenty minutes, she emerges from one of the cabins, with a half-smile at seeing him sitting there in awe of the fishermen, with a mug in his hand. She's dressed, and her hair is wet from her shower.

'Were you up at the flat?' she asks briskly.

'Yes. I had to kick the door in,' he says, so quietly that no one else in the mess can hear. 'The key didn't fit.'

'Well done,' she says, clapping him on the back, as if he were her little brother who's just achieved some kind of good performance, and she smiles, so that he softens again.

'Did you get your pictures?'

She nods, and he turns to Henry, who's sweating after a session in the engine-room.

'We need to talk about the reception after the funeral,' says Mikkel. But Henry has no inclination to talk about receptions just now. He stands wiping his oily hands on a cloth.

'I'll try and get hold of Poul. Ring me in the morning.'

Henry has an absent look as he rings a number on his mobile and disappears up to the bridge.

*

As soon as he has his feet on terra firma he grabs her arm and turns her around to look at him.

'Why didn't you tell me that you know Henry?'

She looks up at him as if she's trying to work out what he means.

'Should I make a list of all the people I know in this town? Is that what you're after? It'll be a long list, I can tell you.'

He isn't asking for a list, but she could do with being a bit more open about things. He'd told her that very first evening about his meeting with Henry and Dorte and the twins, and she hadn't shown the slightest flicker. Why does she treat him like this? He feels like giving her a good shake.

'When I went up there this afternoon my aunt was sitting on a chair,' he says.

'Were you scared?'

He flings his arms wide.

'What the hell do you think? I had to lift her back into bed. There must be a medical diagnosis for people who need to play around with dead bodies.'

'I didn't play around with her. I took some pictures, and Sonny helped me. You wouldn't.'

He'd like to ask what the pictures were, but refrains from enquiring.

'When are you meeting Knud Harber?' he asks instead.

'On Saturday. That's why I had to have the pictures. You know all that.'

When they get near Brøndums Hotel, he stops and kicks the snow a bit.

'I wouldn't mind some of your tea,' he says.

21

After bringing the mugs to the table she goes out through the passage to the scullery. When she returns she has a little white can in her hand.

'I spoke to the caretaker today,' he says. 'He thinks perhaps my aunt had a painting. A valuable painting.' He looks up at her. 'Maybe it was you who nicked it?'

She smiles.

'I don't think the air agrees with you up here. Your aunt was a user. People in that state don't usually hang on to valuable paintings for more than an hour or two.'

He agrees. He simply wanted to hear her opinion.

'Come on,' she says, and goes back through the scullery to the larder. He holds the can while she unlocks the small padlock.

'My little den,' she says.

He's impressed to see how the little larder has been converted into a dark room. Spread out on a long narrow workbench are some black and white portraits of a blonde girl with an awkward smile. He lifts one of them up.

'Who's this?'

'Tine,' she says, reaching up for some plastic bottles of liquid.

Another picture on the bench is out of focus and under-exposed: it shows someone apparently floating in the air amongst some crosses and snow-covered bushes.

'I came over here earlier today,' he says, studying the picture. 'The door was open. A man was in the living-room talking on the phone.'

'That would have been our gardener, Sigvardtsen. He looks after the house.'

He watches as she neatly slips a film into a developing tank and pours in the fluid. She's nimble-fingered. He's sure she could do all this in her sleep.

'Why don't you work with digital pictures? This is pretty ancient technology.'

'I've got a digital camera. In fact I've got three. But I like this process. It's delightfully bad for the environment,' she says with a chuckle. She takes a little red hair-dryer from a shelf, plugs it in, and with a gentle whirr plays the air gently over the wet negative.

'What did Sigvardtsen say to you?'

'I don't think he noticed me. I stood in the hall by the open door,' he lies. 'But I reckon I've seen him before. Yesterday evening when I was going back to the hotel, he was standing in the car park by the supermarket, staring at me. But I'm not sure. It might have been someone else.'

Mikkel holds the picture up again and sees that it was taken the same evening and in roughly the same place as the picture of the girl.

'Is this in the churchyard?'

'Yes.'

'It looks a bit spooky,' he says, trying to read a reaction in her features.

'Here,' she says, handing him a reel of tape. 'That door doesn't close properly.'

Glad to be doing something useful, he tapes over the cracks round the door while she fills plastic trays with fluid.

'Would it have been your mother he was talking to?' he asks.

'Bound to have been.'

When he's finished taping up the door she switches off the light, and for a second there's only the sound of her breathing, before she turns on a red lamp over the bench.

It's as if her features become more striking in the dull red light, while she puts the photographic paper under the lamp. Then she carefully takes the negative and holds the strip up to the light. She's evidently sure about which picture she's going to print.

'That's the one,' she says, with cheery menace.

'Count to four,' she says. As he counts, she illuminates the photographic paper until the count of three, then turns off the lamp.

'You were too slow,' she laughs, laying the paper in one of the fluid-filled trays. He stands close behind her, catching an odour of cheap shampoo, and watches the picture slowly emerge. First the rough outline of a head and a badly distorted mouth which surprises him: he thinks he recognises the features. Then the picture begins to form properly and she starts to laugh. It's him. Taken from below, obliquely, at his aunt's table, at the moment he freaked out in the flat.

'This is a good picture,' she says, placing it in the fixer.

'What's good about it?' he asks.

'You're really angry,' she laughs, making the face herself.

'And is it good because it makes me look like an idiot?' he asks blandly.

'No,' she says. 'It's because you're shit scared. I bet you've never had a single picture of yourself when you're scared. You've got one now.'

He knows what she means. Most of the pictures on his laptop are from parties at the business school, in Hanna's flat, or Val d'Isère where they're sitting roasting after a day on the slopes, making V-signs at the camera. But he can do without this particular portrait.

She skilfully rocks the tray to let the fluid wash over the picture, then takes it out and hangs it up to dry over the bench.

'You can go out now,' she says, 'but careful you don't pull all the tape off.'

'I'll behave myself,' he says. 'But I've got a right to see what you did with my aunt.'

She turns to him, and he can see that's not a matter for discussion.

He looks round the living-room, where everything is light and simple. Nothing here would be worth anything to a stranger, yet every piece of furniture has its story, showing the signs of wear from many warm summers of holidays and parties. A badly faded print of a Richard Mortensen is fastened with drawing-pins over the bookshelves. A yellow triangle and a red square against a faintly greenish background, with a few thin streaks that seem to be positioned by chance, as if someone has been sitting in boredom for an hour doodling with a ball-pen.

He recalls the painting his mother bought the year his father was fifty, and remembers how their acquaintances had nodded respectfully over the palette of colours. It was of course made clear that it hadn't exactly come cheap, but on the other hand it was a safe investment. The guests had laughed at this. The Russian artist had his studio in a kind of garden pavilion near the riding school at Klampenborg, and he was popular with the ladies coming home from an outing in the Deer Park. Quite simply, one supported the dissidents when one bought a painting from this fellow Vronsky. As if we were in the middle of the Cold War, and every brick and block of the Berlin Wall was still firmly in place.

Mikkel remembers how his mother changed the living-room curtains twice, and bought a new sofa, to match Vronsky's explosive fireworks. The painting was synonymous with all the falsehood surrounding his parents and their circle of nouveau riche swindlers. They'd ruined his ability to see anything at all in abstract art.

He settles down on the floor and studies the collection of LPs. A whole metre of jazz, which he hasn't the least interest in, and half a metre of classical – with a pair of Beatles albums, *Sergeant Pepper* and *Rubber Soul*, standing like a partition between the two sections.

It feels so cosy here, he thinks. Then the wind suddenly smashes against the windows. The gale has got up again. All day long it's been calm, and people have hardly noticed the frost as long as they've kept walking at a brisk pace. Through the loud sandpaper-like scratching at the windows he can make out the metallic click of the gate.

He gets up, goes over to the window and takes a look from behind the curtain. A gust of wind sends the snow on the rose-bushes into the air in a fine white cloud. It must have been the wind banging the gate.

Scanning the room, he sees that a door to the left of the kitchen leads to some other part of the house. I wonder where the loo is? he thinks, opening the door. He comes into a double bedroom from which another door leads to a passageway with a little limed-oak chest of drawers. Some holiday photographs are pinned on a board above it. Her parents (he guesses) in the garden. A lunch party, with someone addressing the company. A smiling woman in her early forties: Anne Sofie's mother, probably. A blond boy of eleven or twelve who looks directly at the camera in surprise. Anne Sofie as a child with a long dark pony-tail, hanging on to the back of a lanky boy a little older than her. The picture was taken as they were charging round the lawn. The pony-tail stands out like a dark cloud against the blue sky, and the colour of her yellow dress matches the dandelions in the foreground. A nice picture, he thinks.

He sits for half an hour flicking through old magazines. Then he hears her locking the dark-room door. She passes through the living-room without acknowledging his presence, with the anger in her eyes that he's noticed before.

'Is everything OK?' he asks.

She makes no answer but picks up her mobile from the table and goes through to the kitchen. He can hear her footsteps going upstairs and overhead.

She's talking to someone, about something that's clearly no business of his. Her parents? Her mother? Something important must have occurred to her while she was in the dark-room. When she comes down again she's changed her jumper and trousers.

'Shall we go?'

'Where to?'

'Into town.'

'But nothing ever happens there.'

'It's Thursday,' she says. 'They usually come out of their holes on Thursdays.'

'Who were you talking to?' he asks, hoping to learn of some purpose in their trip into town. She smiles to herself as she laces her boots.

'Come on! I'm ready,' she laughs, buttoning her coat and pulling her fur hat into place just above her eyes.

'Just a second. Why the hurry?' he says while she's snatching up her indispensable camera from the table.

22

As they'd passed through the Old Town it had been covered with a thin new layer of fine snow, and was completely deserted, as if an announcement had just been made of a radioactive leak in the vicinity. Past the darkened houses, they'd allowed themselves simply to be carried along by the wind. But now that they're actually in the pub, he finds to his surprise that the place is crammed full of people: a provincial mix of young and old.

He undoes his jacket and shakes it free of snow. It's a quarter to ten. It looks like Andy's Bar in Copenhagen at four in the morning. Middle-aged dockers, ships' officers in uniform, workmen who haven't gone home yet, unemployed people, dreamers; lots of shouting and laughter and girls, for whom this is evidently just the start of a trip to the disco by the harbour.

He gets the feeling that she knows most of the people there. The middle-aged men smile and nod to her, and a drunkard puts a hand on her shoulder as she pushes by. Two loud-mouthed girls in the standard kit – low-cut, tight-fitting trousers, with rings in their navels – fall silent for a moment as she goes past, before sticking their heads together and whispering. At the back stands Henry with a billiard cue in his hand. He hasn't got any further than picking it up.

'Ah, here come the Copenhageners,' he shouts, loud enough for everyone to hear. Mikkel gives a smile at this public recognition.

The barmaid brings a Hof and a cola to their table. They sit in silence for a moment, getting used to the warmth, watching the game. Just behind them a drunk manages to knock all the bottles and glasses off a table before he's pulled to his feet and led out into the snowstorm to a waiting taxi.

'That's the last gasp of the afternoon shift,' observes Anne Sofie drily.

He can see the logic in her remark. The older ones round the billiard table look well and truly sober, and the young people near the bar drinking cheap lager are just warming up. The drunks were the first sitting, which began when the place opened in the afternoon.

'Are you going to join us?' shouts Henry.

Mikkel sees they're starting a new game.

'Sure,' he says, counting on his parents' credit card.

A row suddenly breaks out by the bar. The taxi-driver with the round head and inquisitive eyes who drove him out to Henry's place the first evening has arrived to pick up a fare who's suddenly changed his mind.

'That's enough for today,' shouts the barmaid, taking hold of the man's arm just before he keels over and upsets another table.

Mikkel's perplexed. What does Anne Sofie see in this place? As they'd crossed the railway track he could just hear live music from the other pub. In here it's almost impossible to make oneself heard.

'What are we doing here?' he laughs.

She looks at him with a slightly irritated expression and goes over to the bar, where an old toothless fellow is laughing. It's Poul. Mikkel notices their familiarity as they talk to each other. She holds on to Poul's shirt, and he suddenly looks unsure of himself, lifting a defensive hand. Her expression changes: she looks offended.

'It's your turn,' someone shouts. Mikkel tries to remember what it was that Henry explained to him the first evening, about in-offs and in-or-overs and draw shots and key shots, and whether you should avoid trouble by leaving the red ball alone.

He takes his shot, which turns out quite well.

She's laughing about something now and Poul's holding on to her. Henry calls out that Poul should keep his hands to himself. A laugh goes round the table. There's a back door into the yard, and she picks up her jacket and fur hat and goes out. Poul follows, closing the door behind him.

They evidently want to talk undisturbed. Maybe it was Poul she was talking to upstairs on her mobile, and that's why they've come here. He can see them through the misted-up windows. Poul flings his arms out and talks urgently at some length while she listens.

They come in again, and she comes over to his table. He wants to suggest that they go somewhere else, but she forestalls him.

'I need a pee,' she says, and squeezing through the crowds she disappears in the direction of the toilets.

'I'm Søren,' says his partner, proffering a hand as big as a frying-pan. 'You're one of Krille's family, aren't you?'

'She was my aunt.'

'Do you know Soffi?'

'Well, I met her by chance. Down by the harbour. A place called Kabyssen.'

'I asked if you knew her.'

'A bit,' says Mikkel. 'She's a photographer.'

'That's what she says,' growls Søren, bending over the billiard-table.

When the game is over Mikkel goes to the bar to order the round of lagers. He lost, of course. He realises that she's been away a bit too long. But now he can't avoid talking to Søren, who despite being deaf as a post would like to know if he's got any nice little substances on him, and insists on another game.

The barmaid chuckles.

'She's buggered off, has she?'

He smiles uncertainly. 'Did she say anything about where she was going?'

The barmaid's smile indicates easy-come, easy-go.

He waits a long half hour at the bar, between the two girls in low-cut trousers. The dark one wants to know who he is, where he lives, and what he's doing there, and the blonde wants to know if he'd like to go down to the disco.

They're really rather nice, especially the blonde one with the retroussé nose, and for a second he considers the possibility. But he can't stop thinking about the way Anne Sofie has stood him up, and he certainly doesn't want to complicate his stay in this town.

He squeezes between two middle-aged dodderers hanging round the doorway. Snow is blowing across the high street, and he shoves his hands deep in his pockets.

Down near the chemist's a crowd of teenagers are huddled against the cold. He walks through them without looking up, and out of the corner of his eye he sees one of the youths having trouble lighting a cigarette.

What was it she said? She doesn't come here in summer. That very statement shows there's something wrong with her. What's the problem with summer, sunshine and warmth? And then there's the way she knows all the wrong people in this one-horse town. The idiots. The drunkards. The middle-aged creeps in that shitty bar. Pissed or high, most of them. And all that empty-headed shouting without anyone listening to anything. At the same time there was her attitude of reserve when they first went in, reluctant to be with people her own age – the very ones they should have been sitting with. But what pisses him off most is that complacency of hers when she suddenly appeared on the bridge of the trawler. As if it was her own boat.

As he nears the square, he can hear the music coming from the other pub. He goes into the yard to have a look. It's half-full and there are candles on the tables. A bit different from the hole she took him into before she vanished.

He can't make up his mind. He could go in, or he could bury his foul humour under the duvet back at the hotel. But the hotel is so bloody pretentious that it can't bring itself to offer internet or television: and it's still only eleven o'clock.

For a moment he considers going and getting his things together and checking into the Seamen's Hostel or the Color Hotel. Maybe he'll do that tomorrow.

He'll settle down at the bar in there and kill a bit of time while the music's playing. Maybe later on he'll look in at the disco to see if the pair with the low-cut trousers have shown up, or perhaps there might be some busty fisher-girl who'd be grateful for a lesson in economics.

There's a group at the table just inside the window where he's standing. A barmaid is gathering empty bottles on a tray. As she leaves the table he catches sight of Anne Sofie. She's sitting on the other side of the gangway with Sonny. They look intimate in the candlelight. Sonny's talking to her, leaning across the table to make himself heard against the music. Through the misted window he sees her lay her hand on Sonny's in a gesture of intimacy that he didn't imagine she had with anyone.

The bar's crowded with people and he has to twist his way through them as he marches resolutely towards her table. She looks up at him with indifference.

'I thought we'd come into town together,' he says.

'I'm just talking to Sonny.'

'Why did you sneak off without saying anything?'

'Well I'm sitting here now,' she says, looking at him, her eyes hard. The way she speaks using the slightly shifted vowels of the local accent makes her sound stupid. It's as if the stupidity radiating from Sonny has somehow rubbed off on her.

'Have we got a problem here?' asks Sonny, looking at Anne Sofie.

She shrugs her shoulders.

'That's enough from you,' stammers Mikkel.

She looks straight at him, open-mouthed, and he realises he'll have to get out of this situation himself. Find a way to get to the bar without losing his frostbitten face on Sonny's fist.

'Have we got a problem here?' asks Sonny again.

Mikkel ignores him.

'You just vanish without a word and leave me with all those old farts. Don't you think you owe me an explanation?' he says, trying to force a smile.

'Just piss off,' says Sonny.

He's not used to being talked to like this. Yesterday evening he was humiliated by this idiot. This is enough. He loses his composure entirely and pokes Sonny's shoulder with his finger.

'You keep out of this, Dumbo.'

He doesn't have time to blink. The blow comes without warning. A fist in the middle of his face. He falls over backwards and sees nothing but darkness.

Instinctively he gets to his feet without any sense of direction and immediately gets a kick in the chest which flattens him across the table on the other side of the gangway amid shouts and breaking glass. The music sinks to a moan with some half-hearted beats on the snare-drum. The people nearest to them try to restrain Sonny. Mikkel manages to stand up and orientate himself towards the exit, blood pouring from his nose. He's got to get out. Out into the air and the cold. Just out.

His blood stains the snow red and he puts his head back and for want of anything else uses a corner of his scarf. Someone's shouting inside, remonstrating with Sonny. He can hear them as he totters on to the road, keeping his eyes on the little specks of the stars and the moon hanging low over the harbour.

Turning to look back at the entrance, he sees her appear at the doorway, staring after him with a half-open mouth and expressionless eyes. She doesn't intend to take sides.

Vigga, who's on duty at reception, summons the chambermaid when she sees him standing there pitifully cold and covered in blood.

'What have you been up to?' she asks, shaking her head. She disappears into the little room behind the desk and returns with paper off a kitchen roll.

'Thanks,' he says. He goes up to his room, fumbling with the key until he manages to unlock the door. He looks at himself in the mirror, trying to gauge the extent of the damage. His nose seems to be intact.

There's a knock at the door, and the chambermaid comes in without waiting for an answer. She's small and round, with a milky-white complexion, curly blonde hair and clear blue eyes.

'Come on,' she says, taking his hand and leading him to the bathroom. 'It could be worse.'

He can only agree. He sits on the edge of the bath while she dries his face with a warm damp cloth, as if she's had years of experience with bloody noses. Her voice is round and soft, her hands small and firm, and with a sympathetic frown she carefully surveys the bridge of his nose and his lip. Perhaps it's the care she's taking that makes him shake a little.

'It's not too bad,' she says comfortingly. 'It's not broken. But your lip's pretty swollen.'

'I'll look after myself now,' he whispers, and turning towards him, she sees he wants to be alone.

'Who hit you?' she asks, and he gently shakes his head. Sonny is neither here nor there. Sonny is only a symptom. It's her who causes the pain. Not a trace of empathy, her eyes hard, her mouth half-open. It all comes back to him. He hasn't seen her like that before. He's noticed anger rising up in her, and her contempt for everything and everybody. Her unpredictability. He knew that side of her, and put it down to a kind of immaturity and a touch of envy. But it was almost frightening to observe the slightly slurred local accent and the almost simple-minded expression on her face when she was with Sonny. She was like a chameleon changing colour according to its surroundings.

'She's not right in the head,' he whispers.

'Who isn't?'

'Her name's Anne Sofie.'

The chambermaid takes a step backwards and looks at him.

'I'd stay well away from her, if I were you,' she says with her hands at her sides, as if he were a little boy who's been playing in a busy road. He offers a nod.

'Here's an extra flannel. Try and take a bath.'

'Just a minute – sorry,' he says in a near-whisper as she turns to go. 'Who's Knud Harber?'

She stops in the doorway to have a think.

'He's got something to do with paintings.'

'Could I find him?' asks Mikkel softly.

'Oh yes,' she laughs. 'You won't have any trouble finding him.'

23

Outside the pub Anne Sofie buttons her jacket right up to the neck. Sonny's sitting there in his red Toyota with the engine running, having a smoke with the window down. She goes over to the car and looks into his eyes, but they register only bewilderment. Just like all the times before, there's only bewilderment. He'd like to know what it's all about, and hopes that one day she'll tell him and he'll understand.

'That wasn't very clever, Sonny.'

Something dawns on him suddenly – it's a suddenness she's knows well.

'If he reports me, I'll be back inside,' he says, rubbing the knuckles of his right hand.

'I'll speak to him tomorrow,' she says.

'Will you?'

She nods. He looks at her camera-case and his face lights up in a crooked smile, as if the episode is now banished.

'Are you going off to take some pictures of the airship?'

'Perhaps.

*

She stays there in the road until Sonny has driven away and the sound of the tuned engine has faded into the music from the pub. Then she turns and follows the railway track towards the harbour. Here on the little path the snow is untouched, and she turns round and round on herself a couple of times, making the camera-case swing out from her body. Then she walks back a few paces, retracing her footprints. She can make out a shadow in the darkness over by the pub and she quickens her pace.

The sky overhead is matt black, and in the light spreading from the street-lamps the snowflakes are circling in frantic whirls. The wind whistles in the radio antenna on the roof of the marine college. There hadn't been much telecommunication on Mikkel's part when he stood and glared over the table, she thinks. Nor afterwards. What did he expect?

Now she screws up her eyes. The wind is biting and the snowflakes are sticking to her. She loves this darkness, with the forsaken holiday-homes hoarding their idyllic dreams and their stores of laughter and secrets.

She knows this is where she belongs. She's walked down every path and along every dune on both sides of the headland. She knows where the cranberries ripen in August and where the roe deer have their fawns in May. She learnt everything from Henry, who used to bring fish, seafood and sometimes game to the Permanent Secretary.

The first time he came to fetch her she was six or seven. He arrived while the sky was still red over Grenen Point. Holger and Helene were in their dressing gowns and sandals, sleep still in their eyes. Worry, as well as sleep, because deep down they were against the arrangement.

She remembers how they went off to the harbour hand in hand. Why she was to go with him, she didn't understand. But she felt full of curiosity and safe with her hand in his. The fishermen winked at her, made faces at her and said nice things about her, and Henry set her on a box in the wheelhouse as they sailed out of the harbour so she could see out of the window. While they fished, with the sun standing low over the deck and the boat rolling from side to side, Henry tied a rope round her waist and made it fast to the mast. Then she could walk around as she pleased while the fishermen sorted the seaweed and whitebait and molluscs from the red prawns.

Despite the rope she had a feeling of freedom, and she could hang half over the gunwale and watch the great jellyfish as they glided by with a banner of threads trailing after them. The strength of the bow against the yielding water took her breath away, and she would hang there for half an hour at a time simply looking down into the depths. And she remembers how, as they glided in again between the breakwaters in the evening, everything was blue. The light, the water, and the sky; and there on the quayside stood Helene and Holger in evident relief, as if she were returning from the moon, and behind them was Sonny a snotty nose, his mouth open and his hands in his pockets. He was green with envy.

*

She carries on, following the railway track, so that she's obvious to whoever it is who wants to watch her, and when she gets near the wide harbour area near the fish market, she dances with her head flung back and her eyes to the heavens, letting herself be blown along by the gusts of wind, which are whipping the snowflakes up and around in little whirls.

Breathless, she stops by the shuttered warehouses that look awkward now that the tourists are warming themselves under sunnier skies. From a trawler moored at the end of the pier, light shines from the portholes of the mess. It's red with rust. Before long it will be its turn to come into harbour. No more lingering at the furthest breakwater like an airship. She can hear the rumble of the generator. It just needs its crew. In four hours they'll come trotting out of the darkness from their homes around the outskirts of the town. They'll be silent and fuddled with sleep. The engineer will start the main engines while the first mate casts off the moorings. The cook will have bought fresh rolls at the back door of the baker's and he'll put bags of them on the table as he heats water for the coffee. She knows the whole routine, because she's been out so often with Henry.

When she had her problems as a teenager, he would come uninvited in the morning, waking her by throwing gravel up at her window. He'd woken her the same way this morning – not with gravel but with a hard snowball. She'd got dressed and followed him without protest.

The red shipping container is still there. In her very place. Insolently. The shipyard's being enlarged with a dry-dock, so the harbour beyond the yard has become a huge messy building site. The hulk of a suction dredger lies in dark silhouette in the harbour basin. In the daytime there's a cacophony of noise here. Steel being cut, the thump of long piles being driven deep into the harbour floor, concrete mixers, welding torches: sometimes even the whirring fans of a refrigerated truck having trouble getting past into the herring factory.

But now it's silent. There's only the wind whistling in the thin antennae and the soft moaning of gulls out beyond the commercial wharf.

'Orange and black,' she whispers.

She forgot that detail when she spoke to Knud Harber. She must tell him about the cathedral when they meet. About the play of light on the surface of the water, which is the real reason for her choice of orange and black. Not absolutely black, of course: absolute black isn't a colour, but a condition. No: black with a slight touch of green and deep, deep blue; and she must tell him about the matt-green oil-drum with Cyrillic characters sticking out of the soft ice against the harbour wall. That drum is somehow a precise complement to the grey ice and the imaginary ideal that the town represents just now.

She stops near Kabyssen and looks out over the harbour. It's not quite the right place to stand, but she stops anyway, while her heart begins to thump.

What does he want? What is he expecting of her? Should she run? Get away from him? Hide? She turns a fraction to look discreetly over towards the warehouses. While she was following the railway tracks, she glimpsed him there behind her in the darkness. She crosses over the quay towards the container and positions herself right out at the edge where the snow lies untouched.

Careful now, she thinks. That water must be cold tonight. Then she shuffles carefully sideways behind the container until she's out of sight.

The *Stella* looks neglected. It's one of the few wooden cutters that hasn't been scrapped. When she stands at one precise spot, she can see the café in the reflection in the wheelhouse windows. She'd noticed that the other day, but hadn't realised what a useful trick it was until tonight. She can keep an eye on him.

She leans ever so slightly over the edge. The water looks black, but that's an illusion. If you keep staring, the lilac and green colours on the surface come into view. This evening the light is perfect.

She lifts her head, and there he is in the *Stella*'s windows like a dark stone statue under the broad lamplight, and her heart begins to beat violently. He's pulled himself right into the shadow around the steps. She releases the clasp and carefully pulls out her camera. The lens is ice-cold and clear. Now it's simply a matter of waiting, while the wind whistles in the *Stella*'s rigging and a loose steel cable keeps striking the mast of the dredger, as if the ship has been abandoned for ever.

Stand absolutely still, she thinks. Absolutely still.

She realises that he can't make out where she's got to. And he'll wait, until he's become quite cold. And she's got all the time in the world.

The cones of light from the headlamps of a car reach her, and she can hear the characteristic hum of Sonny's tuned engine. She clenches her hands with a muttered curse. She'd just fallen into that transcendental peace that excludes anxiety and cold, and she had him beautifully framed in the *Stella*'s window. He disappears from her view at the sound of a car door slamming. Then she hears footsteps and now it's Sonny coming into the reflection, stooping determinedly. He sticks his stupid head round behind the container.

'Have you taken your picture?' he asks.

'No.'

'Well, I'm taking you home now.'

She looks crossly at him but she can see there'll be no discussion about it. He may not be very bright, but he does have his instincts. She doesn't trouble to argue, and puts her camera back in its case. She shuffles carefully back along the container and out onto the quay.

The shadow near Kabyssen has vanished.

She gets into the car looking thoroughly offended, but he doesn't notice. He pulls off at speed with a laugh, happy and a little high.

'The weather's going to be better tomorrow,' he says. 'There'll be a full moon, and the airship won't be flying anywhere.'

He clearly thinks this observation very witty. He bursts out laughing and accelerates so that the car sways ominously from side to side in the slush. Near the warehouse he swerves right out to the edge in an attempt to run over a row of sleepy gulls. They fly off and flap lazily away into the darkness.

24

At the last bend after the wood Holger Strand slows down. There's often ice on this hill between the tall firs. He was late leaving the Department. The clock on the dashboard shows 01.30. He turns into the drive and parks in the car-port. Lights are on all over the house.

He remains a few minutes in his seat, massaging his temples. He has a headache. The last three weeks have been a marathon. There's the whiff of an election in the air and everyone's busy positioning themselves. The opposition is no longer being serious, and the Minister has become self-important. His senior staff are always asking to see him, like a lot of schoolchildren, confused by the contradictory statements of the parties in the current government.

He notices his hands shaking ever so slightly: he recognises the body's final warning before some kind of collapse. From the glovebox he takes half a bar of dark chocolate, snaps a piece off and lets it melt in his mouth while he takes a couple of deep breaths.

'Are you still up?' he calls. He lets fall his heavy briefcase in the passageway to the kitchen, and it lands with a thump on the marble tiles. He takes off his jacket and puts it on a hanger. Gives himself plenty of time. Shoes, tie, top shirt-button. There's no need to hurry. He knows she's been waiting up. And when she sits waiting in the living-room at half past one in the morning, it's because they have to talk, and when they have to talk about something important, it'll be about Anne Sofie.

He just wants to go to sleep at the moment. A quick bath and down under the duvet in the guest room, which has been his bedroom for the past two years. But there's no way out of this, and he puts his glossy black Oxford shoes in their place under the stairs and goes into the living-room where Helene comes to meet him, her head on one side, cracking her knuckles as she often does these days.

'You're home late.'

'There was something I had to finish off before I go to Jutland tomorrow. You know I'll be up there till the weekend.'

'It's so important for you to be there, Holger.'

He realises that she's grappling with some problem. That's the reason for this decisiveness.

'You must have spoken to Sigvardtsen,' he says.

'She's been to the flat.'

'What's wrong with that?'

'She died on Saturday. There's going to be a post mortem, and the body hasn't been taken away yet. And in no time at all Anne Sofie's been there.'

'You're very well informed,' he sighs.

'She's ill, Holger. Your daughter is ill.'

No longer does anything about Anne Sofie's behaviour surprise him, but she certainly isn't ill. He's made up his mind about that. They have a son who is ill – who is in an institution, in fact. But his daughter isn't ill. She's an artist.

'Well, she's got that meeting with Knud Harber,' he says. 'I've spoken to Otto Bremer. He drove up there today. And I shall be there on Saturday. There's a trustees' meeting at the museum.'

Helene wrings her hands.

'I'm worried.'

'You ought to tell Sigvardtsen to stop following her.'

She grabs hold of him, as she's done so many times before.

'Why won't you admit it, Holger?'

He takes her hands, which are cold.

'She's an adult, Helene. She hasn't committed a crime. Nothing she's been charged with, anyway,' he adds, quickly anticipating his wife's response. 'If we treat her like a grown-up person, perhaps she'll behave like one.'

'When have you ever treated her like a grown-up person?' she says tartly. 'You've always spoilt her.'

He looks at his wife and sees that this is as much about him and her as it is about Anne Sofie. He catches a sweetness on her breath and realises she's been drinking.

'Well, yes,' he says thoughtfully. 'I've certainly indulged her, and I've overlooked a few things, but I haven't spoilt her and you haven't spoilt her, Helene. We've done our best, just like all parents.'

'She thinks up whatever ideas she likes.'

'Do we have to discuss this tonight? I don't feel all that well.'

'But you must be aware of what's happening.'

He lets go of his wife's hands.

'We've been through all this so many times. After Mads, we were afraid. But that breaking away, that distance she keeps from us – it came over her much earlier than you think. I realised that the other day when I drove her into town.'

Helene laughs.

'You realised the other day?'

'Yes, it sounds pathetic, but I did. It all began up there that summer when it didn't stop raining. That was two years before we told her. Don't you remember that summer, when she didn't say a word for a whole week? She just sat in the summerhouse in the garden, with her schoolbooks. Have you forgotten?'

She gives a gentle shake of her head.

'She's with him again, if that'll make you feel any better.'

Holger looks at his wife, a slight wince passing over his face.

'You don't listen,' he says. 'Someone might have said something to her that summer. It's a small town. People talk.'

'Said what to her?' she asks, going over to the window, her arms folded as if she felt cold. He watches her as he considers what to say. Although she's turned her back to him, craning her neck towards the lights strung around the patio, he can sense that she's listening. She's frail now. She's changed. She's not the person he fell in love with. He won't say what he thinks. Because it won't make things better. It might make things worse. And then he says it anyway, so that they can move on. He's not even sure if it really is what he thinks. But he says it.

'At some stage you paid Sigvardtsen, behind my back, to make her mother look like an impossible mother.'

Helene turns to him with coldness in her eyes, a coldness only to be seen between two people who've once loved each other, and whose long, tired love has at last withered to nothing.

'She was a drug addict. She wasn't in a fit state to look after a child.'

'How much did you pay him?'

'She was a drug addict.'

'That's not enough!' he suddenly shouts. 'There was more to it than that. There were false, twisted statements from all the neighbours.

And from that drunken doctor who'd gambled away his house and home.'

In the middle of the shouting the new phone rings on the landline. They stiffen, unused to having rows as serious as this. Holger reacts first, grabbing the receiver, listening and beginning to shake.

'No you may not,' he shouts in reply, slamming the receiver down with such force that something breaks and the receiver slips off and falls on to the table. Helene watches with a smile of resignation as he fiddles with the phone in confusion.

'That was him.'

He looks at his hand, where a cut and a dribble of blood have appeared on his finger. His face betrays a flicker of pain.

'She heard something, Helene. Something she never told us. Don't you understand? She knew she was adopted long before we made our confession.'

'Who would have told her anything?'

'And what can they have told her, Helene? Let me hear it from your own mouth. What exactly was the scenario you staged, you and the gardener? Tell me, so at least I'm prepared for disaster.'

She regards him with a cold grimace. The nervousness that has been a permanent feature about her for so many years now seems suddenly to have evaporated. Her eyes flash with pent-up fury.

'You've always been weak. A lazy slimy know-all with useless genes. Without my money and my connections we'd never have got that child. We were hardly in a strong position, with Mads in the house, believe you me. I got Henrik Meyer to fix a diagnosis which made Mads out to be harmless at that stage, and I arranged the rest with Sigvardtsen. And OK, I paid for it, while you went around thinking the adoption was all down to your fearfully important position! You've always been a wimp, Holger. A complete wimp.'

He stares at his wife in shock. This was exactly as he'd feared, but he'd hoped his imaginings had simply been an obsession. One of the many he'd had in recent years.

'I got down on my knees and begged Karen at the adoption service because by some miracle we'd been at university together. And hey presto, we jumped the queue and got the child we longed for. I fought to have that child before she was even born. Was that wrong?'

He looks at her.

'You paid Sigvardtsen to arrange a character-assassination.'

'She was a bloody drug-addict, for heaven's sake.'

'Oh yes, for heaven's sake. She was a pathetic little drug-addict. So it was a piss-easy mission to hand to that stupid arsehole.'

'It isn't Sigvardtsen's fault that she's ... she's turned out as she is.'

Holger gazes at his wife. In a trick of light from the candle on the mantelpiece he can recognise the young woman he fell in love with, and a sudden feeling of despair comes over him as he imagines he can understand her clumsy relationship with Anne Sofie. She can't love her. Not because she's adopted, but because she bought her, with lies and deceit. She must always have been afraid of the moment when it would be her turn to pay for all that. And after that afternoon when her pretty little daughter was involved in a bag-snatching incident and was brought home by the police, her behaviour changed. He hadn't understood at the time. He'd thought it was about Mads and their chronic guilty consciences after they'd given up and put him in an institution.

He turns away from her and goes upstairs to his study, slowly, as if he were counting every step.

Somebody had told his little angel how everything fitted together. Someone who was alone with her that summer when it rained. But who? She was with Sonny from morning to night. They played in the garden, he remembers. They would sit for hours in the summerhouse. She was the school-teacher, and he was the clever pupil. And although Sonny was nearly fourteen, she took all the initiative and Sonny obeyed. He and Helene would stand discreetly in the garden, amused that she could keep that slow-witted boy on the bench for hours at a time. She had had practice at that, they'd agreed, and Sonny was obviously a substitute for Mads, who'd been put away. Thus far they understood her. That was why she loved that strange boy with his learning difficulties.

But where had she been on that disastrous occasion at Sonny's uncle's house? He's been turning it over in his head since they came home from London. It had been during the silly season so the incident was well reported in most of the papers. He'd been into newspaper archives and found the exact date. Then he'd spent nearly an hour up in the loft looking for his old engagement diaries, which he'd hidden in the hope that someone, some day, would ask him to write his autobiography.

They'd been expecting visitors from Copenhagen: that was the day. They'd been busy. Lunch with every delicacy the sea could offer. Friends from the Ministry, and their good friend Otto Bremer. They would have eaten in the garden, but it was pelting down with rain, and they had to get everything ready inside.

Where had she been while they were preparing that lunch?

When the ambulance appeared in the road, followed by a trail of drenched children, he'd hurtled out of the house to look for her, and to his relief there she was, sitting in the summerhouse reading her book. But how long had she been sitting there? That Sonny boy just wasn't normal and had been put away, and in the autumn the uncle's house had been sold to an optician from Ålborg.

Helene had hidden her drawings. Hundreds of drawings she'd done sitting at his desk, or had brought home from school. Fine coloured drawings of Barbie dolls in different dresses, and he remembers that he had to have an opinion about which was the most beautiful: Sabrina, or Erica, or Josefine with the red hair. The sort of drawings all ten-year-old girls draw. The box had been in the loft. He'd brought it down the other day. Here it is: here's what he's looking for. And here she is, around ten years old, and everything is suddenly drawn with much more confident lines. Two people, a little one and a big one, in perspective. One of them against a sunrise, dark and lacking definition. But a woman and a girl in the foreground. There are several. An iceberg in the water and a seal and a woman. There's always a woman in the picture. In the corner or behind a cloud. He stares at the drawings and feels his tears welling up.

Helene appears in the doorway.

'What is it now?' she asks wearily at the sight of her husband sitting on the floor half-buried in a child's drawings.

'Look at this,' he says, and gets to his knees, holding one out to her.

'Look at what?' she asks.

'She's drawn her mother. Can't you see? Look at this one. And this. Look how it changes from innocent dolls to something dark. Branches, clouds, and this woman. Look, in this one she's sitting on a throne, and look, here are some huskies. These drawings were done two years before you ever told her she was adopted. Do you understand? Or don't you want to understand?'

'Oh, the drawings have subjects, Holger. Sometimes the subjects are African. If you looked at a few more you'd find drawings of lions and elephants.'

He shakes his head.

'No,' he says. 'There are no lions or elephants. There are these people. Look at them, for heaven's sake, and think about it. Can't you remember? You were worried that she'd become so silent.'

'You're tired, Holger.'

In desperation he gathers up the drawings and goes over to her.

'Take them and look at them.'

'Now just stop it,' she says, loud and clear.

Holger puts the drawings down on the table.

'I must ring her. I must ring now.'

'Don't do that, Holger.'

He pushes her aside, hurries out of the room and goes downstairs. She follows him.

'Holger, you'll only make it worse,' she shouts. 'Can't you be reasonable?'

He finds his mobile and dials the number of the house in Skagen.

'Holger,' she shouts desperately. 'Holger, get a grip on yourself.'

She goes over to him and tries frantically to snatch his phone, but he fends her off. He stands a long time, tired and miserable, with the ringing tone in his ear. Then he gives up and sits down heavily on the sofa.

'You're tired, Holger. You're stressed. We'll talk about it when you get back from Jutland. I promise. When you're back from Jutland we'll discuss it.'

She sits down beside him and he lets her take his hand.

'Did I ever tell you that Hermansen from the cement works has died?' he asks in a whisper. 'Hermansen came every Tuesday to take him out.'

'Yes,' she says, 'you did tell me.'

'Mads was fond of him.'

'Yes,' she says very quietly.

'They said they noticed a difference when he'd been out to the cement works. As if he'd got some life in his eyes.'

'Yes. That was a good idea, Holger. You've done good things for Mads.'

He stares in front of him.

'Yes,' he says. 'It was good while it lasted.'

'Perhaps there'll be someone else who'll take over.'

He gets up from the sofa. It was Anne Sofie who had brought them to the brink with each other. Not Mads. Mads was ill. That was a fact. With Anne Sofie it was a different matter. Slowly but surely she'd worn them out and they'd drifted away from each other. He looks at his wife and sees that the conversation is over.

'You need some sleep, Holger.'

'Yes.'

25

The advantage of heavy curtains is that they keep the light out – but only if you remember to close them. At the moment the sunlight is firmly settled in sharp squares on the pale floral wallpaper.

Mikkel was in the middle of a strange dream when he was woken by someone running backwards and forwards in the corridor outside. A ridiculous dream that had nothing to do with the previous evening's painful humiliation. A dream in which he accepted an apology from his father. In the dream, they were the same age. In a grey suit and open-necked white shirt, his father stood looking at him with a sad smile on his face. Young and embarrassed, as he remembers him from the wedding photograph that hung in his mother's sewing-room, when they were still living in Vanløse. What his father was apologising for naturally remained, as always in dreams, undisclosed.

He swings his legs out of bed and goes over to the mirror. His lip is slightly swollen and beneath his eye a yellowish-blue bruise has appeared. The whole of one side of his chest is yellow, which explains the pain and the trouble he's had simply getting out of bed. The ancient plumbing warbles when he turns on the tap and carefully rinses his bruised face.

His entire body aches while he gets dressed, and after he's managed with some difficulty to lace up his boots, he rests for a moment on the edge of the bed to wake up properly. What is it in one's subconscious that determines what one dreams? In this case he knows only too well. When he went home to wish them a good journey and to take instructions about his mother's plants, his father had summoned him into his study. They were going to have a man-to-man talk, though a moment later his mother had appeared too and he realised they had something planned. Something they both wanted to confide to him. Something that had to be said before they set off. 'Mikkel,' he heard his father say, rocking slightly on his feet with his hands thrust in his pockets in jocular fashion, 'You really ought to start looking for somewhere else to live.'

He'd turned to his mother, who smiled wistfully, and he saw that this was something they'd agreed between them. 'Why?' he had asked. His father assumed the awkward grin of someone in a provincial casino who's just lost a small sum at roulette. It must be obvious to a young man at the nation's top business school that the flat really had to be sold as soon as possible. 'Don't you read the newspapers, old chap?'

He lifts his arms and stretches until the pain in his chest becomes unbearable. Anne Sofie is a kind of accident, he thinks, a bit like falling off your bike or having a roof-tile come down on your head. But his parents had made careful preparations. The moment had been carefully chosen. There had to be a clear line in the sand, so that they could enjoy their holiday. He had a couple of months, and when they got back, the worst of his indignation would have evaporated.

On that first evening at Henry's, while the smell of meatballs was still coming from the kitchen and Dorte was arguing with her father, it had suddenly occurred to him that he'd spent his entire life trying not to disappoint them. In his project-group with Simon, Jesper and Astrid he'd realised for the first time that life isn't a competition. It was Astrid who had opened his eyes to that, and he was eternally grateful to her. One evening, when he was not entirely sober, he'd been running down whoever was sitting next to him with his sarcastic comments, and she'd asked him if he really needed to work off his frustrations on his friends, and why he found it satisfying to be a complete pain. He'd left the party, shaken and miserable.

Shortly afterwards he'd considered leaving the course, and went to see his supervisor, desperate to talk to an adult. He'd told things as they were, or at least tried to, but didn't get very far. After a few minutes he was sitting in the office crying. That autumn he calmly acknowledged how pathetic it was that his parents worried about their neighbours' grass.

As for Anne Sofie, it's all definitely over with her. She's just a spoilt brat who's gone completely weird because she's had too much attention. That look she'd given him, when he came over to her table. As if they'd never set eyes on each other before. He can't be bothered to think about it again.

*

Green and grey. A thin streak of pale orange across the picture, and blue-black darkness with little flecks of silver.

She hesitates. The picture's come out well, she thinks, but it isn't perfect. She takes hold of the paper with her tweezers and lifts it carefully into the rinsing bath. There's a touch of mist over the Cyrillic characters. This evening she'll try again, with a slightly shorter exposure, she decides, putting it to one side. The pictures from the flat, on the other hand, are decidedly successful.

She gently holds the first one up and examines it carefully. They're lying on the bed. Naked and white. Forehead to forehead, lit in soft white. The lighting and the composition weren't difficult. All that looked after itself. The difficulty was getting Sonny to grasp the deeper meaning.

She fastens the little padlock on the darkroom door and goes through the living-room and upstairs to get changed. She chooses her brown mohair roll-neck sweater and bottle-green trousers.

As she's cleaning her teeth at the kitchen sink she hears the metallic click of the gate closing. She draws the curtain aside. It's Poul with a plastic bag, which he flourishes dramatically when he sees her face at the window. He looks quite stupid with his small eyes and wide mouth. She lets him in, and as he kicks off his boots he gives a broad grin, as if this were an illicit date.

'Look, we've got provisions,' he says, producing a bottle of beer from his plastic bag and opening it boldly with his cigarette lighter before settling down on the old bench. Like all alcoholics he's fairly good at controlling his movements, but it's clear that he's drunk.

'Is this a party, Poul?' she asks, rinsing her mouth out.

'A party? Absolutely. We're having a little party after the funeral,' he says, half-emptying the bottle in a few big thirsty swigs. 'You coming?'

She sits down beside him.

'Maybe.'

'Go on,' he says, doubling up with a large belch. 'I'd appreciate it.'

She's seen his clumsy body-language before, during other winters, and she recognises the fire in his eyes from one meaningless foggy Tuesday night when she'd gone into the pub by the harbour where he has his regular place at the bar. Where Krille, in fact, had her regular place. He's the same age as Holger and Henry, but age is a relative concept. Though his face is worn and his body wasted by over-drinking, there's something boyish about his gestures, and as he sits at the table, blinking in the sunlight falling on him through a gap in the curtains, he's just as she's always remembered him.

'I've got some home-made rye-bread here for you,' he says, struggling a little with the wind in his stomach. 'It smells a bit of beer,' he chuckles, with his nose in the bag. 'And a bit of frozen fish soup.'

Of all the people in the town, she knows he misses Krille more than anyone.

'What else have you got to tell me, Poul,' she asks.

He sits for a long moment staring at his bottle as if he hasn't heard the question.

'The painting.'

'Yes,' she says, looking at him.

He screws up his eyes in an effort to concentrate. Then he leans back and throws out his arms in resignation.

'She sold it to someone for next to nothing,' he whispers to himself.

Some excited children's voices out in the road penetrate the room. Perhaps it's the children's breathless shouting and the sound of their sledge-runners on the gravel in the snow that wake him up.

'Now there's only you,' he says.

Sitting there and drivelling, he irritates her.

'Your grandma was sent over here to learn Danish. It was an experiment.'

'Spare me all that sentimental bullshit,' she says sharply. 'I asked you to find out who bought the painting. That can't be so bloody difficult. Instead you've got yourself pissed.'

She doesn't want to be connected with her grandmother. She has no connection with Greenland. She was brought up in a grand old house near Hillerød amongst beech-trees and mustard-yellow fields. When she looks at her reflection in the mirror, she sees a Danish girl with green eyes. True, she has black hair, but no obvious racial characteristics. She could equally well have had an Italian or French grandmother, and the heart-rending sentimental affection for others that Krille had, and all Greenlanders have, is completely alien to her. She gives him a shake.

'Poul, for heavens' sake. You can't just sit here and bloody well go to sleep.'

He looks up at her, smiling apologetically.

'The caretaker wants to talk to you.'

'About what?'

He shrugs his shoulders.

'Someone's smashed the door in. He thinks it was me who nicked that shitty painting.'

Emptying the rest of his beer he grabs the edge of the table and pulls himself to his feet. Then he stumbles out into the hall and rests his hand on the door-frame while he puts on his boots.

'Henry says I shouldn't give you ideas.'

'Henry can just keep out of it.'

He pulls a face and shakes his head. She opens the door for him and he walks uncertainly towards the gate.

'Poul,' she says, 'wherever she left her coat, that's where the painting is.'

'Really, Soffi?'

'Yes,' she says, 'it's as simple as that.'

The snow in the garden has made a bluish-white crust over the lyme-grass, which sticks through here and there. Poul walks carefully past the rusty swing-seat to the gate, then turns to look at her for one last time.

She realises that behind the film of alcohol, which lies like a thin membrane over all his movements, he's grieving over the loss of a good friend, and it helps a little to present her daughter with a home-baked loaf and a bit of soup.

'Are you going to get you hair cut sometime?' she asks in the impeccable local accent that comes easily to her. 'You look like a horse that's been set on fire.'

He breaks into a toothless grin as he shuts the gate carefully after him.

'And you look more like your mother than you think.'

She stands in the doorway watching him plod down the road. Care for others isn't usually in her, but just now she has a lump in her throat.

26

Mikkel sees his shadow stretch out sharp towards the shallow dunes. The sun hangs low over the town, its light reflected in the snow crystals, making him screw up his eyes. Snow on sand: it's like treading on brown sugar. Not that he's ever trodden on brown sugar, of course, but it must have the heavy consistency he can feel under his boots at every step. His entire body is sore, but it helps to walk.

He can't remember being involved in a fight before, apart from a scene in the sandpit at the nursery in Vanløse. A young man was stabbed in the middle of town just before Christmas, but that was an unlucky chance. The wrong place at the wrong time. Like being struck by lightning. But it hadn't exactly been a lightning strike when he looked in through the windows of the pub yesterday evening. He'd had plenty of time to think about how he should act. He'd made a fool of himself anyway. He'd called him Dumbo, and the payoff had been spectacular.

He walks towards the great grey bunkers, half-submerged in the dunes. The gun-port towards the sea has been blocked up, but someone has since knocked a hole through into the dark interior. He must go over, just to see if there's a couple of German soldiers sitting forgotten inside. He trudges along the edge of the dune and struggles awkwardly on to a path worn by the summer tourists. Inland he can see a deep-frozen campsite with little numbered plots.

Careful not to slip in the snow, he gets a foothold on the concrete lip of the bunker and then manages to worm his way to a little platform, a sharp pain jabbing his chest all the while. He stands slightly breathless, high above the beach, brushing the snow from his trousers. 'Hallo! Anyone in here?'

Still curious, he pushes his torso through the gun-port and has to wait a while before his eyes adjust to the darkness. To his disappointment, all he can see is some sodden toilet-paper and a bit of charred wood. He turns and looks out towards the lighthouse and the sunlight flickering like firelight on the snow. Way out on the horizon a container-ship is making its way into the Kattegat and another is rounding Grenen Point. Further in a trawler is making for harbour accompanied by its following of gulls. Right under the lighthouse a small flock of eider has landed in a little lagoon among the ice-encrusted groynes. 'It's way out of the hunting season,' Dorte had said, turning the meatballs over in frustration as she cooked. But Zeppo, the chef at the hotel in Old Skagen, had spoken up for the eider duck. 'I walked until I couldn't go any further,' Zeppo had chuckled in his heavy Slavic accent when Mikkel had asked him during their game of billiards how he'd ended up here. There was something servile about Zeppo, who had swallowed his pride to gain acceptance by the locals despite his funny accent. But there was also something watchful about him. Careful.

Little by little the sky is gathering itself together in a few blue-grey clouds towards the east, and Mikkel can see that there's more snow to come. Snow and wind. He steps towards the edge of the platform, draws his knees up and lets himself slide carefully down until he regains his foothold on the sharp concrete edge. Then he jumps the last short distance to the sand, with the pain stabbing at his chest again, but he resists it and slithers on his back down the side of the dune. For a second he imagines he's a soldier fighting for the Fatherland, his chest torn by a fragment from a grenade or wounded by a bullet in the back. He stays lying down for a minute looking up at the cloudless blue sky, waiting for the pain to ease slowly away.

It's good to walk. It's easier to forget here, where the light is brilliant and the air tastes of seaweed and salt. He sets off again along the shore, past the groynes near the grey lighthouse and along the water's edge where the massive, unevenly sunken bunkers lie strewn on the beach like a throw of dice. He continues resolutely towards the point where, according to the tourist brochures at reception, the two seas and the whole world meet. Today there's not a breath of wind. Only the smallest ripples on the surface, and hanging in the sky the tern are queuing up to nose-dive into the tiny waves.

He knows how it should look from the paintings. Expansive and majestic, waves breaking in metre-high plumes of spray, the current swirling in every direction, while the wordless lifeboatmen on the shore strain their eyes at the brig that hugs the shore round the point.

He looks along the beach to the west. It's flat here as far as the eye can see, interrupted only by a little crest of low dull-green dunes with a slender white lighthouse in the distance. You could land a jumbo-jet here, he thinks, walking over a fine covering of virgin snow. The only things to catch the eye are a plastic bucket half-buried in the sand, and a few pieces of driftwood. He suddenly understands the uniqueness of the place. Whether you start your journey across Europe in Turkey, or at the toe of Italy, or in Gibraltar with your back to Africa, you'll end up here: so there's only one way to go, and that's back. That was what Zeppo meant. And for Zeppo there's no going back.

Away in the distance, where the coast curves round and the beach and the ocean run together, he can make out three figures coming towards him. After a few minutes' walking he can see that it's a woman and two men. One of the men is a head taller than the other, with a broad-brimmed hat and a stick in his hand, which he uses to point out to sea. Laughter wafts faintly on the breeze, and Mikkel wonders if he should change his own direction and go inland over the levels. What does one do? Does one say hello to strangers? Yes, greeting people must be the normal thing, he decides, because we are all united in being precisely here in this special place.

But he doesn't feel particularly presentable with his black eye, and he makes his mind up to cross over to the levels. He's the one who got landed with a fist in his face last night. The whole ridiculous episode comes back to him with new force. He goes straight inland across the low dunes and reaches a track that has been churned by tractor-tyres, and leads to a big car park. His phone warbles. It's a text from the undertaker.

'Problem with delivery. Please drop by.'

A anaemic little girl is standing in the undertaker's. Fair hair in plaits, and large frightened eyes. For a second he thinks she's an angel. A little Fate risen from one of Jantzen's coffins to have a look around the parlour. She stares at him and he realises that it's the bluish-violet colours under his eye and his swollen lip that fascinate her. Then Jantzen emerges from the back office with a woman who, judging by her complexion and pointed nose, must be the girl's mother. Her hair is long and fine and her quilted jacket is showing signs of wear.

'Ring me,' says the woman, and something fractionally disturbs the set of Jantzen's mouth as she shuts the door after her.

'You got my message,' he says.

'Yes.'

Jantzen takes a deep breath and assumes an expression indicating imminent bad news.

'The coffin you chose isn't in stock, I'm sorry to say. I've had to select another one. It's slightly more expensive, not much more, but it's all we've got available for Saturday.'

'So it'd better be that one.'

'The sexton asked me if you'd like the choir. It wouldn't involve any extra expense. With a bit of support the singing can be really nice.'

'The priest didn't mention a choir.'

Mikkel notices again the slight disturbance to Jantzen's lips, which might be a smile or a wince of pain.

'He did ask me to find out.'

'Well then, that's OK with me.'

At this Jantzen's face brightens with something that is unmistakably a smile.

'Would you like a coffee? I hope you're not too busy?'

No, he's not. He needs to go to the harbour to talk to Henry, but it's still fairly early, and his curiosity to see what Jantzen has hidden in his back office settles the matter.

The window giving on to the yard is barred, indicating that the shop once dealt in some valuable commodity. Along one of the walls packing cases are stacked to the ceiling, and facing them are a worn sofa and two armchairs. There's a table with a coffee-machine by the window, and a CD-player stands on a small bookcase.

He takes off his jacket and chooses the chair which doesn't have springs showing through the upholstery. He's disappointed. He'd hoped the place would be stuffed with coffins, but there are only a few crates packed with ceramic urns, and a few brochures on the bookcase.

Jantzen reminds him of a prisoner reconciled to his fate as he pours a cup of coffee and puts it on the table. Then he seems to be expecting something, as if he's waiting to know what Mikkel thinks of the taste.

It's bitter. Mikkel sips it and looks round the room.

'I've only had this place a year,' says Jantzen. 'I'm not the only undertaker here, but it's always good to have a bit of competition. Our main office is in Hjørring.'

'It must be a strange profession,' says Mikkel.

The set of Jantzen's mouth alters slightly again.

'I remove a problem for people,' he says. 'Death is rather impractical. You're just left with a corpse. The Hindus burn their dead themselves. The ones who can't afford a decent pyre have to make do with an oil-drum. Entertaining to watch, but a bit difficult when it's grandpa in there.'

'Death can be fascinating for an artist,' says Mikkel.

Jantzen's eyebrows flick up and down. Mikkel noticed them last time he was here. Jantzen has two means of expression, and he cherishes them. He has a slight variation in the set of his mouth, which might indicate pain, annoyance or pleasure, and he can raise his eyebrows in situations of surprise, such as the other day when Mikkel insisted on the 'bog-standard' option.

'An artist,' says Jantzen, peering through the window-bars as if he's noticed something interesting in the yard. 'Is that what she is?'

'Who?'

'The girl you were with the other day. The man-from-the-ministry's daughter.'

Jantzen is evidently well informed.

'Some people say so.'

'Maybe you've seen some of her work?'

'Oh yes. Some photographs.'

'Really.'

This is something that clearly impresses the undertaker, and it suddenly gives him the initiative. Mikkel pulls himself together and struggles out of the armchair holding his cup, which he places on the table. The coffee's undrinkable.

'And are they art?' asks Jantzen.

'I don't know. But death plays some kind of role in them. The two of you have something in common there.'

Jantzen has suddenly become more obliging.

'Are they portraits?' he pursues, with a hint of anticipation.

Mikkel furrows his forehead, and with a thoughtful expression he attempts to bring to mind the photographs which he can recall in every detail. They've branded themselves so deeply in his consciousness that he'll remember them for the rest of his life.

'I'm not sure that you could call them portraits.'

'What are they, then?'

'Death runs through them like a theme, I think.'

'In what way?'

Mikkel shrugs his shoulders. He hasn't really thought about this before. Not in this way.

'I think she's looking for something. Isn't that what artists do?'

'Her past, perhaps?' asks Jantzen helpfully.

The fellow's interest takes Mikkel by surprise, but he wouldn't dream of going into the detail of what he's seen.

'Perhaps.'

'But you have seen some of her portraits?'

'Oh yes. One or two.'

Jantzen stands cracking his finger-joints. It's as if he's wondering whether to confide in this young man.

'I met her last winter just after we'd opened this branch. She came in to ask about a coffin. She took a picture of me on that occasion. Has she mentioned me at all?'

'No,' says Mikkel. 'Not in the conversations I've had with her.'

Jantzen gives an embarrassed smile.

'I'd really like to see that picture.'

'Perhaps she didn't even develop it,' teases Mikkel.

'Maybe not,' says Jantzen.

Their talk has taken an unexpected turn. Jantzen is less formal and seems unsure of himself.

'What sort of portrait was it?' asks Mikkel. 'I could ask her. I go and see her once in a while.'

'Do you?'

'Oh yes.'

The corners of Jantzen's mouth twitch slightly as he remembers that afternoon.

'It was nothing special. I just sat on a chair.'

'Why was she after a coffin?'

'She only wanted a look at some brochures. Afterwards it occurred to me that the coffin question was just a pretext.'

He can follow Jantzen part of the way. Anne Sofie chooses her portraits with care. But enough is enough, and the taste of boiled coffee still lingers on his tongue.

'I must get going,' he says, shaking Jantzen's hand.

Jantzen follows him to the door.

'Have you been to the museum?'

'No. I've thought about going in.'

'You could ask her along. She might get inspiration from the old Skagen painters.'

'She's not all that keen on them,' says Mikkel, opening the door.

It's difficult to leave just at this moment. Jantzen's persistence is awkward.

'Isn't keen on them?'

'She calls their paintings biscuit-tin art.'

'Really?' says Jantzen. 'Biscuit-tin art?'

'I've got to go. Thanks for the chat.'

At last he makes his escape. As he crosses the street he glances back at the parlour bedecked with Paw Johansen's sand-sculpted figures, and sees that Jantzen is already talking into his phone.

27

Sigvardtsen stands behind the rose-hedge trying to make out the body language going on behind the half-drawn curtains. That's the Crab, come to see her, and it makes him anxious. What's the Crab talking to her about?

As soon as he senses that departure might be imminent, he crosses the road and lets himself into the neighbour's house opposite. It's another that he looks after. He hangs his cap on a hook, takes off his thick jacket and removes his wooden-soled boots. The living-room floorboards have been planed and one of these days will need to be varnished. The furniture is still gathered in a corner, covered with brown paper.

He fetches a chair and sets it on an old newspaper by the window where he'll get a good view of the gate. He's got plenty of time and he's happy to wait. As a young man he used to go hunting with the butcher, and they'd sit for hours, hardly breathing, on the edge of a clearing while the sun slowly set. From the low brushwood of firs the animals would eventually emerge, stepping carefully, with flared nostrils and sensitive ears, alert for the smallest sound that might not be a hare in the grass or a branch in the wind.

That was what he enjoyed most about hunting. The waiting, and the certainty that at some point the animals would appear out of the undergrowth, driven by hunger. Just the same with that girl over there. Sooner or later she'll come out from behind the rose bushes and disappear down the road.

He lets his gaze rest on a point a little forward of the gate. It doesn't matter whether it's three-quarters of an hour or three hours before she comes out. He's promised Fru Strand that he'll keep an eye on her, and he's not going to miss anything. He gets out his tobacco-tin, takes out just enough to fit on his right thumb-nail, and puts it into his cheek.

The moment the tobacco begins to take effect, he catches sight of someone at the gate. A young man with a thick hooded jacket, who hesitates, looking at the house, puts his hand on the gate, and then changes his mind and goes on down the road.

He knows very well why the boy's after her. That girl is the spitting image of her mother. Years ago he was smitten with the same malady. Krille was eighteen, working down in the fish factory. He was thirty-three, but felt young. He had something to offer: his own carpentry workshop.

One summer evening there was a band playing down by the harbour. She'd had plenty to drink and she looked easy meat, and he'd grabbed her, held her tight and insisted on a dance. But she'd refused. 'Why not?' he'd asked as his blood was rising. She'd looked at him with a wry smile and heavy eyes. 'Because you're so nice.' That's what she'd said, as she pulled herself free and thrown herself into the arms of a distinctly drunk Henry Olsen. She could have said anything else: what she said, and the way she'd looked into his eyes, were unforgettable. 'Because you're so nice.'

Everyone has their share of sorrow and happiness – Fru Strand certainly has. He's known her a long time. A fine woman, who appreciated his workmanship in the old house and garden. The Permanent Secretary had insisted on keeping the wilderness and the hedge of wild roses at the roadside, but even so he'd had no problem finding things to do. An old house suffers a good deal during the winter when the sea-mist lies over the town. Little pieces of cement come loose in a storm and drop from the ridge of the roof, or the chimney needs re-pointing and rendering, or the old window-frames need rubbing down and painting.

Fru Strand has paid him well, and he's had an insight into a good family and the way they live. He's even been present during confidential discussions between the higher ranks of the civil service, sitting there in the shadows, staining the fence or scraping at the window-frames.

Famous people came here. People you read about in magazines. Actors. Television reporters you think you know personally from the daily news bulletin. Artists. For him, Fru Strand has been the doorway to a life that most people only read about. And that's how it's going to carry on. That's exactly how it's going to carry on.

He owes Fru Strand everything. She helped him when his workshop burned down. She testified that he'd been at her house all day. The last time he spoke to her on the phone she was afraid the girl would have some kind of accident, herself and the house too. And she was right to be afraid. Two evenings running she's been down to the harbour, standing right out at the icy edge, staring into nothing. Sooner or later things are going to end badly.

But what can the Crab want to talk to her about? He must have heard something. He knows something. And what the Crab knows, that girl knows.

At a sound from the gate, he lifts his head. There she goes. He must have dozed off for a moment. Stiff-limbed, he takes his jacket and cap from the hook in the hall.

28

The temperature's beginning to drop. As she opens the gate, the snow on the hedge billows up and hits her in the face like a cloud of fine dust. She goes down the road, past the museum, her fur hat pulled well down.

Every so often life becomes so predictable that it's almost depressing. She knows what the caretaker will say if he finds her. 'You've got no business in this flat.' That's what he's going to say, and in a way he's right. But at the moment she can't be concerned with the niceties of the law.

She examines the damaged door and frame. On the table in the living-room lie Sonny's empty beer-cans and the blackened silver paper and crusts of pizza they left behind. The bed is empty. The window has been left open, and frost lies like a thin layer of felt over the panes facing the balcony. She closes the window and turns up the radiators. In one of the kitchen cupboards she finds a plastic sack: she clears the rubbish from the table and wipes it with a cloth.

When she's finished the cleaning, she pulls out the cardboard box from under the sofa, puts to one side the folders of Keldberg family weddings and birthdays, and then empties the remainder over the table, spreading the small colour photographs out and surveying them all.

The first picture she happens to pick up was taken in front of a burger bar: Hirtshals Harbour Grill, says the sign in the background. Krille is there, with two long-haired boys in blue overalls. Another shows a birthday party, complete with cake, in a canteen. The girls are in overalls, their hair in light-blue nets. In a third, a girl-friend, to judge from her smile, appears in pyjamas. This is Krille's entire ordinary life, disordered and accidental in every respect, narrated in pictures that aren't very well exposed. This is Krille's story. The story she was too intoxicated to tell herself. In most of the photos she's high, or drunk, or both.

Anne Sofie straightens in her chair and looks over the table. Holger and Helene are her legal parents. Her life from birth until now. But when she stands in front of a mirror, she knows why her hair is black and smooth, and how she's come by her faintly exotic complexion. What she can't understand is how her biological mother could have been a threat to anyone, why Holger and Helene waited so long to tell her she was adopted, and why she had to go knocking on doors in the registry office to find out a surname.

She starts sorting things according to the first system that occurs to her. The pictures where Krille is drunk and high go in one pile, and the pictures where she's clear-eyed are for herself.

Who can it have been, standing in the road last night? Who followed her down to the harbour? Yesterday evening she'd been afraid. For the first time she'd been really afraid. She was afraid because she realised it wasn't Sigvardtsen. The figure who slowly turned round and disappeared behind the hedge was taller than Sigvardtsen, and he wasn't wearing Sigvardtsen's cap. She stares at the hundreds of small photographs. How does Sigvardtsen fit into all this? Maybe he'll turn up here among these friends and colleagues.

She catches her breath. Is that someone on the stairs? She listens. Someone coughs. A neighbour goes into a flat.

She stands up and goes over to the piano. There she remains for a while, contemplating a tack illuminated in a patch of light on the carpet. She shakes herself free of a thought, goes into the kitchen, opens a drawer and rummages amongst the cutlery until she finds a knife the right size. A fish-cleaning knife with a good handle and a sharp blade. She takes it into the living-room and puts it on the chair under her fur hat.

She carries on searching through the photographs. She decides to start a fourth pile with children in them, and pauses over a black and white portrait. It must be a confirmation picture. On the reverse is the rubber stamp of Jeppesen & Søn, Adelgade 47, Hobro. Krille is sitting in her white confirmation dress, with her Mona Lisa smile, yet looking as if she doesn't quite trust the photographer. Her hair is glossy black and her eyes deep and dark, her lips full. If she showed the picture to a child and asked who it was, she knows what the answer would be.

She sits for a long time turning over picture after picture in the hope that the game of patience will come out. But nothing varies. Party after party. Drinking and flirting. Random snapshots of the beach or of the factory when someone happened to have a camera with them.

Krille's purse is lying on the window-sill. She opens it. Behind the dull plastic is a faded colour photograph. Drawing it out, she studies it. Henry and Krille in younger editions. Between them is a little girl in a pale dress with her hair tied in bows and wearing white sandals. The girl is holding Henry's hand.

She can just remember the occasion. Not what was said, nor the situation as such. But the heat and the smell of warm asphalt and fish, and the beaming lady. Let's have a photograph together, and they stood quite still, as the lady smiled and stroked her hair. She examines the picture intensely. They're all screwing their eyes up against the sun. But they're smiling.

She closes her eyes. The thought is almost unbearable. The thought that Krille always knew who she was. That she would have recognised her as a three-year-old standing with Helene in the queue in the co-op. Or would have watched her on the beach, a ten-year-old playing at the water's edge with Sonny. Or when she was a teenager, half-drunk, high, and shouting her head off, coming into the harbour tavern with Frode. It's absurd, and her resentment at Holger and Helene's silence, their half-truths and their lack of courage, smoulders within her like a pile of embers that refuse to go out.

She'd twice tried in vain to track down her mother, and the message was the same both times. By the time of her third attempt, when she was just eighteen, the rules had been relaxed. She was an adult, and she was given a name after a procedure whereby her biological mother had first been contacted by formal letter and had indicated that she agreed to a meeting.

It hadn't been a surprise to learn that she lived in Skagen. It had been more like a punch in the diaphragm. She'd known that since she was ten. Someone had whispered it in her ear one afternoon. One afternoon when it was raining. She was at Sonny's house with her reading-book. They were sitting in his room, and all of a sudden there he was, standing unsteadily in the doorway. 'The Parrot's little bastard.' Those were the words that issued from his mouth, accompanied by a sweetish stink. One coarse hand on the nape of her neck, and the other under her summer dress. She hadn't understood the words he'd whispered, and there was sweat between her legs.

Sonny had thumped and pounded on his back, and the heavy body turned like an angry bear. Sonny had run off into the scullery with his uncle close behind him. A moment later Sonny had come back into the room with a knife in his hand. 'You'd better go home,' he'd said.

She had straightened her dress, picked up her book, and walked with great care in the scullery so as not to fall over on the newly slippery floor-tiles. She walked towards the door. Out into the rain. She hid her sandals in the dustbin underneath a bag of rubbish, and explained later that she'd left them behind on the beach. With the sandals she also hid the words he'd whispered, and the hand between her legs, and the bad teeth – and the sunken, bloodshot, dead eyes. In the end everything was pushed firmly down under a thick blanket of caring.

She opens the door to the balcony to get some air. At a window on the other side of the street a naked woman is watering some flowers. Down on the pavement in front of the paper-shop the caretaker and one of his assistants are standing beside a mechanised snow-scraper. He turns and looks up at the balcony as if he feels intuitively that he's being watched.

Holger and Helene smoothed everything over with care. Levelled every surface, filled every hollow with oblivion and luxury, and spread a thin varnish of deceit over her inconvenient questions. She was spoilt beyond all bounds. She was the Permanent Secretary's lovely and slightly exotic little princess. She was the child they'd longed for. And Helene was naturally dark, so none of their friends was surprised.

When she eventually met her mother, it was a disappointment. The curtains were closed, and Krille had given herself too much Dutch courage: she just sat in the semi-darkness feeling betrayed. She held her hand and kept telling her she was the most beautiful girl in the world. When she left her that afternoon she felt no clearer about who she was herself, but at least she knew who she wasn't.

Why weren't social services more joined up? Why did they give precisely the same standard package, without discussion, to each and every young single mother? Why the final severance and the impenetrable silence? What were they afraid of? That she'd pack up all her teddy-bears when she was five and come back to live here in Mosegården?

She settles down at the table again and carries on looking. She opens and closes the Kodak envelopes with all the unbearable colour photographs from the first teenage years in the Keldberg family, with Krille sitting with an angry look on her face, as if to signal that the whole thing is a terrible misunderstanding. The pictures nauseate her and she throws the envelopes to the floor with a smack. In another folder are pictures from youthful years at parties in clubs in Hirtshals, and later in Skagen. Blurred pictures taken in fogs of hash and junk, but at least they're of Krille on good days and bad. Krille smiling through her highs. But at least she's smiling.

She hears the entrance door bang down below, and a draught from the stairwell blows the bedroom door to with a squeak. She gets up from the table and listens. She can hear slightly dragging footsteps on the stairs: she goes back to the table and seizes the knife. Then she sits down on the sofa to wait, the coffee table a kind of barricade in front of her, holding her breath as the sound of the footsteps becomes clearer. Then silence out in the hallway. A soft whistling. He's examining the door. Then he steps over the bead curtain spread out on the floor, and suddenly appears with his hand on the doorframe and the beginnings of a smile on his face.

'And who have we here?' he says, out of breath from his climb up the stairs.

'I thought you must be someone else,' she says with relief, slipping the knife discreetly back between the cushions.

The caretaker looks at her briefly before turning to the table. He picks up a picture at random and considers it before putting it back.

'There've been a few well-oiled parties here over the years,' he mumbles.

She makes no comment on this remark, but simply stares forward, offended. She was in the middle of something and he's interrupted her.

'How are you then?' he asks, sitting down at the table.

Still no answer, and he nods to himself.

'I got hold of the Crab this morning. Your mother had a painting hanging above the piano. Of course he knew nothing about it.'

'She sold it because she was short of cash.'

'Is that what he says?'

'Yes.'

'Do you believe it?'

'Yes.'

'Who would she have sold it to?'

She shrugs her shoulders.

'Someone she owed money to, perhaps.'

He sits and shuffles the pictures with one finger, as if he too is playing patience with them.

'Until a year ago, Grete Sigvardtsen used to live in the flat next door. Her son did her shopping for her. He's friendly with your adoptive mother, isn't he – could there be any kind of connection there?' he says, pretending to look at a picture on the table.

She can tell from his tone that he hasn't come here to be officious or unpleasant. He's trying to tell her something without making difficulties for himself. If you're the caretaker of several blocks of flats you have to be cautious about what you hear, and especially about what you say.

'What do you mean?'

'Well, he's always running round doing jobs for the posh people. Maybe he's heard something. Someone must have bought that picture. And if they were from round here, somebody else will know about it. You know how people talk.'

The caretaker holds a photo and stares at it for a while, before smiling and putting it down.

'I really liked your mother,' he says, getting up from the table.

She remains motionless in the hope that he'll say more, but realises that he's on his way somewhere else.

'Do you take pictures yourself?' he asks with a glance at the camera-case.

'Yes,' she says, with sudden energy. 'And I'd like a picture of you for my collection before you go.'

He smiles.

'For your collection?'

'Krøyer and Ancher painted all the characters in the town. I'm photographing all the biggest idiots around here. A little project on the side.'

He laughs.

'Could I be having a little tinkle on the piano while you take it?'

'If you like.'

He's in his early fifties, and has dark curly hair; he's solid without being fat. He looks like someone who's had a good life. Someone who doesn't owe anyone anything. Someone who feels he doesn't need anything beyond a good supper.

'There's an amazing crisp sound in this old Joanna,' he says, sitting down at it. He can't wait to get playing.

Everyone has a touch of vanity. Even a caretaker. But he's untouchable now, painstakingly drawing everything he can out of the music which fills the room. She gets up and goes into the bedroom, opens the wardrobe and lets her hand run through the contents until she finds what she's looking for. A lilac-coloured silk shirt trimmed with lace over the front and at the cuffs. While the caretaker is off in his different world, she takes off her sweater and changes into her mother's lilac shirt, buttoning it with care. She closes the wardrobe and looks in the mirror. She runs her fingers through her short black hair. Half turns. It fits perfectly. Then she returns to the table and takes out her camera. She sits on the edge of the coffee table without disturbing him, her finger on the shutter.

His face has the tranquillity of a child at rest, while his thick fingers dance over the keyboard as if he's never done anything else in his life. When the last chord slowly fades away and the neighbour's television can be heard again, he remains sitting there for a minute staring ahead of him before turning on the piano-stool and looking at her.

'Mozart,' she says with a little smile.

He nods and notices that she's wearing her mother's lilac shirt with the lace. There was something he'd been going to say, just as he turned to her, but now he casts his eyes down and sits lost in thought for a while before lifting his head and looking her in the eye.

'Forget all that about the painting,' he says. 'I was just talking nonsense.'

'It's too late now.'

He shakes his head and there's another long silence.

'If you found that someone nicked it, or bought it for next to nothing, it wouldn't make your life any better. It wouldn't make the slightest difference,' he says.

She holds up her camera and takes a picture of him while he tries to remember what was on his mind.

'You've got a family, haven't you?' he says, indifferent to the camera. 'A good family. You're a privileged young woman. If you just put all this behind you and start to behave normally...'

'Normally,' she interrupts with a sneer on her face. 'What's normal? Is it normal to go round sweeping the streets when you're as musical as you are?'

He gets up from the piano.

'I don't sweep the streets. I have other people to do that.'

'Maybe you should go in for one of these talent shows, "be a star for an evening". That would be normal, with your talent.'

'Look after yourself,' he says, going out into the hall and taking a last look at the door-frame before he gathers up the bead curtain. She can hear the rattle of a thousand beads as he lays it on the kitchen table. Then he goes.

Fru Sigvardtsen, she ponders. Fru Sigvardtsen used to live next door. Her son was often around here. That was why the caretaker came. Not because of the painting, but to talk about Sigvardtsen. She gets up and runs out to the landing and shouts down the stairwell.

'Look after yourself too. Make sure you don't become normal. You'd only end up in a sodding "star for an evening" programme. Bingo! You've won a tube of KY jelly. Before you know where you are, you'll be getting your dick into the presenter – on camera.'

She hears him laugh on his way out.

She stands with her hands clamped to the banisters, looking down into the stairwell, when the door opposite suddenly opens and an obese woman comes out onto the landing.

'Oh my God,' cries the woman in fright, her hand on her breast. 'I thought...'

The woman stops herself from saying more and edges hurriedly along the wall down the stairs.

'You old shit,' Anne Sofie's shout echoes round the entrance hall. 'For every fucking time you've gone and complained about the parties, I'm going to wake you up and stare into your fat face. You hear me? Into your fat face.'

The door below on the first floor crashes open this time, and a man's hoarse voice resounds up the stairwell.

'Will you shut up, Krille!'

'I thought she was dead,' wails the woman as she goes past him.

She tries to slam the door hard as she goes back into the flat, but it's not hanging properly, and the effect is lost.

She feels hot now. It quickens your pulse if you shout a bit. Where did she put the little photo with Henry and Krille? The one she found in the purse. There it is on the window-sill.

The shadow of the photographer lies in the foreground. It was a stolen moment, she can see. Time for the family portrait. We won't mention it to anyone.

29

As soon as she has her hand on the gate she notices that one of the small panes in the front door has been broken, and the snow on the path is trampled and grey.

She steps carefully over the splinters of glass in the hall. Then she stands in the living-room with her heart thumping. The chest of drawers has been emptied of its contents: postcards, coloured pencils, Christmas candles, and everything else that gets forgotten as a year goes by in a holiday house. They're all spread over the floor. She looks towards the kitchen door, holds her breath and listens. Just a faint hum from the radiator, but there's a sharp smell in here. The smell of an unfamiliar, slightly bitter aftershave.

She goes through the scullery to her darkroom and sees that the lock has been broken. For a dizzy second everything goes black in front of her eyes. She runs out into the kitchen and almost flies up the staircase to her room in the loft.

Breathlessly she clicks open the lock on her red suitcase and searches frantically through her underclothes, until she finds the negatives.

The landline rings in the living-room. She stiffens. Who can it be? And why now? Heart still pounding, she goes downstairs to the phone. She stands staring at it hesitantly. Then she lifts the receiver.

'Anne Sofie,' she says. She doesn't breathe.

'It's Ole here. The caretaker.'

She breathes again in relief.

'Yes?'

'The only person who might be able to tell you something you don't already know is Fru Schaumburg. She was director of social services then. It's four or five years since she retired.'

'What do you mean by "then"?' she says.

At the other end of the line there's a silence, as if he regrets making the call. She can hear people talking quietly in the background. Plates being put into a dishwasher. Music from a radio.

'Hallo?' she says.

'When you were born.'

Now it's her turn to have to think. She's evidently underestimated the caretaker.

'Fru Schaumberg?'

'Yes. My wife thinks she lives up by the woods. In the sheltered housing.'

She thanks him for ringing and hangs up. Then she closes the thin curtains in the living-room and goes back to the darkroom.

Everything looks as it should be. She gazes at the picture of the green oil drum in the half-formed ice. She's soon lost in thought.

There was someone standing in the darkness near Kabyssen, where the light didn't reach. What was he waiting for? When Sonny picked her up he was gone.

She stretches up to a shelf to reach the cardboard box where she keeps the black and white photographs from the night in the churchyard. There he is. Like a ghost with a cross in the foreground. But as far as she can remember, the pictures were stored in a different order. The portraits of Tine were on top: now they're the other way round. He must have got them out of the box and put them on the table one by one, and then gathered them up like a pack of cards before putting them back. That way their order was reversed.

Fru Schaumberg. She must go and see her. Not tomorrow, but now.

The door is opened by the home-help, flushed and stressed, sweat glistening on her upper lip, eager to collect her children from nursery. She stares irritably at the young woman with the fur hat and black coat. She's only just dried the hall floor, and now the snow is melting off the girl's boots in a puddle around her feet.

'I'm off now,' she calls out towards the living-room, and hurries out.

Anne Sofie takes her time. She takes off her coat, hangs it up, and bends down to unlace her boots.

Fru Schaumberg is rather tall and thin, with eyes like two little black glass beads behind her glasses. She's doing some embroidery. With a slightly shaky hand she slips her needle in and out through some thin brown fabric. Anne Sofie settles herself opposite her in a plush armchair and observes the embroidered half-timbered English house with roses in the front garden.

'Your parents have a house in Østerby, did you say?'

'That's right.'

'And who are your parents, actually?'

Fru Schaumberg looks up from her embroidery, her dark eyes shining with alertness. From her smile it would seem that she's known in advance what sort of visit this is.

'My father's name is Holger Strand. He's a Permanent Secretary in the civil service, and my mother, Helene, is an interior designer.'

'And your parents are fond of coming here?'

'Yes, they come every summer.'

Fru Schaumberg nods.

'The summers are getting a touch too noisy these days. But the countryside round about hasn't changed.'

'I agree. Did you work at the town hall?'

Fru Schaumberg gives another nod.

'For twenty-three years. Twenty-three good years, I may say.'

'And you were director of social services?'

'Yes. I came here in eighty-one. I'd had a position in Vejle. I lost my husband early, and the year afterwards I moved here. You have to do something drastic. I like the silence and darkness here in the winter months, and there's the strange feeling that Skagen is somehow where everything ends. It all gave me the peace I needed to carry on with my life.'

'Yes. It can be silent here.'

'And you must tell me a bit more.'

Anne Sofie sits up in her chair. She glimpses a smile again on the old lady's face.

'Well, you haven't walked here in this weather just to hear about me,' laughs Fru Schaumberg, picking up her embroidery. 'How can I help you?'

'My biological mother died last week. Ellen Kristine Keldberg. I was put out for adoption more or less as soon as I was born. I've been told that my mother wasn't in a fit state to look after me. They say she was a drug-addict.'

Fru Schaumberg puts down her embroidery in her lap and scrutinises the young woman opposite her.

'It's not every day that a newborn baby is taken into care. I well remember the case. Clearly it was you. That much is obvious.'

'What happened to me?'

'The same as usual in your situation. You stayed in hospital for five days, and then you were transferred to Lykkeborg. There you were looked after for three months. That's a legal requirement. The adoption service has a list of couples who want to adopt, and after three months they choose a couple who come and fetch you, and you begin your life in your new family.'

'Was it you who decided that my mother was an unsuitable person to look after me?'

'I had the ultimate responsibility for that.'

Fru Schaumberg gets up with some difficulty and puts her embroidery down on the table.

'I'm going to make a pot of tea.'

Anne Sofie looks out of the big picture-window at the slender white birches and the snow lying on the path. It's silent here. Just the ticking of the clock on the chest of drawers and the sound of an electric kettle bubbling away in the kitchen.

Fru Schaumberg is in no hurry. She gets the cups and sugar bowl from the cupboard, then the little silver dish for the obligatory pastries. She potters about at her own calm pace.

'I can see you like paintings,' says Anne Sofie, looking at the walls covered with scenes of Old Skagen. Winter: dull yellow houses, sky, sea, grey snow-covered streets.

'I'm very fond of Secher. His pictures have clean lines and you never have the distraction of people in them. Are you a photographer?' she asks, nodding at the camera-case.

'Yes I am.'

Fru Schaumberg gives a laugh.

'I had the idea that the Sechers would make my old age a bit easier, once they'd appreciated in value – as I knew they would. But now I can't part with them.'

Fru Schauberg puts the teapot on the table and settles down again, gesturing to Anne Sofie to serve herself.

'What convinced you at the time?'

Fru Schaumberg smiles.

'Do you take milk?'

'No thank you.'

Anne Sofie pours a cup for Fru Schaumberg and another for herself. She sees that she won't get any further with the old lady before the tea ceremony is over, so taking the little silver tongs, she lifts a lump of cane sugar from the bowl and lets it dissolve in her tea. She knows that Fru Schaumberg is watching her every movement and has already formed a picture of the family she comes from. She blows gently over the delicate cup and lays the teaspoon on the saucer, looking at Fru Schaumberg and her indulgent smile. She takes it as a sign that she's successfully passed some kind of test of good manners, dating from another era. She raises her cup and slightly exaggerates the angle of her little finger. She sips the tea and replaces the cup in the saucer almost without a sound.

'I well remember the case,' says Fru Schaumberg, taking up her embroidery again. 'It was my first serious case since I became director. Your mother had been adopted herself, but she'd had no contact with her family at that stage.'

'Was that what decided you?'

'With that sort of decision a lot of reports are taken into account. They come from all the relevant experts – your mother's doctor, for example – and from conversations with the family and the neighbours. You build up a picture of the situation from an overall assessment. Above all it's about the child's best interests, because obviously it's a very grave matter to deprive a mother of her right to her child.'

'Did my mother not accept the decision?'

Fru Schaumberg sits for a moment thinking over the question, drawing her needle through the material.

'That I don't remember.'

'When is that sort of thing decided? When she's pregnant?'

'Yes, in your mother's case it was decided late in her pregnancy. She fell downstairs while she was in her ninth month. Her neighbour found her.'

'Fru Sigvardtsen?'

Fru Schaumberg's breathing pauses for a second, and she looks up from her work.

'That's right.'

'Was it because of what Fru Sigvardtsen said I was taken away?'

'No. As I said before, it always comes from an overall assessment. There was your mother's doctor, Dr Meinertsen, who died a while ago, and other people too. I remember the reports were quite decisive.'

'Who might the "other people" have been?'

The old lady considers her answer, as if she's suddenly realised that the young woman with the intense gaze has already reached a conclusion and is simply looking for the supporting evidence.

'Well, there were the other neighbours in the flats, and people in the town, and the social services staff who had paid out benefits to your mother.'

Anne Sofie looks out at the woods, lost in thought. Fru Schaumberg lays her embroidery in her lap and smiles.

'And how did it turn out for you?' she asks. Then Anne Sofie tells Fru Schaumberg what she imagines she wants to hear: that things have gone well in her life, that she still lives with her parents, that she's interested in art and hopes to get a place at the academy; and about Thomas, who's taught her how to take photographs, and about her summers in Skagen with her parents, and her familiarity with the town and the coast, and the friends she's made here since she was a child.

Fru Schaumberg nods and listens, and time passes. It's beginning to get dark, and Anne Sofie thanks her for the tea and the useful chat. Fru Schaumberg stays sitting in her living-room while she puts on her boots in the hall.

'Is Fru Sigvardtsen still alive, do you know?' she asks casually, as she pulls her fur hat down over her forehead.

Fru Schaumberg looks over to her.

'I think she died about six months ago. I'm sorry. But why don't you talk to her son? He'll remember best. And I believe he tried to get your mother out of her habit. As far as I remember, he was the one who alerted us that things weren't right.'

'I've no idea where he lives.'

Fru Schaumberg laughs, and gets up from her chair.

'Wait a moment. I'll get the phone book.'

*

She walks along the edge of the wood, bowed down against the wind, which has freshened. Fru Sigvardtsen found her. She'd fallen downstairs. Fru Sigvardtsen's son had been the first to raise the alarm.

She feels hurt now, and anger flushes her cheeks. They're all dead anyway. Dr Meinertsen, and old Fru Sigvardtsen, and the neighbour downstairs. What was it the caretaker had said? That Sigvardtsen and Helene were friends. She hadn't reacted, but the remark had stung her. What had he meant by 'friends'? She remembers now the warm days in the garden, when Sigvardtsen had sat up on the ridge of the roof with his trowel and his mortar-board. The weeks when Holger was travelling. When he was away he sent her cards. Nice cards: she remembers one particularly, which when you opened it, played a tune. Which tune it was, exactly, she suddenly can't recall.

She wishes she could smash something to pieces.

The darkness is gathering from the north over the town and the floodlighting over the yellow walls of St Laurence's church is thick with swirling snow. Just in front of the church door there's a bench. A bench where you can sit if you feel like it. Or if you can't manage to walk any further because you're full of dope and oblivious to the cold.

As Anne Sofie stands looking at the bench, it suddenly occurs to her that it was a real stroke of luck that she met Mikkel. Mikkel was able to tell her that his aunt's body was still there because there had to be a post mortem, so she was able to take her pictures. She remembers that Knud Harber has only seen a fraction of her work. She warms to that thought, and a sudden feeling of happiness flows through her.

The portraits she showed Harber are only the intimation of a much broader symphony. That's really what it is, she muses. Now, with the bench in front of her, things fall into place. For the first time it all falls into place like the pieces of a jigsaw, and that was what she'd been hoping for when she took the train up here: that things would come to her. Things you can't bring about deliberately. It began with the dull green oil drum with the Cyrillic characters, which she's going to enlarge so it covers one of the end walls, with the grain so coarse that it looks like pebbles on the beach. That's going to be the first picture you see when you enter the gallery. Immediately afterwards, the indefinable moments of pain against a blue-black and orange background. Herself.

When she left Fru Schaumberg's house, everything had been black. Completely black. Now, as the snow tumbles out of the darkness, she's filled with a prickling joy.

30

'There's a young lady in reception who'd like to talk to you.'

Merriment in the voice. A bit too much merriment. Vigga evidently has her own sense of humour.

He'd walked down to the harbour after seeing the undertaker. Henry and a fitter were busy with a problem in the engine-room. Henry seemed irritable and didn't mention the bruises on his face, but gave him to understand that Poul would be organising the reception after the funeral, and it would be held at the Seamen's Union in Kappelborgvej. On his way back to the hotel he'd gone into Café Jacobs and hung about the bar with the waitress and a fellow who worked in the accounts department of the shipyard. They believed him when he said he'd slipped on the pavement and hit his head on a road-sign, or at least they acted as if they did. After a bit of aimless talk and a beer, which the accountant guy insisted on paying for, he'd carried on back to the hotel to get his laptop.

'Who is it?' he enquires, though judging from Vigga's tone of voice it can only be one person.

'Frøken Strand.'

'Would you please ask her to piss off.'

A silence follows, as if the line's gone dead.

'We don't use that kind of language in this hotel.'

'Well, tell her to go to hell.'

'Not that sort of thing, either. But I could say that you're not to be disturbed.'

'No, hang on,' he says. 'I'll come down.'

She's leaning back on a sofa in a pale lilac shirt trimmed with lace, rosy-cheeked from the cold and slightly out of breath. She's thrown her coat over the armchair beside her.

'What do you want?' he asks.

'I wanted to say hi from Sonny. And to say sorry.'

That's the last thing he needs to hear.

'I'm finished with you,' he says, looking at her more in disappointment than anger. She sighs, as if he hasn't understood anything. Then her face brightens and she smiles.

'This is where they used to sit having a good time in the old days.'

'Who?'

'The biscuit-tin painters.'

'Look, you do need to show a minimum of talent before you can run down a whole generation,' he says. In the middle of his anger and disappointment it dawns on him where he's seen her lilac-coloured shirt before. In the shared kitchen back in Simon's student residence, there's a poster of Jimi Hendrix. It's the same shirt, with the prominent lace on the chest and around the sleeves – or almost the same. What's she up to now? Her black velvet trousers have a gold-embroidered waistband, and he notices for the first time a touch of green mascara on her lashes. But despite the uneasy feeling in his stomach, and a faint electricity running through his body, it's all finished with her. The funeral's arranged, and tomorrow, before anyone in the congregation has had time to blink, he'll be on the train enjoying the winter-white landscape. This week will have become nothing more than an entertaining anecdote for a Friday evening at the Business School.

Meanwhile he sits down on the chair furthest from her. She can jolly well make a comment on his bruised face before he leaves for good: she may as well see what sort of psychopath she goes around with. But before she manages to say anything, a waiter appears at the table exuding an exaggerated politeness, as if Mikkel has sat down with the crown princess. It's obvious from his sickly smile that Johansen, as his name-badge announces him to be, has been in cahoots with Vigga, and knows very well how Mikkel made a somewhat bloodstained entry into reception yesterday evening.

'I'll have a hot chocolate and a slice of cake,' Anne Sofie says, with the innocent look on her face that he'd seen on the train journey, when the woman in the gangway became hysterical. 'It can go on the account.'

'The account?' queries Johansen, still standing there.

'My father's account. The head of the Ministry of Culture. Our house is down in Østerby.'

The waiter nods submissively and darts an inquiring look at Mikkel, who raises a warning hand as he departs.

'How do I look?' Mikkel asks.

She sits up in the sofa and studies his face for a moment before leaning back again with a sigh as if at a loss for words.

'He's sorry he went a bit too far.'

'A bit too far? He's completely brain-dead. He's not fit to be with normal people. He ought to be put away.'

She nods, as if she's heard this description of her best friend before.

'And what do you think of this shirt?' she asks with a smile.

'Enjoy your cake,' he says, getting up.

He just wants to go now, but on the other hand he has rather missed her. He couldn't stop thinking about her while he was tramping round Grenen Point that morning; and in the biting cold and endless whiteness he'd come to the conclusion that it was really his own fault that everything had gone wrong the day before.

'You know something?' he says sitting down again on the edge of the chair. 'For a moment I began to have my doubts, after yesterday evening.'

He shakes his head. He's about to say something about her letting him down, leaving him in the lurch when he'd been beaten up, but he senses that it would sound hollow: after all, she's never made any commitments to him.

'Your aunt was my mother,' she says.

'Goodbye,' he says pointedly, getting up again.

'Ask Henry. Here's my mobile: ring him.'

She skims her mobile across the table like a chip in a poker-game.

'Your mother,' he repeats in bafflement, looking thoughtfully at the phone.

'We might have been cousins. Sort of cousins. But your parents were careful to keep their distance from her pregnancy. They didn't want to be associated with her little bastard.'

'Luckily for you,' he finds himself saying.

He immediately regrets making that remark, because his feelings for his parents are of no concern to her. In the silence that follows a laugh can be heard from the dining-room. A spark from the open fire flies like a comet out of the fireplace and burns out on the floor.

'I have a brother who's sick,' she says, as the laughter from the neighbouring room subsides. 'My parents, Holger Strand and Helene I mean, were advised not to have any more children. They heard about a young woman up here who was pregnant. Their gardener told them.'

She leans across the table, as if to tell him a secret, and he sees the fire reflected in her green eyes.

'It was that gardener who did the dirty work. Do you get that? They stole me. And now he's up to something else. I don't know what it is, but I'm certain it was him who came into the house while I was out. He broke a window to make it look like a burglary, but I know it was him. It couldn't have been anyone else.'

'You're paranoid,' he replies, but he says it uncertainly, because there is some funny business going on. He can still feel the pain in his back from the nail in the chimney. That must have been the man she's talking about.

She smiles bitterly, as if she's a teenager in the middle of the character-assassination of a friend.

'I've decided he's going to be part of my art,' she whispers.

Leaning over the table she gives him the feeling that what she's about to say is profoundly confidential. Anger shows again in her green eyes and a deep line runs across her forehead.

'In every work of art there's darkness and light,' she whispers. 'He's going to be the light.'

'All that about your dad getting his throat cut in a fight,' he says in a low voice, looking quickly around the lounge to make sure they're still alone. 'It just isn't true. Why do you say things like that?'

'The darkness and the light,' she repeats to herself, as if at that very moment something's just fallen into place. Her eyes are shining.

'Why?' he asks again.

For a second her thoughts seem to be elsewhere. Then she looks at him.

'That was my feeling, until two hours ago.'

'This is complete crap. How do you expect me to take you seriously, when you sit there giving me bullshit like that?'

The waiter returns with a steaming cup of hot chocolate and a large slice of cake on a silver salver.

'Thank you,' she says, saying nothing more until the waiter has gone. At the sight of the cake he rather regrets not having ordered something himself. It's too late now.

'Just think, we could have been relatives,' she laughs, trying a taste of the whipped cream. 'Your parents must be really nice. Nice people. You look like someone who has nice parents.'

'My parents are the kind of people who don't get on too well with the neighbours,' he says. 'My father has a factory down in Køge, where they make hand basins and bathroom fittings. He's been having a run-in with the union because he's underpaying his Polish workers.'

'A factory,' she repeats. 'That sounds really great. And if the Poles could get a better deal where they come from, they wouldn't be working for your father.'

She hasn't understood a word, he thinks, staring, hurt, into the fire.

'My mother, Krille I mean, was a model for a few painters when she was young,' she says. 'They hung out at Knud Harber's house in the Old Town. He'd just bought the house, and there was a really big party. You know, like in the Krøyer lunch-party painting, and all that shit. Krille was the dessert. Poul found her early the next day. She was sitting in the phone-box, half-naked and very much the worse for wear.'

'Another of your sick stories,' he says.

She shakes her head.

'Henry told me, the other day.'

'When you went out to sea with him?'

She nods. 'I told him I would be going to have dinner with Knud Harber, and he was pretty worried. I've never seen him worried about anything before.' She gives a laugh and concentrates on the cream with its glacé cherry on top. Then she quickly wipes her mouth on a napkin and looks at him.

'You've no idea how lovely the sky is on a winter morning like that. When the sun's just below the horizon, shining over the edge of the sea. Only the fishermen know about that. They don't see that kind of beauty in the pictures in the museum. That's why they never go there.'

'What's lovely about it?' he asks, hypnotised by her beauty.

'To begin with everything is lilac-coloured loops, just like my mother's shirt,' she says, smiling. 'Then the sky goes dark red, but still with that lilac in the background. The light shines in golden swirls.'

She raises her hand and draws an S in the air with her teaspoon, and looks at him, knowing perfectly well that he won't know what she means.

'Is that why you want to see Knud Harber?' he asks. 'Because he abused your mother?'

She leans back in the sofa with a wry smile, licking a speck of cream from her lip with the tip of her tongue.

'He didn't abuse my mother any more than she abused him and his friends.'

'So?'

'He's agreed to show my pictures if I have dinner with him.'

She bends over the table, turning her attention to the chocolate, which by now has reached the kind of temperature when it doesn't burn your tongue.

'Harber won't remember her anyway, that's for sure.'

He watches as she sips her chocolate. This girl is a non-person in the Keldberg family's superficial set of nouveau riche swindlers. This crazy girl in strange clothes speaks with a refined Copenhagen accent when she deems it appropriate.

'You can't be sure that it was the night at Knud Harber's that your mother got pregnant.'

She looks up in surprise. Then gives a short laugh.

'When my mother was modelling for Knud Harber's friends, I was five or six.'

He watches her carefully guiding a teaspoon of cake to her mouth.

'What about Henry?'

She suddenly smiles.

'It suits you, that multi-coloured look.'

He has to give a grin too in response, with a painful tightening around his lips. At last she's recognised the beating he's had, though it matters less now than in did half an hour ago.

'How's your project going, by the way?' she asks, giving quite a good impression of being interested. 'Is it finished now?'

The first evening, when they'd made their way together through the darkness towards the flat, he'd held forth about various economic models and how they affected ordinary people. Apparently that lecture is less important now than the sugar content of the glacé cherry that she's very carefully eating round.

Just as he's shrugging his shoulders at the question, a wind-blown group of people bursts into the room. It's the trio he saw on the beach in the morning. One of them, a tall, grey-bearded man in a large dark cloak and broad-brimmed hat, is laughing noisily. All three seem the worse for wear from the biting frost, but invigorated by their walk. The woman pulls off her gloves and goes to warm her hands at the fire.

'Skagen used to be different: it was better then, perhaps,' hisses Anne Sofie as she looks down at her cake in a vain attempt at making herself invisible.

'Frøken Strand!' rings out a high baritone voice across the lounge, and she looks up in irritation from her plate. Mikkel gets up automatically from his chair as the man in the cloak comes over to their table, smiling broadly.

'I spy a mauve orchid gracing these historic surroundings.'

The man throws his cloak aside and holds out his hand to Mikkel.

'You must be Thomas,' he says, with a wide friendly smile.

'This Thomas is called Mikkel,' she comments crisply.

Mikkel gives a little bow.

'And the person trying to impersonate the painter Holger Drachmann is Otto Bremer,' she says, still giving full attention to her cake. 'Otto is a homosexual, as you can guess. At Christmas every year Otto goes off to Asia to screw under-age boys. That's how he manages to get through the rest of the winter.'

With this acid comment she whisks the cherry off with her spoon and pops it in her mouth. Mikkel cringes and a flush comes over his cheeks. Otto Bremer lays a reassuring hand on his shoulder and looks down at Anne Sofie.

'Have you spoken to Knud Harber?'

'Only briefly,' she replies, ostentatiously scraping the last of the cream from her plate. Otto tries to work out what lies behind that answer.

'And so...' he says emphatically, with sudden seriousness.

'We're going to meet.'

'Oh good,' he says, reverting to his cheery attitude. 'If it won't disturb you too much, we'd like to get a bit nearer the fire. We could do with some warmth. And a bit of alcohol in our coffee.'

'We're just going,' she says, getting up.

As she's picking up her coat, Otto Bremer's guests come over to the table. The woman, who's got some life back into her fingers, directs a friendly smile to Anne Sofie, who snatches up her fur hat with a 'let's go' glance to Mikkel.

'This is Anne Sofie Strand,' says Otto.

The woman smiles politely.

Without wasting so much as a look at Otto Bremer's guests, Anne Sofie heads towards the door as if she has a train to catch.

'Sorry,' says Mikkel to the little group, hurrying from the room.

Outside, he finds her buttoning her coat with an aggrieved look.

'A little courtesy doesn't cost anything,' he says.

She glares at him.

'It costs everything, you idiot. Everything. When are you going to learn that?'

Mikkel realises that he's standing there in his T-shirt. He's come out without his coat.

'Hang on a minute,' he says.

There are so many questions he hasn't had an answer to. He's forgotten to ask her if she's coming to the funeral, or about her relationship with her mother and with Henry and Dorte. What about his own parents, who are so guilty of betrayal? There are hundreds of questions. They were interrupted by Otto before he could ask anything.

'I need one more picture,' she says, starting to walk. 'But maybe I'll get to the reception.'

'Hang on,' he says. 'Wait a minute.'

31

By the time he's scrambled out of the hotel with his coat half-on, she's vanished, and a new layer of fine snow has come down on the road. There was so much he wanted to ask her, and now she's gone. Why the hurry now, when they've found they're almost cousins? Or are they? Was all that story about Krille just another of her inventions? He gets out his mobile and calls Henry's home number. After a couple of rings it answers.

'Dorte here.'

'Hi, this is Mikkel. I've met a girl called Anne Sofie Strand. She reckons my aunt was her mother.'

A silence follows.

'Are you still there?'

'Tell me something: don't you ever talk to your parents?'

She has him there.

Someone laughs down at the gate of the museum. A group of people are coming out. He goes over to see how long it is until closing time. 'Biscuit-tin painters' she'd said, and he'd jumped in with both feet and allowed himself to be annoyed.

The attendant steps aside for him with a friendly smile. It's too late now to change his mind. The last time he was in a gallery was a school trip. They'd wandered round in a daze of indifference. Then someone went and stuck a cap on one of the exhibits. At the time it was side-splittingly funny.

He senses an exaggerated feeling of attention around him. Three women in turn give him a smiling welcome. First the dark woman with the heart-shaped face who sells him his ticket, then the older one who pops out from the gift shop for no apparent reason, other than to take a look at the last visitor of the day, and then the young blonde attendant with the broad forehead and the rather sulky mouth. He has an idea he's seen her before, but in the flurry of making his entrance he can't think where.

Where are you supposed to start? How long do you have to look at a picture before you can say you've seen it? Because that's the idea, isn't it? He walks around a bit, going from room to room. He stops and takes a look at the garden with its thin covering of snow. He can almost feel its frozen crust, glistening like icing. The deep holes left by a cat's difficult traverse run across it. Turning to a beach scene he peers at it, unable to forget Anne Sofie's words. 'Your aunt was my mother,' she'd said. Why hadn't she mentioned that earlier? Why had she been secretive about it? Even in the pub? Everyone must know. It's completely absurd. He'd been the only one round the billiard table who hadn't known who she was.

One evening long ago in the living-room, as he lay under the table playing with a car, he'd heard his parents talking in low voices about his aunt. Certain words had caught his attention and interrupted his game. It was all about something that didn't concern him. Something they were keeping to themselves, and for that very reason he stopped and listened for a moment. 'It was bound to happen.' 'It's just what you'd expect.' Something was the matter with this aunt, he gathered from the heavy atmosphere. But what it was that you'd expect, and what was bound to happen, remained a mystery to him.

The beach scene makes no impression on him, so he goes over to the big room reserved for special exhibitions. It has cone-shaped windows in the ceiling.

And what about Henry, who'd stood on the bridge with his hand on her shoulder, as if they'd known each other for ever.

This room must be a new extension. His gaze wanders upwards to the incoming daylight and he notices the careful system of tiny video cameras, discreetly and strategically placed. It's interesting, he muses, that the cost of a museum's security system must be in a very simple relation to the cost of its insurance. Simon had suggested they should write about insurance companies. "Overcoming moral hazard in insurance policies." But since none of them had any intention of becoming an insurance broker, the idea had been shot down. And here, as everywhere else, the little surveillance cameras can help spot a vandal but can't avert a catastrophe: so you can hardly call it a win-win situation for the insurance company and the museum. Though perhaps it's a win-win for the insurance company and the police.

Mikkel pulls himself together and looks at the pictures, which is after all what he has paid for. He observes that the people in the pictures have lived here in the town, and he turns to a portrait of a girl set against a dark brown background. Her name is evidently Tine, and she shows an astonishing resemblance to the young attendant who took his ticket. The same sulky thoughtfulness, the same broad forehead and blonde hair. She must have lived here and modelled for the artist Carl Madsen. Maybe she did it for a laugh alongside all the other things she was doing, or maybe she simply wanted to make a bit of money. As he looks at her he wonders whether she felt flattered at being painted or found it a complete pain. Did this Carl fellow behave himself? There's no way of knowing.

He recognises some of the paintings from postcards and posters. In her college room Hanna has a copy of the girl with the straw-coloured plaits, and he sees that the original a good deal smaller than the poster. That's bit of a let-down, he thinks, and turns on his heels so that his shoes squeak on the newly-polished floor. He's suddenly captivated by the vast, dark, painting on the end wall. The women sitting in the white steam from their ironing seem to be looking past him. He puts himself close to the canvas and examines the brush-strokes. Then, restless, he turns into the next room, where he finds the famous painting of the drowned fisherman lying on a table lit by daylight from a window, with everyone around him dumbstruck with grief. There's his widow, and his young son, and his mate with a dewdrop dangling from his nose. Another picture just inside the door shows a boy leaning out of a shed on one extended arm, looking out to sea. Krohg is the painter's name, and although he's never heard of him, he can see that Krohg has his own way of painting. Sharper, he thinks, as if he's turned the paintbrush round and painted with the handle instead of the brush. It's cold in the picture, but the boy's wearing only a shirt and thin trousers held up by a length of rope.

'Time to get out,' he mumbles to himself, and bends to tie his bootlace. He's beginning to roast in his thick jacket; he takes it off and sits on a bench in the middle of the room, lost in thought.

Henry and Dorte, the toothless Poul, Aunt Ellen, the twins and the eider duck. They're all here in the pictures, if you look carefully. He's even spotted the idiot who was standing by the hot-dog van in his blue

Helly Hansen kit. And the young attendant with the blonde hair and clear blue eyes is here too, hung in the room on the left. He's even noticed Jantzen the undertaker at the back of a crowd of anxious fishermen at the grocer's shop. Are they coming in, or are they going to stay outside? Between those two eventualities stands a good deal of money. Especially if you're an undertaker, he thinks with a sigh.

The only reason he's sitting here with his head in his hands after paying good money for a ticket is his fear of looking weird if he goes out again ten minutes later. His boots are in a terrible state after his walk to Grenen Point. He must see if he can get hold of some water-resistant spray. He hears firm steps across the floor. Firm steps on high heels. The acoustic in the gallery is unforgiving. A pair of firm legs, and black shoes. Nice ankles, and dark tights (it is winter, after all), and then a blue skirt. They come to a halt in front of him. He's been sitting there dreaming, and now he looks up in embarrassment into her blue eyes.

'Have you seen the drawings upstairs?' she asks. She speaks with the local accent and glances quickly towards the entrance. He looks at her in amazement. For a long time. What is she asking about? The drawings. What drawings?

He slowly shakes his head. He hasn't seen the drawings upstairs: he stands up, puts his jacket over his arm and follows her into another room and up some stairs to a kind of covered exterior corridor. As she walks in front, her skirt swings from side to side, and he follows her right to the far end, where three steps lead up to a door. She turns to him before they go in.

'Are you an art student?'

He shakes his head.

'I'm a student at CBS. It's a business school. In Copenhagen: in Frederiksberg.'

'I thought you must be an art student.'

He suddenly remembers where he's seen her before. In a picture in Anne Sofie's dark-room.

'Sorry,' he says. 'I'm more of a numbers man.'

There's a seriousness about her, just as she appeared in the picture.

'The archive is down below. Art students are allowed in the archive. But actually the most interesting things are up here.'

'I'd like to see them,' he says.

She produces a key and opens the door. Four steps lead down inside, and he can see that they've come into the roof space of the old building. Thick pipes run along the walls, and they have to duck under some cables to get in. He notices some old archive boxes.

'Spooky,' he says in the gloom. She turns a switch, and a solitary lightbulb gives a yellow glow from a rafter.

She whispers: 'There's not enough space down in the archive. This is a temporary store for stuff that's useful for researchers and students even though we can't exhibit it.'

Opening a box, she pulls out a sketch.

'Look,' she says, letting her finger run gently over the drawing. The ring from a coffee-cup is visible in one corner, and he puts a hand on her shoulder.

'Is that from a coffee-cup?' he whispers, carefully feeling the rough texture of the paper. He's not sure why they're whispering, but she started it, and the place seems to call for it.

'That's right,' she says, blushing. 'Krøyer was sitting at a table with a cup of coffee while he was playing around with an idea.'

'How much would a drawing like this be worth?' he asks, and she turns to him, letting her fingers gently stroke the roughness of his bluish-yellow cheek and lip, while her breasts rise and fall under her rather tight uniform jacket. There's no misunderstanding this situation. Neither of them leading, and neither of them being led. Up here in the roof space there's gentle yellow light, and warmth, and the sound of breathing, and he turns to her, and she lets her head fall back with a sigh, and he kisses her open mouth, and her fingers feel frantically for his belt, while he unbuttons her jacket, silver button by silver button.

'Come over here,' she whispers, drawing him further along the roof space and down onto her on a pile of folded archive boxes on the floor, where they hastily undo such of their garments as are necessary.

'The drawings,' she whispers as he pushes himself into her, and she stifles a cry, and they hold on to each other desperately, and time stands still, and when he comes it's powerful and painful, she's sweet with a taste of acid-drops.

'Tine, someone's calling you.' They stiffen like animals and listen, and he can hear her heart beating.

'Tiiiine.'

Hurriedly they get to their feet, and he hits his head on a rafter as they dress frenziedly on the spot. Tine turns off the light and he follows her towards the light beyond, towards the door, towards the stairway with the four steps, disorientated, sweating, with his jacket screwed up into a bundle. When they reach the open corridor they hastily straighten their clothes.

Down in the gallery stands a woman, looking severe.

'He asked about the drawings,' says Tine, blushing in her attempt to control her breathing.

'Mikkel,' he says. 'Mikkel's my name.'

'Mikkel,' repeats Tine, holding her breath.

The woman isn't wearing uniform and must be the duty officer. She looks up at them in surprise.

'Would you be kind enough to come down?'

As Tine brushes past him, he notices something in his hand. A crumpled piece of paper that he stuffs into his pocket. He follows her down and sees that her hair is a real mess down at her neck, and he almost stops her in her tracks as he straightens the worst tangle with his fingers. They go down the stairs and into the gallery.

'If Mikkel has seen what he wanted to see, I think we'll lock up,' says the woman, and he feels a drop of sweat trickle from his temple. He hastily mops it with a corner of his jacket.

'Thank you,' he says as Tine avoids his glance. 'Thank you very much.'

'You're welcome.'

The last of the daylight has been swallowed up by darkness as he leaves the museum. Feeling confused, and intoxicated by her perfume, which is stronger in the ice-cold air, he walks over to the hotel.

Not until he's just outside the entrance, standing in the light from the dining-room, does he stop and retrieve from his pocket the crumpled, and by now rather fluffy, piece of paper. He opens it out: a drawing of a dog with a ball, with a brown stain from a coffee-cup in the corner, and a signature.

32

The thought that Sigvardtsen has a home, and a bed that he sleeps in, and a table that he sits and eats at, has never struck her before. He used to turn up every day, the weeks when she was alone with Helene in the house. Whenever they arrived, he'd be standing in the garden with his shears or his paint-pot, and he'd raise his cap at the gate as they drove away.

Fru Schaumberg had looked him up. There were several Sigvardtsens in the town: Bent Ole Sigvardtsen, electrician, and Tove Sigvardtsen, teacher, and then K. Sigvardtsen, carpenter.

It's a terrace of low houses, with a kind of grey cement roofing. The beech hedge running along the pavement isn't thick, and through its foliage she glimpses the gardens with their rotary clothes lines, kit-built greenhouses, neglected fruit trees, snow-covered garden furniture, rusting bicycles and the occasional empty rabbit-hutch.

Sigvardtsen lives in the house at the end nearest the car park. She walks past the garages and up the path to the door. A few doors along, two youths are trying to kick-start a moped.

A Christmas wreath hangs in the kitchen window. The lights are off. He's not at home. To be on the safe side she walks across to the garages, out of the wind, and rings his number. It gives two rings. 'Sigvardtsen,' comes a crackled reply. She can tell he's somewhere out of doors: someone's talking in the background; a car drives past.

'Hallo,' he says a couple of times, before hanging up.

To the left of the door is a small wooden shed: the sort of place people use for bikes and garden tools. On the roof over the shed door are a weathervane and a gull made of plywood, as if they somehow have something to do with each other.

She glances over at the two boys. They've managed to get some life into the moped, which coughs and spews a white fog over the path. With all that going on, you could stage an open-air play here without anyone noticing. She opens the door and goes into the shed. His overalls are hanging on the wall. In the corner is a workbench where he makes gulls, gnomes and weathervanes to sell to anyone sufficiently lacking in taste. She switches on the light and looks around. Where would you hide a spare key? Somewhere out of sight, but within easy reach.

Seeing a pair of old wooden-soled boots on the floor, she shakes them one at a time. No: too fanciful. What about the shelf with all those paint-brushes and pots. On tiptoe she lets her hand slide along the edge. Nothing but dust. A woman calls to a child outside, and she freezes until the voice dies away. The garden hose is neatly rolled up. Brooms, shovels, a power saw. Sigvardtsen's a tidy man. In the corner hang several hooks strung out on a line, with some of those green glass floats that fishermen used to use to mark the position of their nets. Every tool has its own place, and the spare house-key must have its place too. But where? She squats down and peers under the table. More boots, a can of weedkiller, and an old red Carlsberg beer-crate. She pulls it out into the light and looks inside. It's full of small brown cardboard boxes. Screws and nails, evidently. That's why it was so heavy. Trying to slide it back into place, she finds that it's more difficult than dragging it out. There's so much friction against the concrete floor. But it has to go back: he'll notice immediately if it's even slightly out of position. She has to get on her knees to push it right in under the table.

It's hopeless. She brushes the dust off her trousers, and then notices, in front of the beer-crate, a narrow white scratch in the grey concrete. She kneels down again and lifts one end of the crate. And there's the key.

All along the terrace there are lights in the windows. Some children have gathered round the moped. She puts the key in the front door. It turns, and she goes into the hall and locks the door after her.

The place smells of fish. Fried fish. On the left is the kitchen with a window looking out onto the path. To the right is a toilet, and a little further on, the open door to the living-room. She has difficulty finding her way, and she'll have to turn on the light if she's going to see anything at all. But how long will it be before he comes back? She walks firmly over to the verandah door to the garden. It's warped, and she has to push it with her shoulder until it gives with a dry thud.

Though the hedge can be seen through, it looks as if it's continuous all the way round. She needs an escape route, and steps out into the crunchy crust of the deep snow. Right over by the dark-stained tool-shed near the group of garages the hedge thins a bit, leaving a gap just big enough for her to wriggle through if necessary. Back inside, she puts her camera-case down on the table, leaves the door to the hall ajar, and switches on the lamp over the armchair in the corner.

The furniture is heavy and dark. A tall dresser stands on one side of the room, some blue plates hanging in a curve on the wall above it. There's a crossword puzzle on the dining-table. She opens the door to the bedroom. An unmade bed, and a bedside table with some bottles of pills. Above the bed is a large biblical scene of a shepherd in a landscape strewn with thorn-bushes, a lamb in his arms. 'The Good Shepherd', it says in small print in the corner. On a bookshelf are a couple of feet of old porn films and above them a framed picture of a middle-aged woman with grey hair.

Sigvardtsen is someone just like everyone else, and Mum is the best mother in the world, she thinks, getting out an old photograph album. Black and white photos. People out in the country. A farm photographed from the air, its ornamental garden decked with triangular rose-beds. Portraits of people from another era. Sepia. She guesses this must be Fru Sigvardtsen's album, and puts it back on the shelf. In one of the dresser drawers she finds tobacco, pipes and pipe-cleaners and a box of buttons and sewing things. In the other one are some old crosswords, supermarket receipts and bank-statements. She opens the doors at the bottom of the dresser. Table linen. What had she been expecting? A painting? A large overcoat with a faint scent of perfume?

Switching off the light, she goes into the kitchen. The light from the lamp-post on the path outside is enough for her to find her way around. On the wall beside the small kitchen table, where he evidently eats, hangs a notice-board. A newspaper cutting with a picture of a hunting-party out on the heath. A full-colour advertisement for coffee. A photograph. She takes that down and opens the fridge to get more light. A youthful Helene in the garden with a bouquet of roses in her arms and a wide smile. Helene is smiling at whoever's taking the picture. She knows who took the picture. She took it herself. With her first camera, when she was twelve.

She puts Helene back on the notice-board and moves into the living-room to shut the verandah door. The moment she picks up her camera-case from the table, there's a knock at the front door. Hard, firm knocking. Then whoever it is finds the doorbell and rings. She can make out the outline of a man through the frosted glass and she flattens herself against the wall and slides along to the kitchen. He seems to be peering in from the darkness outside, and she freezes on tiptoe. He's wearing a long woollen coat and scarf, but no hat. Straight black hair and a ring in his ear. He turns slightly and looks at his watch, banging again impatiently at the door.

There's something familiar about him. Where has she seen him before? Then she remembers: at the undertaker's last winter. It's the undertaker she photographed.

She squats down below the window as he rings the bell for the third time. Then there's a moment's silence before the telephone rings in the living-room. She can see his shadow on the ceiling. She has the feeling that he's standing and staring in through the kitchen window. She holds her breath.

Then at last all is quiet. She stays sitting there for a while before she risks standing up to look out. She feels like throwing the key away and simply running off. But she goes into the shed and puts it back where it belongs.

She hurries away from the house with her heart pounding, walking in the opposite direction from the way she came. She didn't find a painting hidden in the house, but she did see a picture of the Permanent Secretary's smiling wife. And a good friend came by to say hello. She feels sick now, and her anger grows with every step she takes.

On the road along the western shore the constant passage of refrigerated lorries has crushed the snow into a yellowish mass, which sticks to the wooden soles of his boots as he crosses from one side to the other. He's been out to the harbour to get plaice, and he's already looking forward to his dinner. A couple of little plaice, potatoes, herring pickled with cowberries and HP sauce, all with the juices from the pan. As he trudges down past the Swedish church, he decides to grill the little plaice hard, so that the bones are crunchy and crisp. The ten he's bought cost only five kroner each.

Yesterday he'd bought dab. Peter, whose nets they came from, said dab was good at this time of year, at least as good as plaice. But he was wrong about that. Dab has a bit more of a watery taste, and the flesh isn't so firm.

He's kicking the snow off his boots when he hears the telephone ring in the living-room. He doesn't often get phone calls at this time of year. The houses he looks after are all closed up for the winter while his holiday-makers go south for the sun. From November until well into March it all looks after itself. Then this sudden snow and confounded cold which upsets his rheumatism, and he has to go down and clear the snow from the pavement in front of the engineer's house in Trindelvej. It's the only house he looks after with a pavement in front of it. In most of the Old Town, fortunately, there are no pavements, and the council sees to the clearing and salting.

He quickly takes off his boots and hurries to the phone.

'Sigvardtsen,' he says, sitting down rather breathlessly. One of his socks has come off in the boot, and he sits gazing at his bare white foot.

He thinks he can hear a faint sound of breath before whoever it is hangs up. That's the second time today he's been rung up without the caller saying who they are. It worries him. Then the phone rings again. He considers just letting it ring, before picking it up.

'Hallo.'

'Is that Sigvardtsen?'

'Good evening, Fru Strand.'

He fancies she takes a breath during the pause that follows. As if she's searching for the right way to begin what she wants to say.

'Please forgive my husband's behaviour last night.'

'I quite understand.'

'When is the funeral?'

'On Saturday.'

He senses a sort of desperation.

'What's the weather like?'

'It's been calm for a couple of days, but there's more snow and wind on the way. It's five or more degrees below. It's not exactly a Copenhagen summer here.'

She pauses again. He sits down again and begins to scratch patiently at the eczema on his heel. Little flakes of dead skin drop gently down to his polished floor.

'I'm worried,' she whispers.

'What's the old saying, Fru Strand? "Happiness and grief often go together"?'

Once again there's no sound from the receiver, and he takes a look at his skin. It's worse in winter. Skin needs light. He can hear Fru Strand taking deep breaths.

'I hope I'm not being too personal.'

'You can trust me, Fru Strand.'

'My husband ... doesn't think it's all that bad ... but ... well, I'm worried.'

'Of course.'

'Did you ring last night?'

'Yes. She stood for nearly an hour staring at the water in the harbour. I can't take the responsibility any longer, Fru Strand.'

'My husband will be there tomorrow. He'll try to get her to come home with him.'

'Of course,' he says. 'That would be best.'

'Yes,' she says.

'I've spoken to Fru Schaumberg. She rang me just before I went down to the harbour. She's had a visit from a young woman.'

'Fru Schaumberg?'

Sigvardtsen notices that Fru Strand is quite good at forgetting certain things.

'Fru Schaumberg was director of social services then.'

'Oh God! Is she going into all that?'

He hears the line go dead and hangs up. He goes into the kitchen and looks at the plastic bag with the little plaice. They're still alive, twitching in the confined space of the bag in instinctive hope of escape. He gets out his chopping board and fish-cleaning knife. As he cuts the head off the first one, gutting it with one sharp tug, he realises that he forgot to ask what time the Permanent Secretary will arrive.

Fru Strand is worried, and with good reason. Last night the girl was standing on the edge of the quay staring out into the darkness. She's reaching out for the limit. Playing with fire. If Sonny hadn't arrived, it might have turned out badly. Sooner or later it'll turn out badly, he's certain. It'll all go wrong. And he's trying to fathom what's going on with her. What did that toothless Poul want to talk to her about? What does that drunkard know? What did Krille tell him over the years? What did she say to him? Poul knows something. Something about the painting.

She behaved as if nothing was the matter when he turned up the other day. And now she's sniffing around in Krille's flat, which is nothing to do with her. And she's picked up that young fellow from Copenhagen who's come here so he can go to the funeral, as far as he can make out. People in this town talk. Krille has died, and the rumours are flying around. Who hung up on him? It could have been Jantzen. It would be just like that bastard to hang up. Was that today? Yes, it was today. You're going senile, he thinks, and notices that the heavy curtains in the living-room are closed.

33

A truck with a trailer shudders over the clods of ice on the quay, and he has to move right over to the edge as it goes past. Above him are the gulls, and out in the harbour a trawler makes its way between the red and green lights into the darkness.

The whole town shuts itself down around you, he muses. The people who live here are gathered together in a thin, transparent net. And yet it's impossible for outsiders to see through it. The townspeople seem to be trapped – trapped in a shared resignation about the darkness, which creeps up imperceptibly from the harbour as soon as the last tourist has packed their bags. Scared, he takes a step backwards. He's stood a little too long looking down at the tempting black water. Tine had stepped out of the picture and come over to him. That's how he'll remember her. His heart thumps, and even the stink of fish is beautiful.

His daydream is shattered by the sound of a fist banging on a window from inside the dockers' café. A man's beckoning to him. It's Poul, standing waving a newspaper.

It's like a hot-house inside. At a table in the corner sit four middle-aged men with lined faces, half-naked after a session in the sauna. There's something boyish about their carefree attitude. They've unloaded their ship and now they're playing cards. Poul's sitting on his own, grinning broadly with the few teeth he has. He picks the newspaper up from the table.

'Have you seen this?' he asks, pointing to the deaths column.

Mikkel reads:

Ellen Kristine Keldberg. Born 27 May 1969. Died 7 January 2007.

Krille to her friends. The Parrot to her enemies.

Funeral at the Chapel Saturday 14 January at 14.00

Drinks at the Seamen's Union afterwards.

'Did you put this in?' Mikkel asks, embarrassed by the grins coming from the direction of the card-table. He can tell that Poul is drunk, and apparently here only for the warmth.

'Well, you've got enough to do as it is.'

He hasn't been asked if he'd like a beer, but there it is, already opened. He thanks Poul for it.

'That's a nice birthmark you've got there,' remarks a sharp-nosed pirate with a ring in his ear. He realises that they know all about his spectacular stunt yesterday evening.

He feels like asking why on earth Anne Sofie has any interest in that Sonny character, but he restrains himself. Maybe because he doesn't really want to know. Instead he knocks back his beer and leaves the bottle in a crate by the fridge. He wants to get out. The smell of chlorine, sweat and sour sauna hangs in his nostrils, and the radiators along the windows towards the street are at full blast. The only person in the whole place who's the same age as him is a lanky boy with something of a hare lip. Despite his youth his body looks prematurely aged. He gets up and gazes at Mikkel, his mouth half-open while he searches for words locked away somewhere in his head. Then he manages to smile and the words are released while he adjusts the towel round his waist.

'The group playing at the p-p-pub tonight are p-p-pretty good,' he stammers, glancing quickly at the card-table, as if he has reservations about launching this verbal ambush.

Mikkel points to the bruise under his eye.

'I'll only run into Sonny again.'

'He's been b-b-banned, so you'll be all right,' says the young man with a misty stare and a sudden laugh as if he's high on something. 'Anyway – if you haven't got anything else to do.'

Getting beaten up by Sonny yesterday seems to have won him some kind of acceptance by the locals. The mention of the music is a discreet courtesy from someone his own age, and it's an invitation he's delighted to accept, especially considering the alternatives on offer. It's his last evening in the town, and he feels mildly elated following his visit to the museum and his encounter with the girl whose perfume still lingers on his clothes. He's no idea what this guy's called – and he'd like to ask but it would seem strangely intimate, seeing that he's wearing nothing but a towel. As for himself, he's in no doubt that Poul has already explained to everyone present who he is and why he's here and how he was frozen off by Anne Sofie yesterday, like so many before him.

'Will you come to the funeral?' he asks instead.

The guy takes another quick look at the card-table.

'I didn't know her all that well. But my dad's going.'

'Who's your dad?'

'You went for a meal at his house on Monday.'

'Is Henry your dad?'

'Yes.'

'And Dorte. Is Dorte your sister?'

'My half-sister.'

'Henry's always been generous with his spunk,' comes a dry comment from the card-table.

Now he sees the likeness with Henry. Thin with long limbs, and with a slightly crooked smile exactly like Dorte's.

'Great, so maybe we'll see each other there,' he says.

'I'm Erik.'

'Mikkel. My name's Mikkel.'

The moment he steps out of the café he sees a bright white light at the harbour mouth. It's the *Fjordö* on its way back in, heavy as a whale. He pulls his hood over his head and walks towards the town.

Tine. There was something decisive about her as she led him up the stairs and along the corridor. If he didn't have the crumpled drawing sitting in his hotel room, he might have thought it was all a mixed-up memory of last summer on the beach. But in contrast to the tanned Swedish girls he can scarcely remember, Tine had a seriousness in her face when she suddenly set herself in front of him. As if she'd been waiting for him ever since he got off the train.

A blue coach is parked a little further off in the darkness. "Jøhnson's Tours", it proclaims on the side. He walks past a party of grey-haired pensioners who are buttoning up their coats with frozen fingers while the local guide's patter tells them about the warehouses and the architect Bindesbøl and his inspiration from Bergen. They're shivering, longing to be back in their warm coach.

As he reaches the Warehouse restaurant there's something going on: at the service entrance stands a black Porsche Cayenne the size of a small bungalow. A man in his early forties with dark curly hair and stubble on his cheeks emerges from the kitchen.

It's Zeppo, the chef he met the first evening when he was playing billiards with Henry and Poul. The very Zeppo who's going to serve up Henry's eider duck at a dinner on Sunday. Zeppo stops suddenly when he realises he's being watched. He stands alert, as if assessing the situation and sizing up the person in the darkness; then he suddenly smiles.

'Well I never, it's you sneaking around there,' he says, pronouncing the words in the Slavic accent he'll never shake off, even if he lives to be a hundred. Zeppo opens the car door and gets in.

'Nice car,' laughs Mikkel.

'It certainly is. Hop in,' says Zeppo, and he doesn't demur. Kabyssen with its grilled chicken can wait.

They drive off beside the shipyard. Zeppo ostentatiously gives the accelerator one small push, the turbo hums, and they grin like two little boys.

'This is Knud Harber's car,' chuckles Zeppo. 'I went to Ålborg airport to meet him. He doesn't dare drive up here in this weather.'

'Where are we going?' asks Mikkel as they curve past the shipyard in the direction of the outer harbour.

'There's something I need to fix up. It'll be useful to have you with me,' says Zeppo darkly.

They turn along the furthest quay, and Mikkel sees a little marina and a small harbour for dinghies on the right, as well as some tall buildings that he takes to be another shipyard. He hasn't been to this part of the harbour before, and he sees the town in a completely new perspective from the opposite side of the basin. Far inland shines the spire of the church, and out across the water lie the warehouses where Zeppo picked him up. A strange rusty coaster is moored way out by the harbour entrance. The only light comes from small portholes at the deepest level below decks.

Zeppo stops and turns off the engine.

NATASHA STREMOVA – KALININGRAD

Welders' cables and power lines hang frozen over the side and snake down like living things into the snow lying on the quay. The gangway looks as if it's covered in icing. On the bridge someone stands having a smoke in the dark.

'I'm glad to have a little company,' says Zeppo, pulling a bundle of euro-notes from his inside pocket. 'Here,' he says, handing Mikkel half of the notes. 'I'm going on board. Can you get out and stand by the car, so he can see I'm not on my own?'

'Sure,' says Mikkel. 'You haven't got a gun you could lend me?'

Zeppo gives a wave to the sailor and goes over to the gangway. Mikkel can hear them speaking in Russian before Zeppo more or less hauls himself across the slippery gangway and disappears into the ship with the sailor.

As he waits the headlights of a car flash along the quay, blinding him for a moment before it turns towards the marina and parks beside an elderly Saab. Although the shipyard has closed for the night, he can see the sparks from a bit of welding going on in the darkness. Someone's doing overtime. Lovers are clearly meeting over at the marina. Faint sounds of laughter drift on the wind.

The cold comes creeping under the soles of his feet, and he has to jump up and down to keep warm. What the hell is Zeppo up to? What is all this? He walks up and down a bit on the quay while he waits. Ten minutes seems an eternity when you're stuck on a remote quayside while a Serb you hardly know vanishes on board an old Russian rustbucket – especially when you're about to die of hypothermia with a wad of crisp new euro-notes in your pocket. At last the door opens with a creak and Zeppo comes back along the deck and on to the gangway. He has something in his hand: a folded plastic bag. He slithers cautiously across the slippery gangway on to the quay.

'Jump in,' he says. Mikkel gets in and hands Zeppo the bundle of notes. Zeppo puts the cash back in his pocket without counting it, shoves his hand into the plastic bag and pulls out a large flat tin.

'Look,' he says, beaming. 'Beluga. The real stuff.'

Mikkel begins to understand Zeppo's breathless enthusiasm.

'They haven't all turned into oligarchs,' grins Zeppo.

'How much did they scorch you for that?'

'It's OK. Harber's paying.'

Zeppo turns the Porsche round, and they drive slowly back across the bridge. One of the parked cars has Swedish plates, Mikkel notices.

'What's going on here?' he asks.

'I don't know, but they haven't come to buy plaice,' chuckles Zeppo.

Mikkel leans back in the leather seat, enjoying the sound of the engine. Tomorrow is aunt Ellen's funeral, then off on the train home.

The priest had rung him that morning, just before he left the hotel. She sounded as cheerful as she was when he met her, and she suggested three hymns: 'Watch now the rising sun', 'I am tired and seek my rest', 'Always carefree when you walk'. She pointed out that it was a very traditional choice, but they were hymns that Krille's friends knew and could sing. He had made no objections. There's nothing more for him to do now except be there at a quarter to two and sit down in the front row. The question of who's going to carry the coffin out to the hearse is for Henry to deal with. And this evening he'll go down to the pub by the harbour. He'll just sit down and listen to the music, which Henry's son Erik has said will be worth hearing.

He thanks Zeppo for the drive, wishes him luck for the dinner on Sunday and goes into Kabyssen for chicken and chips. Cheered by the thought of being with a crowd of people his own age just drinking together, he hangs his jacket over the back of a chair and goes up to the counter.

It was bog-standard at the undertaker's, and it's the bog-standard menu here in Kabyssen, but at the pub tonight he'll be generous with his parents' credit card, and he hopes that Erik will have his friends, and his friends' friends with him.

34

Lights are on in the living-room and he can make out a shadow behind the curtain. He has a moment of doubt. He should go back to the hotel and leave her be. After all, tomorrow's the day of her mother's funeral, and it's the day she's going to meet Knud Harber. But there are so many things he wants to ask her. He'll invite her down to the pub tonight. It's simple. That's what he'll do.

He opens the gate and walks up the little path to the door. Something crunches beneath his boots. He's treading on tiny splinters of glass: then he notices that one of the small panes in the door has been broken. She mentioned this afternoon that she'd had a break-in.

To his great surprise, the Drachmann look-alike opens the door. He's without his cloak and broad-brimmed hat, but still with that look of keen interest, and smiling through his tangled grey beard. Otto Bremer invites him in with a wave of his hand, as if he could just do with some company.

'Someone's been visiting without a key,' says Bremer. 'There was quite a puddle on the floor. And the drawers had been half-emptied. I ventured to tidy up.'

There's something disarming about Bremer. His eyes are mild and intelligent, and on this occasion he's dispensed with the relentless merriment that Mikkel remembers from their brief encounter at the hotel. Bremer has been busy with something. Beside the teapot and mug on the table sit his briefcase and a sheaf of papers.

'Where's Anne Sofie?'

'I don't know. The door was open when I got here.'

Bremer goes into the kitchen and returns with a mug.

'Your name's Mikkel, isn't it?'

'That's right.'

Mikkel gathers that the mug is for him. With a thank you, he takes off his jacket. Otto Bremer reminds him of one of the professors at the Business School, a man called Hjort, on whom the students had bestowed lousy scores in the annual evaluation. He'd felt sorry for the old professor, who'd found suddenly that he was past it without the School management being aware of it. Otto Bremer has the same long stooping back and wild grey hair and beard. But there the likeness ends. Bremer doesn't look the least bit senile. There's a curiosity in his eyes and something lively in his smile. He pushes the mug across the table and fills it with steaming tea.

'I gather from that little exchange this afternoon that you know Anne Sofie quite well,' says Mikkel.

Bremer leans back on the bench and laughs. He seems to judge the remark a bit of a cheek, but spot on.

'Anne Sofie's father asked me to drop by. They worry about her because she doesn't answer the phone. And she certainly has her little ways.'

'Excuse me a moment,' says Mikkel. 'I'll just take a look and see if she's asleep.'

This Otto Bremer character seems OK, though he's just a little too relaxed about everything. Who broke the glass in the door, and where can Anne Sofie have gone? Mikkel goes purposefully into the kitchen and up the narrow stairs. Her thin brown roll-neck sweater and black velvet trousers are lying on the bed, and her red suitcase is standing by the window. So she hasn't left, he concludes, with mixed feelings of relief and anxiety.

Otto Bremer is sitting waiting for him in the living-room when he comes down. He's put his pages of notes into his briefcase.

'You're a good friend of hers?'

Mikkel merely nods.

'A photographer too?'

'I'm a student at the Copenhagen Business School.'

Bremer scratches his beard and smiles, as if he senses a youthful bashfulness in the younger man.

'You'll just have to make do with me, I'm afraid. My name's Otto Bremer. I'm an artist, and a professor at the Academy. As I said, I'm a good friend of the family. And as Anne Sofie so elegantly expressed it this afternoon, I'm a homosexual, so you really ought to watch out.'

Mikkel smiles, embarrassed.

'What brings a young man up here at this time of year?'

'My aunt has died. Her funeral's tomorrow.'

Bremer gives a nod.

'How about you?' asks Mikkel.

'A meeting of the museum trustees. Have you had time to look at the museum?'

'I was there this afternoon.'

'A little too dusty for you, perhaps?'

'No. I quite liked it. The portrait that really struck me was painted by someone called Carl Madsen. I'd never heard of him. It was a portrait of a girl. Tine, she's called. Anne Sofie took some pictures of her the other night in the churchyard. She's an attendant at the museum.'

Bremer laughs. He pauses for a moment as if he's trying to work out why an intelligent young man should talk such rubbish. Then he replies: 'Yes, I think I know what you mean.'

Mikkel sips his tea. Now he's talked about it, almost the way it is. Maybe this professor was at the museum this afternoon and heard something. Back in his hotel room is a drawing by P S Krøyer, which is probably worth a fortune. Maybe he'll be accused of theft. He can picture everything that's going to happen. He's charged with the crime. Sensation at the Copenhagen Business School. Young economics student steals priceless drawing from Skagen Museum. But it was Tine who stuck the bloody thing into his hand, because she didn't know what else to do with it.

'Tine,' says Bremer, scratching thoughtfully at his beard. 'A fine little portrait.'

Mikkel nods. 'Yes. So there's a meeting of the trustees tomorrow?'

Bremer smiles.

'Yes, it gave me a good excuse to come up here for a couple of days to get a blast of fresh air. In that respect I'm very much like Anne Sofie. She has a great fondness for this town too, once the fairy-lights have been switched off. And now here we are chatting away together.'

This causes Mikkel to smile. Bremer reminds him of a nineteenth-century actor during the interval of a play. Silk shirt and brown waistcoat. He's pretty sure Bremer must have his own tailor.

'Frankly this place bores my arse off,' he says with sudden defiance. 'Tomorrow I'm going back to Copenhagen, and I couldn't be more delighted to get away. I don't know Anne Sofie that well. I happened to meet her down by the harbour on Wednesday. I just came round to see if she wanted to come and hear a group at the pub tonight.'

Bremer purses his lips.

'You don't know her?'

'No. She's not someone who's easily understood.'

'You don't think so?'

Mikkel wonders if he's said something rather stupid. He's tempted to unload all the frustrations he's suffered here: Bremer would be the ideal recipient. Call it perhaps a kind of trust. He doesn't understand it at all. He could mention his bewilderment about the funeral. Or Anne Sofie's many personalities, and the fact, which he discovered rather late in the day, that her biological mother was his aunt: though this Bremer character has possibly worked that out already. Despite the unanswered questions it feels good to be sitting here in the living-room with someone who is friendliness itself.

'I ought to be on a skiing trip with my mates,' he says. 'But then my aunt died, while my parents are away on their travels.'

Bremer smiles. 'Death always comes at an inconvenient moment.'

Mikkel nods. 'I'm just surprised how miserable it is here.'

'There's the sky and the sea: you can get high on that combination,' laughs Bremer.

'High?' exclaims Mikkel. 'This place is a hole in the ground. A very unimportant hole full of half-wits in my opinion.'

Bremer screws up his eyes and leans over the table.

'Skagen is what lies between the houses when the mist comes down like a silken curtain and makes pillars out of light,' he says with a theatrical flourish.

Mikkel smiles at this. 'Yes, and the filthy smell of fish.'

'Exactly,' says Bremer, banging his fist on the table and making the mugs jump. 'Skagen is the sound of the fog-horn out on the breakwater and the endless shrieking of the gulls.'

'And a Serb running away from his own shadow,' adds Mikkel, to keep the game going.

Bremer rolls his eyes.

'And Skagen's the furthest sandbank where the shouts of the dead rise out of the surf, and a lonely walker suddenly appears in your face out of nowhere.'

'And saying the wrong thing in the wrong place,' grins Mikkel, pointing to his bruised cheek.

Bremer sits with a smile on his face, then suddenly looks at his watch, gets up and grabs his cloak and fedora.

'Skagen's a condition, my boy. A condition. That's what you're about to learn.'

He adjusts his hat with a touch of vanity.

'I have to go now, I'm sorry to say,' he says. 'It's been a pleasure to meet you. Why don't you sit here for a bit and see if Anne Sofie shows up.'

'Thanks,' says Mikkel.

Bremer looks at him, detecting his slight anxiety.

'I don't think you need to worry. She has her haunts.'

Mikkel follows him out to the hall and stays standing in the doorway until the tall man in the cloak and broad-brimmed hat is indistinguishable from the darkness.

35

Sigvardtsen rattles the door to the undertaker's. It's locked, but through the window he can see light from a half-open door inside, and music can be heard from the back of the shop. He opens the side-gate and goes into the yard. The snow has been blown into half-metre drifts, and he has to clamber through them to knock at the barred window. A pale face appears at the grille and vanishes again. The music is turned down and some packing cases are moved before the back door is unlocked.

'We said we were going to meet,' mutters Jantzen irritably. 'I went round to your place.'

'What time?'

'Late this afternoon. You weren't answering your phone. You must sleep pretty soundly.'

'I was out at the marina. I'm here now.'

'Yes, I can see you are,' says Jantzen, opening the door with some reluctance.

A young woman is sitting across an easy chair, her legs dangling over the arm. Her blonde, greasy hair falls over one of her eyes, while the other surveys without expression the man in the cap. She looks like a tart, thinks Sigvardtsen, giving Jantzen an offended look.

'She's just going,' says Jantzen with a dazed sort of smile.

The girl gets to her feet with a lazy movement and gathers her keys and cigarettes from the table. Jantzen hands her her quilted jacket and she slips into it, brushing her hair from her forehead.

'You can call me,' she drawls in a nasal voice.

'Of course,' smiles Jantzen, following her through to the front door.

Sigvardtsen casts his eye over the coffee table between the easy chairs. A cola and a glass. A lighted candle. An ashtray filled with cigarette ash and a disposable syringe. He can hear them whispering together in the funeral parlour. Then the front door opens and closes and Jantzen returns. He looks at Sigvardtsen with a blissful smile.

'Have you ever thought of buying yourself a new cap?' he enquires cheerfully.

'Have you ever thought of shooting yourself in the head?' answers Sigvardtsen, pointing at the table. 'What's all this stuff?'

Jantzen glances down at the syringe in the ashtray.

'She's diabetic.'

'How much does she know?'

'Nothing.'

'Where does she come from?'

'Frederikshavn.'

'Who is she?'

'My cousin.'

'You look so like each other.'

Jantzen regards Sigvardtsen in surprise. This guy actually has a fraction of a sense of humour hidden away somewehere. The ghost of a smile appears on his face.

'Have a seat,' he says, scratching at his arm.

'Have you got the money?'

Jantzen moves a packing case away from a chest of drawers and slides a drawer open. He brings out an envelope and hands it to Sigvardtsen, who thrusts it quickly into his pocket as if it were hot.

'Aren't you going to count it?'

'I don't need to. I know where you live. What did you tell him?'

'The truth.'

Sigvardtsen feels uneasy about the undertaker, who once again has a far-away look in his eyes and seems distracted. He bitterly regrets having anything to do with this petty criminal, but there's no going back now. The envelope presses on his heart like a millstone.

'I'd like to hear your version of the truth.'

Jantzen sits down heavily and closes his eyes for a second. Then he looks at his companion.

'I told him I bought the painting from a drug addict who'd inherited it a couple of years ago from a friend who died of cirrhosis. He took a copy of the receipt which the Parrot signed to authenticate the sale.'

Sigvardtsen considers this explanation.

'You told him she was a drug addict?'

'Of course I bloody well did. Any normal person would have auctioned it. The man's not a fool.'

'Didn't he ask why you didn't get it auctioned yourself?'

'He can work that out, you idiot. He only wanted the receipt to cover his back.'

'The Crab's running round looking for her coat.'

'She left it behind when she left.'

'Left it behind?'

'Yes.'

'And where is it now?'

'In a black bin-bag at the charity shop. That's where she bought it. It's probably on its way to Africa by now.'

Jantzen smiles at the thought.

'And she never got her money.'

Spreading out his arms in appeal, he adds:

'It's hardly my fault that she just sat down and died before we'd settled up with her.'

Sigvardtsen wonders whether he should hit Jantzen over the head with the claw-hammer he's just noticed on the shelf by the window.

'Why did she fall asleep?'

Jantzen sighs, as if the question were irrelevant.

'Now why do people fall asleep? People fall asleep because they're tired.'

Sigvardtsen is middle-aged. If he allowed his beard to grow, it would be white. But all his life he's lived on fresh air, fresh fish and fresh vegetables, and he's worked with his hands since he was thirteen, so his body is supple and tough. He takes a step forward, pulls Jantzen from his chair and flattens him against the packing-cases with such force that something inside them breaks.

'The Crab's going round talking,' he hisses. 'This afternoon he was down at the girl's house.'

'What girl?' gasps Jantzen.

Sigvardtsen crushes him against the boxes again, his crooked fingers working their way behind the collar of Jantzen's jacket until he has him by the neck and his colour changes from pale yellow to blue.

'Now listen, you bastard,' he says between his teeth. 'If that girl gets to hear it was me who helped you with that painting, I'm going to break your bloody neck.'

Jantzen gasps for air and things begin to darken in front of his eyes.

'And how's the Permanent Secretary's wife these days?' he has just enough breath to whisper, his hands reaching for his neck.

Sigvardtsen lets him go and walks to the door. He's doesn't know what to do. It pains him that he's become involved with this psychopath. But he can tell that the undertaker knows something. Something about his relationship with Fru Strand. Something about the girl. Krille must have told him something while she was under the influence, ingratiating herself to get some of his bloody drugs.

'What does Fru Strand think about her daughter gadding about in the churchyard at night?' croaks Jantzen.

Sigvardtsen stands and thinks about the question for a while. Not because it's complicated, but because he can't think clearly at the moment. The whole business has moved in a totally unexpected direction. Jantzen had asked him to find a buyer, but that was when Krille was doing fine. Now all of a sudden she's dead, and people are asking questions.

'Well, she's worried about her,' he mumbles.

'Aren't mothers always worried?'

'She's afraid she's going to harm herself. She's done it before.'

Jantzen's face is beginning to regain its normal colour. He sits down in the chair again.

'A young man came to see me,' he says. 'Very mean with his money. He's seen her pictures. She's obsessed with death. She's even taken a picture of herself with the Parrot. The two of them lying side by side in bed stark naked.'

'How do you know that?'

Just for a moment Jantzen sits thinking about the question.

'The young fellow told me. She's fascinated by death.'

He's had the same kind of idea himself. He can't work out what Anne Sofie might be up to.

'Tuesday and Wednesday nights, both nights, she just stood and gazed at the water in the harbour,' he whispers. 'Fru Strand told me to keep an eye on her. I was sure she was going to jump. I stood there waiting to hear the splash. She went to the same place both times. There's something about the place that means something to her.'

Jantzen has lit a butt from the ashtray and he holds it between two fingers while he takes a drag. A vague, sour smell spreads over the room.

'Where exactly does she go and stand?'

Sigvardtsen looks down at his boots. Once upon a time everything was simple. Summer would come, and with it would come laughter and light. Fru Strand opened like a rose. Important people would come to stay. They would eat in the garden. The girl was small and easy to deal with and the Permanent Secretary was friendly and distracted. Sigvardtsen would drop by every day and give them a hand. Sometimes he'd even be invited to eat with them. He was on first-name terms with famous people and enjoyed their respect. These days it's all gone wrong, he thinks. It's all gone wrong now.

'Near Kabyssen,' he says, clearing his throat. 'They've dumped a container out there. She goes and stands behind the container.'

Jantzen closes his eyes and smiles.

36

The lock on the dark-room door has been wrenched off and the hasp and staple are flapping on the door, leaving four dusty little screw-holes in the door-frame. It was easy for whoever broke in. All too easy. Did she think that little lock was sufficient protection for her vulnerable creativity? Didn't she see there ought to be a bit more to it?

The first thing Mikkel sees on the table is the set of portraits of Tine. In one of them her face is half in shadow. She's looking down as if she can't quite decide whether to cooperate. In the next one she's looking up at the sky, caught perfectly in the moonlight, smiling, as if she's given in. As if she's embarrassed by her own beauty.

As soon as he's put Tine down he sees another photograph. A black and white portrait of a small masculine-looking woman with short blonde bobbed hair, half-moon spectacles and heavy ear-rings. He has a feeling he's seen her before. She's smiling, holding something in front of her with two fingers. Picking up the photograph, he can see that it's a ticket: a train ticket.

He hears the slam of a car door and hurries out to the living-room. She's stamping the snow off her boots when she catches sight of him.

'What are you doing here?' she asks in the local accent, which she's adopted since he last spoke to her.

'I came to invite you down to the pub. There's going to be music there tonight.'

'Who else has been here?' she says, glancing rapidly at the table top.

'The professor. The fellow with the hat. Bremer. He was here when I arrived.'

'Heaven preserve us,' she says, throwing her coat over a chair and pulling her fur hat off. 'So you've been sitting here deep in refined conversation with the Drachmann.'

'We talked about the pictures in the museum.'

He'd like to ask her about the portrait of the woman on the train, but clearly this isn't the right moment.

She turns in the doorway to the kitchen and smiles a broad smile.

'Ah yes: you were at the museum today, weren't you?'

'How do you know?'

She laughs. 'A bit of juicy news travels faster round here than you can send a text.'

Her whole body shakes as she doubles up with laughter.

The little idiot hasn't been able to keep her mouth shut. They've been out together somewhere and now Anne Sofie is either high or drunk. Or both.

'I can't imagine what you're talking about,' he says.

'No,' she says, going out to the kitchen and opening the fridge. She pulls out a carton of milk and takes such large swigs from it that the milk runs down her chin. Wiping her mouth on her sleeve she spins round and looks angrily at him.

'What was it you said at the hotel? What is it that your dear father makes? What got him rich? Was it sanitary ware? Sanitary ware!' she shrieks, and creases up again, as if it were so funny that it makes her stomach ache. 'People are queueing up for Keldberg's sanitary ware. You ought to suggest that slogan to him when he comes home from his beach holiday. Or what about this one: "There's always a queue for Keldberg's sanitary ware."'

'What the hell are you on this evening?' he asks.

She stands looking at him, while the laughter subsides to a smile.

'Did you smash the window?'

'You know perfectly well I didn't.'

'What about Bremer? Did he suck your dick?'

'No.'

'But did he want to?'

'It makes me sick to listen to you.'

'Now, about your father. Let's discuss this sanitary ware.'

Mikkel shakes his head. 'No, but we can talk about you. How you're just a pissed-up little rich-girl with an identity crisis.'

She cranes her neck to indicate how impressed she is.

'Identity! How very bloody perceptive. Now is there a cute little psychologist hidden away in this person? Are you sure you shouldn't change the course you're doing?'

'Yes, that's something I am bloody sure of, because if I did, I'd be doing work on idiots like you. And I really wouldn't want that.'

She disappears into the kitchen and returns with a breadknife in her hand.

'You're quite right,' she whispers. 'I am just a touch psychotic. I could cut your throat right here and I wouldn't give a shit.'

She gestures with the knife in front of him and he draws back on to the bench.

'Just calm down please,' he says.

'Unbutton your shirt.'

'Just cool it.'

'Come on, do it now.'

'Would you please put that knife down.'

'Not before you tell me why your parents have such poorly-developed minds, and why you think you haven't inherited their stupidity. Tell me: why do you think you're better than that petit-bourgeois jerk, your father, who wouldn't have anything to do with my mother, and wouldn't be associated with me.'

She takes a step towards the table brandishing the knife.

'You're so bloody naïve it's embarrassing,' she shouts in his face, 'and oh so careful not to do the slightest evil in the whole wide world.'

Still shouting, she sticks the knife into the table in front of him, leaving it there quivering.

'You can stick it into yourself,' he yells in despair, pulling the knife from the table and hurling it across the room.

'You're pathetic,' she hisses, and goes back into the kitchen. She turns on the tap and drinks from it.

He has to get out of here. She's off her rocker at the moment. But he can't move. He can hear her going up the stairs now, then her footsteps pound over the ceiling. He sits for a long time in shock, the words still stinging him. He knows what she meant. His parents forgot to tell him one little detail when they sent him here with their credit card and their warm encouragement to deal with all the bequests and debts. One significant little detail by the name of Anne Sofie.

He can hear her again now overhead, then her steps creaking on the stairs. She sticks her head through the door, a summer bonnet on her head. A dusty bonnet with flowers and a bow. On her hands are long black silk gloves.

'Excuse me,' she simpers. 'Do we know you in the neighbourhood?'

Her eyes are shining and a smile hovers on her red-lipsticked mouth.

'That would be telling,' he says.

'Couldn't you say just a little?'

'Can't you just give over with this shit?' he says, looking straight in front of him.

She turns a fraction and takes a cautious step into the room.

'I arrived on Tuesday. It's beautiful here in the winter,' she says, pursing her lips.

'Do you think so?'

'Oh yes,' she says, throwing out her arms as if addressing a big audience. 'When all the razzamatazz is over. I come twice a year. Once in late August, when the water on the south beach is nice and warm, and once in January. I like January best. What about you, young man?'

He leans back on the bench watching her. What does she think she's up to? Five minutes ago she was flourishing a knife.

'What about you, young man?' she repeats.

'I came up here to bury my aunt,' he says, his voice expressionless.

'But that's not the reason for your unhappiness,' she says. 'And who might she be?'

'My aunt?'

She lays a hand on her breast and laughs theatrically.

'No, no, not your aunt, young man. She who has made you unhappy.'

She may well be a good photographer, thinks Mikkel, but as an actor she's absolutely useless.

'I only know her name,' he says.

'Her name?'

'Yes.'

'And your aunt's called Ellen Kristine Keldberg?'

'She's dead, in case you've forgotten.'

'Ah! Just think: she's dead. Someone of my acquaintance painted her when she was young. She was certainly a rare beauty. The gentlemen would give their right arms for her when she appeared down at the harbour in the summer. Oh yes. Those were the days.'

He listens to the drama while his fingernails flick at the splinter in the table-top where the knife was stuck in.

'And now it's a young lady who's making you unhappy. One whom you met here?'

'Yes,' he says.

'It's important that one remembers to enjoy it.'

He has to smile at this.

'Enjoy being unhappy?'

'Yes. In fact that feeling runs very deep in me. Being in love is rather superficial.'

'And who's being superficial at the moment?' he enquires.

She takes off the bonnet and shakes some of the dust off. She smiles to herself, then looks at him.

'Is there going to be music at the pub?'

He nods.

'That's really great,' she says, pulling off the long black gloves. 'Were you really scared of me?'

'I'm going now,' he says, not moving from his seat.

'I'm coming too,' she says.

He doesn't know what to say. He can't bring himself to get up and get his jacket. He contents himself with a shrug of his shoulders, as if he couldn't care what she decides.

'Tine's boyfriend is quite jealous,' she says in the silence that follows.

'Does he know something?' he asks, glancing at her.

She smiles, and he feels humiliated. That's what she's been fishing for: confirmation of what she's heard. And he jumped in with both feet.

'I'm going to have a bath,' she says. 'Will you wait for me?'

He doesn't know whether he'll wait or not. He can't think why he should wait for her. Tomorrow is the funeral, and then home. Finished with this place. With her. With everything up here. For ever.

37

He does wait for her, and they go down through Østerby. She's full of energy, dancing around in the road. All the anger she brought into the living-room and the ridiculous play-acting have completely evaporated.

She takes hold of his arm and tells him that this evening, the second Friday in January, is a special occasion. When he wants to know more, she explains that the most talented of the musicians who've played here in the summer meet up again on the second Friday in January, when there isn't a single tourist in the town. He smiles. This evening he's going to forget his project report, his parents, the ski trip and the party at Astrid's. He'll just drink through it. She stops suddenly and looks past him down the road.

'What's the matter?' he asks, looking in the same direction.

She turns to him, smiling.

'I've never taken a proper picture of you.'

'Of me?' he asks, feeling suddenly hot.

'Yes.'

'Well, go ahead.'

'Look,' she says, pointing at a newly-refurbished house at the end of a garden. 'They didn't skimp on the yellow limewash there.'

'No,' he replies. 'And that's not Skagen. At any rate not what Otto Bremer would call Skagen. His definition of Skagen is what lies between the houses.'

'He's got a point,' she says, opening the gate. 'Come on through.'

'Is this the place for the photo-shoot?'

'Yes,' she says. 'Right now and right here.'

He places himself in front of the house wearing a tense smile while she gets out her camera. She stands for a long time watching him, her mouth half-open.

'Is this OK?' he asks.

'You'll have to take your clothes off.'

'What?'

'Take your clothes off.'

'I'll do no such thing.'

She looks affronted.

'Because it's cold, or because you're embarrassed?'

'I can't be arsed to stand around in a garden stark naked, when it's minus five, just because you think it would look nice.'

'What do you mean, you can't be arsed? And who said it would look nice?'

'Forget it,' he says, walking back towards her. She blocks his path, grabs his jacket and looks up at him.

'Why don't you believe in me?' she whispers.

He hesitates. That seriousness has come over her. Despair burns in her eyes.

'Where shall I put my clothes?'

'Put them down on your jacket.'

'You've got thirty seconds,' he says, spreading his jacket on the snow. Then he hurriedly removes his clothes and drops them on the jacket. He knows she'll just turn round and leave if he suggests keeping his underpants on.

He steps across the snow, naked as the day he was born. It's a strange sensation in the freezing air, but he doesn't feel the cold. She looks at him, and it doesn't bother him. He's aware of the cold like a thin membrane. Snow begins to fall in fine flakes as if she'd ordered it specially. It sticks to his warm skin. He can't remember feeling so relaxed in front of a camera.

She turns and looks up at the full moon and waits a moment until a cloud has cleared it. She focuses, glances quickly through the camera, makes an adjustment, her little finger extended, moves a metre to the left and raises the camera again. Then she remains absolutely still for several seconds.

A 'squeee-eak' is heard. She lowers the camera and laughs. He gets dressed again, exhilarated by the cold. It's a bit of a balancing act getting his trousers on – she has to steady him, and they end up laughing.

They struggle on down the road, making tracks in the fresh snow. She runs ahead and slides on the thin white covering. He's happy and pleased about the little test of his masculinity. He picks her up. She doesn't weigh much, and he swings her round.

They reach Firenze on the harbour road. They can hear a guitar being played, seemingly laughing and weeping alternately.

'Someone around here has nimble fingers.'

'Yes,' she says breathlessly. 'That's Kim, the caretaker's son.'

*

Down in front of the stage the music's so loud that all verbal communication is impossible. Rosy-cheeked and invigorated by the cold, they squeeze between the crowds and up the steps behind the bar into the next room. Henry's son Erik has managed to seize a table. Mikkel catches sight of the girl with mauve hair who works in the fast-food restaurant, the one who explained that he just needed to keep on 'over there'. The blonde one and the dark one from the harbour tavern are here too, as well as Henry's daughter Dorte, whom he doesn't recognise at first. Tonight she looks like a film-star from the fifties, with waved blonde hair and red lips. Tine, over by the window, avoids his glance, and he sees that she's there with her boyfriend.

'Where's Soffi?' shouts Frode through the wall of sound.

Mikkel points to a table near the door where a crowd of middle-aged men from the harbour are sitting. She's sitting on Poul's knee having a quick word.

Then Zeppo comes in with snow in his hair and a woman on each arm. Their arrival is clearly the continuation of a party they've already been to. They must have ducked under a fence to get to the door on the less crowded side of the room.

For the first time, everything is as he expected. From where he sits he can see Dorte opposite, and Tine by the window with her boyfriend, and now he notices Sonny out in the street. According to Erik he's been banned, and he presses his nose flat against the window. Mikkel knows that in a minute Sonny will come in and throw himself down at a table. It's a safe bet that it was Anne Sofie who rang and invited him, and that'll be good enough for him to be allowed in.

He decides that it's time for Keldberg the sanitary-ware magnate to buy a round. He gets up and orders two bottles of rum, some ice and cola.

'Anything else?' smiles the barmaid.

'Yes, peanuts and crisps and some more glasses.'

A few louts are hanging about in their shirtsleeves in the snow outside. They're busy setting off some rather late New Year fireworks, shooting rockets along the white line in the middle of the road. Sonny's in charge of the game. The first rocket hits a road-sign fifty metres away and explodes like a grenade in an inferno of fireballs. The gang gives a roar of enthusiasm.

Mikkel steps outside with half a bottle of Cuban rum in his hand. He's seen Anne Sofie about to slip away.

'Where are you off to?' he asks.

'A little walk round the harbour. I'll be coming back.'

'I'll come too.'

'No,' she says.

'Wait,' he replies, fuddled with happiness and alcohol, but she goes off anyway, and he follows like a pet dog. She stops and takes his arm, and he holds onto her, the wound on his back hurting in the cold as if it's been torn open.

He has a moment of doubt. She turns to him.

'Go back,' she says. 'You're not too good at the moment.'

He sways slightly. She'd like a drink from the bottle he's holding. He replies that she won't be able to take it. She takes a swig anyway. On the other side of the road, at the door of the discotheque, a few fifteen-year-olds are flirting with the bouncer.

'Come on,' she says, taking his arm. She wants to show him something, and they set off past the fish market until they're far out at the end of the first pier.

'Look,' she says, pointing to the cathedral-like shipyard on the other side of the harbour. 'Look, there's an airship.'

He can see what she means. It seems to hang floating in the darkness. For a long while they look at the airship in silence as small snowflakes materialise out of the night. Then she takes his arm again and they walk back towards the Warehouse restaurant and the town.

That was all she wanted to show him. He stops and holds her, but she holds her hand over his mouth.

'What would Tine say?' she laughs. 'Or Dorte?'

Then she looks at him with her green eyes and a worried frown on her forehead.

'Will you do something for me?'

'Jump in the harbour?' he laughs.

'Will you go back to the others?'

'I'm not leaving you out here on your own,' he says, taking a step backwards to recover his balance.

'I'll be along in a minute. They'll be wondering where you are. Go on,' she says, laughing.

'You won't do anything stupid, will you?'

'I'm not daft. I just need another picture.'

'You always need another picture,' he says, feeling dizzy and slightly unwell. 'What sort of picture?'

'My green oil-drum,' she grins.

'What are you talking about? Come here now.'

'I've only got this evening,' she says, kissing him on the cheek.

He walks back towards the pub and the harbour road, where red emergency flares are exploding against fences and walls of houses in a kind of alternative New Year display. In his drunken state he's happy and afraid at the same time.

As he draws near the fish market he can see someone in the shadows behind a refrigerated trailer. He stops and stares at the figure half-turning its back to him as if lighting a cigarette. Between the houses, Bremer had said. Or between the big trailers. Then the cold and the sick-feeling in his stomach come over him and he carries on over the railway line and past the Seamen's Hostel.

She wanted to be alone. He comforts himself with the thought that she has every reason to be alive. She was so happy the afternoon she showed him the portraits of herself. She's got some kind of plan for those pictures.

In a storm of fireballs that he barely notices he turns into Kappelborgvej. At the back of Firenze he sticks a finger down his throat. It's all been too much.

She stands in the middle of the open space until Mikkel has reached the Seamen's Hostel. She sees him stop for a while, staring at the refrigerated trucks.

This evening she has to get her picture. The warmth of the rum is running through her and she can feel her own pulse beating. She swings right round in a kind of dance and notices someone amongst the trucks.

A truck pulls out from the shipyard and she moves behind the warehouse until it's gone. Then she sets off quietly and calmly right down to Kabyssen. There she waits a little before crossing the quay to the container.

Where's he gone? Is he behind the factory now? In that case things are going well. With the full moon, and the reflection off the snow, the light is astonishing. She moves right out to the edge at the end of the container and listens. She hears the soft dry noise somewhere of a lump of ice beneath a shoe. He's not quite so good this time, she thinks, taking her camera from its case.

The *Stella* lies at its berth. A gull takes off from the wheelhouse, disturbed by her movement, and flies with a few lazy wingbeats out over the harbour. She looks along the quay. In this perfect light, as long as she uses the right lens, she'll get the Cyrillic characters without losing depth, nor the detail of the grey mush of sea-ice.

She edges carefully sideways along the long side of the container, until she can see Kabyssen reflected in the *Stella*'s windows. She can hear the sound of a car, and cones of light sweep out towards the sand-dredger. It's Friday night. There are people who just drive around because they have nothing else to do. In the lights of the car she senses his movement, just as he disappears into the storm-porch of Kabyssen. He's indistinct – just a shadow in the *Stella*'s windows.

She keeps absolutely still. Is he coming? She's not sure. Then a slight movement in the window and she takes a deep breath. She recognises the drawn-in feeling in her belly and the spasms of anxiety from the dormitory at Søgården, after lights-out, when the director had done her last round with a jangle of keys. She knows that the violence of boys can be rough and heartless, but it's nothing to the demonic power girls can wield. Carefully taught, choreographed wickedness. Practised, tested and adjusted until the effect is perfect. Who's out for a walk? Here they come in their ankle-length nighties, stealthy on bare feet in the blue light from the high windows, chanting their rhymes, until one of the new girls, who hasn't yet learned to control her breathing, suddenly sits up in bed with a look of terror on her face.

She holds her breath.

He's coming out of the porch now, she can tell. Slowly and carefully, like a blurred shadow in the window, he takes a couple of steps forward. In the reflection she can make out a movement indicating that he's looking around. Then he continues the last few steps towards the container, the snow crunching under his boots. He's hunched and cautious, as if he feels intuitively that it might be a trap, and just before he disappears from sight in the *Stella*'s glass, she creeps out on the opposite side.

Everything's absolutely quiet now. The fireworks in town have stopped. The snow along the side of the container is fine and soft to tread in. She keeps one hand on the catch of her camera-case so that it doesn't rattle as she takes the few steps to the corner.

There he is. The same ghost that floated among the crosses in the churchyard. The same long thin body that stood in the drive of Gahm's villa. The heavy coat hangs off him, as if his shoulders are too narrow. He looks clumsy and confused, like Holger when he stepped into her room in his dressing-gown. Hidden somewhere in her memory is the picture of a red beach-ball against a blue sky and the smell of the sweat in his armpits, and his soft voice reading from the book he held in his hands as she leant back against his chest, as if snuggled in a great warm hand.

Thin snowflakes whirl in the dark. He's standing, slightly stooped, looking down the quay. His body-language is asking: Where's she gone?

All he can see is slush-ice and a green plastic drum in the water. The only thing he can hear is the wind getting up, making the *Stella*'s ultra-thin aerial wires sing, and the only thing he feels is a soft hand, and a gentle push between the shoulder-blades.

Sigvardtsen stands at the bar, uneasy at the level of noise and the youngsters' hysterical happiness around him. He looks impatiently at his watch. He's unbuttoned the neck of his boiler-suit and bought himself a beer. It's too hot in here. Sweat stands on his temples.

The young fellow comes into the pub in a loose-fitting shirt, despite the cold. He recognises him by his untidy spiky hair. He's come back alone. The girl's gone off by herself. She's always gone off by herself.

It's all been with the best of intentions. He owed Fru Strand a favour, but things have gone wrong. He's learnt that it's never a good idea to get involved in the fate of others. There's always a price to pay. Fru Strand was worried at what he'd said, and not without reason. She feared the worst. One says a little too much, he thinks to himself, and then, like Judas while Jesus was breaking the bread, one hopes for forgiveness. You never really know what people intend or what they want. It may well end badly. But when the summer comes, everything will be as it was.

He takes his time drinking his beer. It's dark, frothy and bitter. The fellow the girl's been hanging around with the last couple of days has got matey with the other loud young people at the table in the corner. He takes his cap off the bar and squeezes through to the door. He's waited long enough. He's said hello to the barman. He's had a beer. Now he's off home.

The moment he steps out on to the pavement, she's there right in front of him. The shock is like a blow on the head with a hammer.

'Is that you?' he blurts out through the noise of a wailing guitar and the young people's heedless laughter, as if he can't believe his eyes.

'Who did you think it was?' she replies, carrying on towards the high street and paying no attention to the party going on inside. The glance she sends him just before she turns the corner makes him freeze on the spot.

38

The finding of the post mortem is that Ellen Kristine Keldberg died of an overdose of heroin. It comes as no surprise to her friends, her social worker, nor to the Frederikshavn police, who were aware she was a user. For long periods she'd managed to keep to the booze, but she'd had her lapses.

The white coffin stands in the chapel bedecked with flowers, and flower-arrangements run all along the central aisle. Everything is as it should be for a funeral. Almost – but when the coffin arrived by hearse from Ålborg early that morning, the undertaker, who had been expected to receive it, hadn't been there to meet them. The sexton had been to his house, while the gravedigger saw to the flowers. Had Jantzen made a mistake about the time? The priest has to explain to the small gathering that it hasn't been possible to book another hearse at such short notice, so the coffin can't be taken to the crematorium until Monday morning.

Mikkel looks round. He counts fifteen people sitting there, scattered in twos and threes.

Henry and Dorte are there with the washed and tidied twins between them. Dorte looks over to him: he returns her glance and she smiles. He smiles too. She whispers something to one of the twins and Svupper breaks into a gappy grin and gives a wave. He waves back.

Sonny is sitting with Poul. Mikkel doesn't know any of the others. Middle-aged men and women. Ah yes, he recognises the caretaker. He was the last to arrive and sat just inside the door. And he knows someone in the choir. He caught a brief glimpse of Tine when she leaned over the balcony and looked down at the congregation. She looks like an angel, he thinks. An angel with a hangover. An angel who tastes of mint.

When he'd woken up, she'd already gone, leaving a note on the chest of drawers. 'Maybe you can help Dorte with her move on Monday.' What was he to make of that? Did it mean that she would be helping Dorte move? Did it mean that if he helped, they'd see each other on Monday? He leans back a little in his seat and looks up to the choir, but all he can see is the conductor's back.

Tine's boyfriend had gone off to the disco with some people Mikkel didn't know, and he'd been standing in the cold outside the pub, concluding that Anne Sofie wasn't going to keep her promise, when Tine came up to him. She'd reminded him about the drawing by Krøyer of the dog with a ball that he'd taken out of the museum by mistake. It had to go back into the archive of course, they absolutely agreed, and since they probably wouldn't be seeing each other again, she went back with him to the hotel.

'See now the sun is setting', the choir is singing, and he mulls over his disappointment that Anne Sofie has stayed away from her own mother's funeral. He can't concentrate on the priest's sermon. It's about charity, and how Ellen Kristine Keldberg will long be remembered in the town. One or two people in his pew nod and venture a smile. Sonny turns on the tap: his tears run down his seam-like tattoo.

'From dust you are and to dust you shall return. From dust you shall arise again' comes clearly and firmly from the priest.

One entire wall is covered with portraits of men in uniform. He looks at the pictures. He recognises Henry and Poul there, Henry with his wry smile and Poul with his round head and protruding ears. They're only boys here, he thinks, and studies the other pictures. Some had evidently found their way into the Norwegian navy, others to the Royal Navy. In this place everyone's bound up with the sea, so it's the navy you join.

He turns to look at the gathering. Three times as many people have turned up here than were in the chapel congregation, maybe because Poul has announced that the bar is free. He greets some of those he recognises from the service, introducing himself and explaining the family relationship. A little Greenlandish woman stands and smiles, as if she hasn't quite understood his relation to her recently-deceased friend.

'You're a good person,' she declares.

'Thank you,' he replies in surprise, while others around him break into a laugh.

People are sitting eating in small groups; some hang around the bar. Most of them don't know who he is, nor why on earth he should have turned up at the funeral. Here there's no eulogy nor music. Just a steamy hubbub of voices in a thick fog of tobacco-smoke.

He looks about him. Poul is standing at the table where the buffet is laid out. He looks a sick man, and sober. This is his party: it was his friend they mourned this afternoon, and this initiative must have made some inroads into his pension. Dorte's going off with the twins, he sees. She's talking to Henry while she gets their coats on. Then she waves to him and gestures that she'll give him a ring. He nods and goes over to Poul.

'This is a very good do, Poul. Delicious smørrebrød.'

Poul takes a deep breath and looks at Mikkel.

'You think so?'

'Yes. Definitely.'

'I hear your parents are away on their travels,' says Poul.

'Yes. In the end it was up to me to meet Krille's friends. My parents are sorry they couldn't come to the funeral. I've just talked to them, actually. My father rang. He insists on paying for this occasion. He believes that's the right thing.'

Poul considers this proposition, before looking up at Mikkel to say: 'Then we'll have our funeral luncheon with a drop of the hard stuff.'

He nods.

'Anne Sofie didn't come,' he says when they've found an empty table. Poul shakes his head.

'Why not?'

'It's all too much for her. Not to mention what isn't being said out loud.'

'What isn't being said out loud?' he asks. 'About her coat? Or about the painting?'

Poul shakes his head again and casts a glance towards Henry.

'We mustn't give her any false hopes.'

'Hopes?' he smiles.

'Yes.'

'What do you mean?'

Poul shakes his head once more. No more is going to be said.

He lasts out until the end of the afternoon in Poul's company, then makes his apologies, saying he must go back to the hotel to pack.

As he's zipping up his jacket, he decides to go over to Anne Sofie's. Tomorrow he needs to speak to the caretaker before he sets off, and he's remembered that they haven't discussed what should be done with all Krille's furniture and clothes. And what about all her photos? They are really her history. Her life. Maybe he should just forget about them. But maybe Anne Sofie would be grateful to him later.

When he goes outside into the cold, the wind has got up. It's blowing a veritable storm, with the snow blowing like dust off the drifts, and the halyard of the flagstaff lashing against the mast. It's as if aunt Krille is having the last word. Just reminding him of the sort of life she lived.

39

Knud Harber glances at his watch. Anne Sofie Strand accepted the dinner invitation. She'll be here in good time. The white wine is chilling and the sole ready to go in the oven.

He's just spent the afternoon on a little lecture, writing a draft and listing the key points. He'll be presenting it to his young Scandinavians tomorrow at Ruth's restaurant. After that, true to character, Željko Popović will provide a stupendous dinner. It will be nicely finished off later in the evening, while the burgundy is still flowing in the bloodstream, with a private view at the museum followed by a light supper; and to add an element of surprise, Fru Groth will sit at the grand piano in the large gallery dressed as Marie Krøyer.

Then off to New York on Monday morning. The forecast promises a change in the weather, with warm air from the west, but the wind's still howling outside and that worries him. If it carries on like this all night the flights from Ålborg will almost certainly be cancelled.

Apart from the storm crashing against the windows, he's content with the way things are. Everything at the gallery is more or less in place. The builders are well into the job, and the architect's directing the project himself. He's going to celebrate the opening with a party, no expense spared; and when all the rumpus has subsided, the money will be pouring in.

Lemon sole in white wine and butter. It'll go in the oven in an hour. He has butterflies in his stomach as he pops a Viagra from its foil and washes it down with a last mouthful of gin and tonic. If there's going to be a party, let it be a party, he mutters to himself.

Otto Bremer has hinted that the young woman has an awkward temperament, which isn't necessarily a bad thing in an artist engaged in the creative process, though perhaps not perfect for tonight's little soirée. But Bremer had only mentioned it in passing, so it's not something he needs to dwell on. She was lovely standing there in the gallery, slim and neat as a ballerina, and he recalls the portraits she made of herself, like a Madonna by Munch under the surface of the water.

Apart from the draft of tomorrow's presentation at Ruth's, his thoughts this afternoon have been occupied by his dinner with this little mimosa. He'd stood at the top of the dunes for an hour in the wind, to get a good blast of oxygen to his brain. Snow fell from a grey-black sky, and the sea was like liquid lead until it broke into waves, smashing against the rim of the ice with a heavy, hollow boom. He'd looked over to the Sunset snack bar. People spend the warm summer evenings there while their children eat ice-creams or skim stones at the water's edge. It struck him how merciless and brutal the sea is when it awakes in winter. He'd turned his back on the heaving predator and trodden carefully across the snow-covered dunes into the warm.

He's prepared like a youth getting ready for his first date. He's going to entertain her. He'll talk of the new trends in American visual art, and about the first events of the summer at his new gallery. When she's settled, and the dessert wine has begun to do its work, he'll let her talk. He'll listen attentively to what she has in mind. He'll discreetly allow her to open up gradually, while the wine takes effect. He'll keep all the options open by praising her concept, whatever the hell it turns out to be. It looks like a pubertal visual protest against a life of affluence.

From what Bremer said, it was a young man she knows who took the pictures. What the guy felt he can only guess, but one thing's for sure. She must have a profound influence on him.

But going one step further and calling it art ... He has a clear idea of when a picture can be considered art. It's his special gift and it's made him rich. If you jump out of a window on the twenty-fifth floor and manage to capture the moment when you hit the asphalt, that isn't necessarily art. She's too sure of her direction, too uncompromising, however absurd that may sound. Her output is like a child's drawing: its spontaneity embraces everything that defines a work of art, but it's never going to be more than a drawing done by a child.

The gallery down by the harbour has a roof-space. He's thought of using it as a store that can be converted in the summer into a sort of incubator studio. Like a little annex. Invite a couple of young artists from the Academy. The youthful hopes for the future. Something along those lines. That was how he was thinking as he laid the sole in the white wine and dressed them with finely-chopped dill. But he doubts that she'll be satisfied with that. She wants her show in the main exhibition space or in the Bredgade gallery in Copenhagen. That's out of the question.

Well, he can always lie. Promise what she wants, and break the promise. Yet one of the rules he's followed throughout his career has been absolutely to keep his word. It's a sensitive profession, and for that very reason one has to be straight as a die.

He pours himself one more gin and tonic. His favourite tipple. Sweet and simple. It's his third, and he has to smile. 'Are you going to drink yourself into it, you old bastard?' he thinks, and then realises that he hasn't got candles on the table, nor any background music. He needs something classical – something quiet and subdued to disguise the pauses and the predator thundering against the dunes.

He's put out some art magazines so that she can look at them while he's laying the table. He won't lay it yet, before she comes, so it'll seem as if he hasn't had time. As if he's had other things to deal with. As if he's almost forgotten that she'll be coming.

40

She's wearing the blue silk dress. With its tight fit, narrow stiff collar and close-fitting waist, it gives her something of the air of a concubine. Mikkel brushes snow from his hair and leans against the doorframe.

'Aren't you off this evening?' she asks.

'I've decided to stay a bit longer. Why didn't you come?'

'There's tea if you like,' she replies, and he wishes he hadn't asked. He takes off his coat and removes his boots, trying to avoid the puddle that's already gathered on the hall floor.

He settles down on the bench as she takes an eyeliner from her make-up bag. She goes out to the kitchen, where a little oval mirror hangs on the wall.

'The undertaker didn't turn up. He was going to take the coffin to the crematorium in Frederikshavn,' he says, looking over to her. 'The grave-digger and sexton went all over the place looking for him. So we left the chapel straight after the service.'

She's concentrating on her face. He considers the element of the absurd in the situation.

'I ordered the cheapest coffin. Because of what you said. Do you know what he called it?'

'No.'

'Bog standard.'

She smiles.

'Do you know him?' he asks.

She holds her breath as she draws a dark line under her left eye. She stands examining the result, and blinks a couple of times.

'Sonny says coffins aren't the only thing he deals in.'

She turns from the mirror and looks over to him. She's put a slight touch of green on her eyelids. She looks like a pretty sixth-former off to a party.

'You seem a bit jittery about this,' he says.

'I am a bit,' she says, disappearing upstairs. He can hear her footsteps overhead. He looks round the room. It's cosy here, and he'd like to relax, but he has a distinctly uneasy feeling. Once more he hears her overhead, and her hurried little steps down the narrow stairs, and then she's back.

'Skagen is what lies between the houses,' he mutters like an amateur philosopher. 'Or what's in the dead window-panes.'

'My father's on his way,' she says, putting her mobile down on the kitchen table.

'Henry?'

She straightens suddenly and looks at him as if he's a complete idiot. 'The Permanent Secretary. He's coming for a meal with Otto Bremer and the director of the museum. He's one of the trustees.'

He nods. Of course her father would be one of the trustees. He imagines the first topic of conversation at the dinner. The disappearance of the totally irreplaceable sketch *Dog with ball*, by P S Krøyer. Just as well Tine took it with her when she crept away down the corridor last night.

'I think he's on fifteen or twenty boards,' she remarks absently, perching on the edge of the bench while she laces her boots. He can feel that she's tense, as if the door into the exam room is about to be opened.

'How are you going to get there?' he asks.

'There's a bus from the station.'

'If they're still running,' he says. 'The weather's getting a bit wild.'

On go her coat and scarf, and her indispensable fur hat, which she insists she took off a Russian sailor who was washed ashore one winter. That's obviously complete baloney. She seizes her black portfolio and waits while he zips up his jacket.

It feels just as bitterly cold as it did the first evening when he stood at the station and gazed about him. The wind's blowing in howling gusts and they're bent double as they walk in silence down the road towards Brøndums Hotel.

He'd like to go in and take a hot bath. Later maybe take a walk round the town. Perhaps Dorte will show up, if she can persuade Henry to look after the twins. Or Tine. He's decided that Dorte can have the piano when she moves into her flat. The caretaker is OK about that.

'Good luck with your meeting,' he says.

'Thanks.'

She goes on past the museum. A little snow-trooper engaged in her own winter warfare. He never mentioned his feelings about her. His musings are interrupted by the thought of Tine and her taste of mint. And Dorte's smile in the chapel: he could make whatever he liked of that. It ought to hurt when people look at the pictures, Anne Sofie had said. Right now it hurts just seeing her getting smaller in the darkness, leaving nothing behind her but her footprints and a brief cloud of snow as she passes through a drift. Well, she'll sell herself as dearly as she can, he's convinced of that. Just before she reaches the high street, a car turns the corner and catches her in its lights.

*

Holger Strand had rung as soon as he was through the Limfjord tunnel. Anne Sofie didn't pick up; but then, she never did. He pulled into a petrol station and sent her a text. I wonder if she ever got the message that I'd be coming this evening, he asks himself, relieved to have got here at last. After he'd passed Frederikshavn the road was so slippery that he'd had to drive at a snail's pace.

He'd had lunch with the board of the Vordrupgård home, and then he'd taken Mads for a long walk in the woods. Mads seemed to enjoy his company. He'd borrowed a pair of binoculars from the home, and Mads was interested in them. And, heaven be praised, a roe-deer appeared at the edge of the trees, and he could show his son how to focus the lenses.

As he turns the car towards the museum he notices a girl walking through the snowstorm. A small figure with green eyes, a fur hat and an angry look on her face. He stops and lowers the window.

'Where can I take you?'

She considers the offer.

'To Old Skagen. I'm going to meet Knud Harber.'

She gets into the back seat as usual and they go past the museum, turn left at Brøndums Hotel and drive up towards the memorial.

'Are you nervous?' he asks. The heavy Mercedes sinks a fraction lower in its suspension as he accelerates noiselessly along Markvej, snowflakes whirling in the beams of the headlights.

'Yes,' she says, rummaging in the side-pocket of her portfolio.

'Did you go to the funeral today?'

'No.'

'Did you have a word with Henry?'

'Early on. He came round this morning. He wanted to know when I was going to meet Knud Harber. I went out with him on the trawler on Thursday, by the way. He threw snowballs at my window at four in the morning. There was no getting out of it.'

He smiles. 'I didn't know he was still fishing.'

'He's a relief skipper. The regular one's in Thailand.'

They drive along the salted roads past forlorn detached houses and on to the main road. He can see her holding tight to her leather portfolio, as if afraid someone might steal her precious photos. He'd bought it for her just after her confirmation, when they were in New York. She'd flirted shamelessly with the Puerto Rican taxi-drivers and the waiters in Greenwich Village, and they sent conspiratorial faxes home to Helene, who hadn't been able to come. It was the summer she most looked and behaved like other teenagers. Then in the autumn her character had changed.

'Goodnight,' she'd said one evening, and they could hear the television on in her bedroom. But she'd gone out, lured by the drifters who hung around the town centre. When she was fourteen she'd been involved in a bag-snatching. They'd had to go and fetch her from Hillerød police station; and the very next week she'd stuck a pair of scissors into her art-teacher's stomach. Helene had wept, and protested. He was head of section then, Helene was a respected architect, and it was obvious that her teachers and social workers were completely bewildered.

'Why did you do it?' her caseworker had asked.

'Because he has no talent.'

That was the most painful part: her insistence on being punished. If she'd simply cried in despair and said that she couldn't remember anything about it, she would have been given treatment and they could have kept her at home. But she didn't want treatment, and she was placed in Søgården.

He takes a look at her in the rear-view mirror. She's sitting concentrating on her meeting, he can see. He slows the car a little and turns out towards Højen.

'I've just been to see Mads. I've been wickedly corrupt and sent the home a bit more grant.'

She simply stares out of the window, but he knows she'll be listening if it's something about Mads.

'Just ring if Bremer turns up and starts putting his arms around Harber,' he jokes. She rolls her eyes, so she must have enjoyed that little joke.

'I shall need a bit of money.' A quietly-spoken comment from the rear seat as they approach Old Skagen. 'For the printers. They want a deposit.'

'I've ordered a credit card for you,' he says casually.

She nods, and in the mirror he can see from her exaggerated observation of the darkness through the window that he's managed to surprise her.

'We must be here', he says, bringing the car to a halt by a little snowed-up lane that winds between low houses clothed in darkness. 'How will you get home?'

'I'll call a cab.'

He waits in the car watching her struggle through the drifts in a cloud of fine snow. Then he drives further on to the roundabout and back towards town. There's a dinner at the Warehouse by the harbour with Bremer and the board of trustees. He's looking forward to a glass of good red wine and a talk with Bremer.

41

'Come on in,' says Knud Harber as the front door is almost blown in by the storm. She has to use all her strength to shut it behind her. He can't help smiling at the small figure standing before him in the hall, covered in snow and with her fur hat pulled down so low that only her eyes are visible. In her arms she holds a black leather portfolio.

She brushes the snow from her coat before taking it off. He gives her a hand, hanging up first her coat, then her fur hat and scarf. She puts the portfolio down on a small chest of drawers and bends almost double to pull her sweater over her head before making a slight adjustment to her dress and running her fingers through her short hair.

'There,' she says, with the suggestion of a nervous smile.

'Incredible weather,' he chuckles as she takes off her boots. 'And you've brought your portfolio.'

'Yes,' she says, showing a slight wariness as she moves into the living-room. 'Yes, I've brought the latest pictures. The ones I mentioned. I'm quite pleased with them.'

'The ones expressing release,' he says, going into the kitchen to turn the oven down. She's arrived precisely on time, and the fish still needs another quarter of an hour. Fifteen minutes for her to get acclimatised.

'Sit yourself down,' he says.

She stands in her fine blue silk dress and looks around. Every chair and lamp is exquisitely designed. A burglar would hardly notice the small pictures hanging above the sofa. Unaware of their value, he'd run off with the art deco lamps and the stereo system.

While Harber is opening the oven to add a little cream to the fish, she leans over the sofa. A sweet little pencil drawing by Max Ernst. Above the French commode, which must itself be worth a fortune, hangs a small portrait by Christian Krohg. A boy. A boy with wild blond hair. Red cheeks and pure blue eyes. A boy with a cold, with a dewdrop hanging from his nose, in the raw weather of March or April. While she's looking at the picture he comes into the room in his apron, sweating slightly from the heat in the low-ceilinged kitchen.

'Ah yes,' he says. 'The Krohg is a recent acquisition. I bought it a couple of weeks ago. A little masterpiece.'

'Aren't you worried about leaving it on display?'

'Of course I am,' he laughs. 'I shall take it home with me.'

She studies the picture carefully.

'It's been well and truly smoked, wherever it was before,' she comments, allowing a finger to slide over the canvas.

'Take it down if you like,' he calls from the kitchen, and she lifts it from its hook and examines it to the sound of ice-cubes clinking into glasses. Harber returns, round and ruddy like a pig before Christmas.

'What do you think of it?' he asks, setting an aperitif before her on the coffee-table.

'I think it's crap,' she says.

Harber goes back into the kitchen. He's actually rather satisfied with her reply. Bremer is mistaken, he decides, both about the value of the picture and in his assessment of her.

'Why is it crap?' he laughs.

'It's been painted with the sort of enthusiasm you'd have if you were painting a fence. It was probably a commission. Someone at a beach party must have wanted his son preserved for posterity. The snot dripping from his nose is Christian Krohg's subtle protest. He hated commissions.'

She puts the picture down on the coffee-table and sits on the sofa with one of the art magazines while Harber busies himself in the kitchen.

He chuckles as he carefully carries the piping-hot dish of sole to the table.

'All the same, it's one of his better pieces in my opinion. They all painted to order. That's how they made their living. I hope you're hungry?'

'I haven't had a hot meal since I got off the train five days ago.'

'*Voilà*,' he says, and they sit down. He takes her plate and serves her.

'How did you get here?' is his first question as they begin to eat.

'I took the bus.'

He admits that it's been fearsomely cold here, and describes his walk over the dunes earlier that afternoon, and the thoughts he'd had about the carefree summer visitors who have no idea of the violence of the sea at this time of year.

'It's greedy, the sea,' he says.

'The locals would say it's generous,' she replies.

'Greedy as well as generous,' he laughs, and tells her about the house and how everything around here was badly dilapidated when he bought it.

She listens as she eats, and he realises that he's doing all the talking. He should have resisted that last gin and tonic.

'Did I tell you we're setting up a little gallery here? I'm thinking of showing a few things by the young people. Kirsten Hjort and Nils Peter from the Academy. Do you know them?'

With nothing more than a slight shake of her head, she concentrates on her sole.

'Downstairs, in the main room, I'm going to open with Sabrine Holm and Tobias Dahlmann and Jannick Søderholm. Later on there'll be Harald Eskelund and August Joensen. Do you know any of them?'

'I've heard a bit about Sabrine Holm. Everyone knows Harald Eskelund of course.'

'All five of them are rocketing up. Young and ambitious. Happy to make the necessary compromises. All artists have to compromise,' he explains. 'You have to crawl before you can walk.'

'You've got a gallery in Bredgade in Copenhagen, too,' she says, discreetly placing a small fishbone at the edge of her plate.

'I'm going to have to abandon Bredgade. I lost a court case about the rent. They're going to turn it into a gym.'

They eat. For a moment neither of them speaks.

'I've produced a catalogue for my Scandinavians. If you'd like to see them, that is, and what's going to be happening next in the art world,' he says to fill the silence.

'I've come to show you my new pictures, not to admire your high-achievers.'

'High-achievers,' he chuckles, considering the expression. Something's going wrong. She's the one who should be talking, he thinks, prolonging his smile.

'If I'm going to make some kind of judgement about your pictures, I need to know who you are. Tell me a bit about yourself,' he says, pouring more wine into her glass.

'You've no doubt spoken to Otto Bremer,' she says, with a smile. It's the first time she's smiled since she took off her coat.

'Maybe Otto's version isn't quite the truth?'

'It's true for Otto, and you can be satisfied with that.'

'I'm interested in knowing what drives you,' he says with a laugh, noticing a little sweat round his neck and feeling the wine flushing his cheeks. She puts down her knife and fork and goes out to the hall to fetch her portfolio.

'The truth,' she says, sitting down in the sofa. 'Well, here is the truth, or a little bit of it.'

She takes out the pictures and lays them carefully on the coffee-table. 'As I said down at the factory, they're going to be printed on tissue-paper, one metre by two.'

Harber is still sitting at his meal. He'd hoped she'd open up a bit after the wine, but she hasn't touched it. Now she's settled on the sofa, defiantly waiting for him to get up and give his opinion.

'One thing at a time, Frøken Strand,' he says, draining his glass. He remains seated for a couple of minutes before getting up and taking the two plates out to the kitchen. When he returns he feels slightly unsteady on his legs. He stops in the middle of the room and scratches his elbow.

'You're most certainly a gifted young woman,' he says.

She watches him from the sofa.

'I think I made myself quite clear down at the gallery.'

'Absolutely,' she says. 'You invited me to dinner and said we'd talk about it. That's why I'm here. Here I am with my latest pictures. The last pictures.'

He doesn't want to look at her pictures. The moment he sits down to look at them the balance of power will be upset. So he remains on his feet. He picks up a picture.

'Do you recognise that little woman?' she asks.

He's confused for a moment. A small woman is sitting reading a magazine.

'Her name's Ellen. Her funeral was this afternoon. Were you there?'

'Should I have been?' he inquires, going over to the French commode, where he takes out a bottle and pours himself a stiff whisky.

This isn't the same girl he met at the factory three days ago. This one is about to go berserk, he decides, regretting the entire arrangement. He was deceived by her delicate appearance. At the moment it feels as if he's got a panther lying there on his sofa. An untamed dark little beast of prey. He half-fills his glass and drinks. It burns his throat, and he returns to the coffee-table and holds up the picture. He puts it down and picks up another. It's the same woman. She's lying with a young girl on a white sheet. They're both naked. He realises that the older woman is dead.

'How the hell did you get these pictures?' he asks, throwing them down on the table. 'They're most unsavoury.'

'I was afraid you'd find it sentimental.'

Harber looks at her.

'I can let you show your pictures upstairs in my gallery in June, while I've got a show by a couple of young people from the Academy, provided that ... you stay here for the night.'

He smiles at this. He's succeeded in saying it, so it's clearly understood.

'As I said, it's a series,' she says. 'They'll be enlarged and printed on tissue paper, and I'll touch them up with oil paint in blue-black and orange.'

He picks one of the pictures up again and looks at it. He gives a laugh.

'Well, well, it's the Parrot.'

'That's my mother,' she says.

For an instant Harber's breath is quite taken away. But he can see the likeness now. It's obvious. It's quite clear once you know. He laughs.

'And now you're sitting here wearing her dress, I see.'

'That's part of the time-series I was talking about. It's about consequences. And pain. And betrayal. I'm the work of art, and you yourself are part of it, if you like.'

That's how it had taken form for her the other day as she stood next to St Laurence's church looking at the bench where her mother had died. That was where she had realised there was a pattern of events, that she herself could control. Her picture had painted itself, so to speak. She would express herself in one way, and others would express themselves differently, and those who did so differently would necessarily be part of the picture. For better or for worse. When she'd moved on through the town, she'd thought it would be Sigvardtsen who'd be painting with her. Later she realised it would be someone else.

Harber watches her as she carefully rearranges her pictures. He's dizzy. Something comes to him. A dinner many years ago, when he'd only just bought the house. She'd been beautiful, the young girl they'd met down at the harbour. They'd wanted to paint her. And, yes, it had become a little violent.

'I think I've made myself clear,' he announces, tipping back his glass again. 'You're aware of the conditions.'

She looks up at him, a little wrinkle between her eyebrows.

'What's missing for you? What more do you want?'

He realises that she's referring to the pictures.

'Look here,' he says. 'This isn't art, just because you cut your own wrist. Nor, for that matter, because you photograph yourself in bed with your dead mother.'

A sudden anger comes over him. It was Bremer, that sentimental fool, who'd introduced her to him. Bremer's got him into this painful situation and now it's too late to get out of it without losing face. What's been said is said, and her very appearance is highly provocative. Both in her portraits and here in real life.

'Art is something you can't put into words,' he says. 'What you've got here is a protest. It needs something else before it can become art. Something you don't expect. Something new. Something that hits you in the face. You can't even tell that she's dead, unless you know already. And now you must go. I need to get something ready for tomorrow.'

'Something like this?' she asks, holding up another picture.

He takes it and is about to throw it back down when his eyes are suddenly wide with amazement.

'How on earth?' he asks, dropping it as if it's hot. All desire has gone from him. He's in shock. She's sitting there like a wildcat, as persistent as a defiant child. Everything's swirling around him. He's angry with himself. Angry that he hasn't managed to control the conversation. He'd prepared himself but he's lost control and everything's taking place on her terms.

'How did you get that picture?' he whispers.

'Is it someone you know, perhaps?'

He stands, unable to move, looking sidelong at the picture on the table. The disturbance in the water, the hands and the eyes, caught during the few seconds of sudden awareness, filled with anguish. Is it a trick photograph? He doesn't dare ask. What you don't know...

'There were four or five of you against my mother,' she says. 'That's why you refuse to look at her. You're afraid.'

That's enough. He brings his glass down hard on the table.

'You're completely sick. You're disturbed. I know nothing about her. Except that she was known as the Parrot.'

'But you all raped her.'

'Is that why you've come here?' he says. 'Is this an infantile attempt to pressurise me? Listen, your mother was so debauched that a whole regiment could have raped her without anyone lifting a finger. And as for this,' he says, seizing the picture from the table between his finger and thumb and waving it around, 'This is sick. Criminal. And now you have to go. Right now. I'm sorry.'

'This is art, if you think it is,' she says. 'If that's your opinion.'

'Oh yes,' he says. 'You're right about that. If I decide this is art, then it's art. But I've decided that it's sick.'

'And I've decided that Christian Krohg is sick too,' she says, grabbing the painting. Before Harber can react, she takes a knife from the dining-table, thrusts it into the picture and makes a long slash across the canvas.

'There,' she says. 'Out with the crap. Out with it all.'

Harber stands, swaying slightly, a little drunk, and feeling as shocked as if she'd stuck the knife in his chest. It's unforgivable. The picture is irreplaceable.

'What the hell are you doing?' he whispers, completely paralysed.

'And this isn't art, either,' she says, tearing his Max Ernst down from the wall and screwing it up.

She doesn't manage to throw it on the floor before he's on her with all his hundred and forty kilos. He hurls her off the sofa with one savage movement.

'Are you out of your mind?' he roars, flinging her across the room. This is it. This had to happen. Now he's incensed. Now there's an account to settle, it's bloody well going to be settled.

'Come here,' he hisses, as she darts like lightning under the dining-table. He gets hold of her ankle, pulls her out, and throws her on the table. He seizes the collar of her dress and pulls it half off her. Three slaps in the face and she goes quiet. He turns her onto her stomach and pulls down her tights. In blind rage his right arm sweeps the sauceboat, and everything else, from the table to the floor.

'You little tart,' he hisses. 'I'm going to bloody teach you what art is.'

She screams when he forces himself into her, and he grabs her by the hair and bangs her head hard against the table. Then she's quiet and the chemistry begins to work. He pushes in dumb anger until he's out of breath, and realises he's not going to come even if he's at it until morning. He pulls himself out and gasps for breath. He gathers his painting up from the floor. A work of art lost to posterity.

She crawls down from the table and over to her pictures. He turns to her bitterly.

'You can just get out, you little devil,' he roars, seizing her arms and pulling her across the room. 'Out with you,' he hisses, flinging open the door and dragging her out into the cold like a bag of rubbish.

She's bleeding from one eyebrow, and she's conscious that she's lost a corner of one of her front teeth. She can't feel her mouth. The leather portfolio flies out and hits her in the face. Then her coat, sweater, fur hat and boots, before he slams the door.

She sits in the middle of the snowstorm, blinded by the blood from her eyebrow, not registering the cold. He didn't come, she thinks in surprise, pulling up her tights. Then she crawls over to the door, gets to her knees and pushes it open.

'Give me my pictures,' she screams.

Knud Harber's reaction is immediate. He snatches up the pictures from the table and stumbles out into the hall.

'Here's all your shit,' he hisses, tearing them in half and throwing them at her head. They flutter away like leaves in the storm as he bangs the door shut again.

She gets to her feet. One side of her dress is torn from top to bottom. She picks up her sweater and pulls it over her head. Her coat and hat lie just outside the doorway, her boots further away in the darkness. She manages to get her clothes on, and embarks mechanically on gathering her half-pictures together. Most of them are caught in the rose-bushes on the edge of the dunes. She scrambles round for a long time trying to find the last one, then gives up and walks off towards the road. Her fingers have no feeling in them and the wind has swept the snow into knee-high drifts. Every step throws up a cloud of blinding flakes.

When she reaches the road she gets out her phone. It's wet. She crouches under a street-lamp and dials his number. She manages to get a connection and hears the ring-tone once before the phone gives out. She puts it back in her pocket and begins to walk towards town. Where the storm has blown the snow off the road, she runs. It's a matter of keeping her pulse-rate as high as possible. No resting. She can't feel her feet. Just run, where she can; otherwise walk and avoid stopping.

Near where the railway track crosses the road she sees a car coming towards her. She recognises it and gives a wave. He stops and she gets in.

'What happened?' he asks, looking at her face, her swollen lips, and the blood frozen in a crust across her cheek.

'Just drive,' she whispers. 'Take me home.'

'Don't you think I should get you to a doctor?'

She shakes her head.

'Just take me home.'

He turns the car and drives back to town. She hasn't got words to describe what's happened. And he doesn't need any. She sits, silent, huddled in her coat as they drive down the high street. The traffic-lights at the cross-roads sway in the storm. Some young people in quilted jackets, hoods awry, are giving themselves a brisk blast of wind as they make their way down to the disco.

She drops her coat and fur hat on the table and gets undressed in the middle of the living-room. Panting slightly, and with shaking hands, she holds her dress up in front of her, wondering in confusion whether it might be possible to sew it together again. She lays it carefully over a chair, goes into the bathroom and turns on the taps. She adjusts the temperature carefully to what she can stand.

She looks in a mirror for the first time. Her face is swollen, and a piece has been chipped from one of her incisors. She begins to cry. She can't remember when she last cried, but it feels good. As she slips into the warm water she hears the front door shut. She closes her eyes.

42

The drive is so snowed up that he has to leave the car and walk down to the house through the drifts. When he gets there, it's a blaze of light, and he stands in the storm considering what to do. At the door a piece of white paper has stuck to the threshold. It's a picture that's been torn in half. He takes a look at it in the light from a window. She's lying on her side, as if asleep. She's naked, and the slim arms of a girl are holding her. He puts it in the inner pocket of his jacket.

He tries the door. It isn't locked, but he doesn't go in. He stands for a moment, recovering himself. He allows his pulse to fall back to normal and briefly surveys the garden. Then he goes down to a fence made of rough grey wood and wrenches off one of the thin round palings. Some nails come with it at one end. He swings this stick a couple of times as if he were getting ready for a game of rounders. Then he walks back to the house. Music comes from the living-room. He opens the door carefully and goes in.

Knud Harber has taken a bath. He's sitting naked as a hippopotamus by the coffee-table, busy cutting his toe-nails.

The first blow smashes into his back, and he has to twist the stick to pull the nails out of his shoulder. Harber gives a roar of pain and topples towards him with all his massive deadweight. He has to take a quick step sideways to avoid being flattened on the table.

Harber corrects the direction of his movement and hurtles out of the door, slips over in the snow, but gets to his feet again. The fear of death has made him unusually swift and he's part-way over the dune before the next blow falls on his back. He's as strong as an ox and doesn't miss a step before the third blow comes down on his neck. He lets out a roar of fear as he reaches the top of the dune and meets the icy wind and the thunder of the sea. Another blow falls hard on his back, and with every blow two small drops of blood ooze from his fat body, but his cries for help are drowned in the hollow rumble of the surf.

A solitary gull drifts sideways inland over the place where, on summer evenings, the people of Skagen give a round of applause as the sun finally sets.

Snow is blowing across the road, and he dips the headlights to see his way more easily. He feels bad. He has a bad stomach, and bad memories of everything they could have done differently. Of everything he could have done differently himself. Instead he'd pretended. Pretended that he didn't understand the detail. From the first white lie to Helene's grotesque confession. That's how he had betrayed not only his daughter, but Helene too. It's too late now. Their love had died among their feelings of guilt about Anne Sofie, the girl they'd chosen, but who hadn't chosen them.

He switches back to full beam, unsure which lets you see further in this weather. His hands shake with anger, and once again he dips the lights. Anger at Bremer, who'd recommended this gallery-owner. She'd come up here full of hope with her photographs.

He can make out flashes of red light further away in the snowstorm. Red reflectors. A car is parked at the top of the drive. He slows down and stops behind it, gets out and tramps determinedly through the drifts. Then he stands in amazement for a moment.

Every light in the house is on and the door's wide open. He looks into the hall, where a small drift has been accumulating inside. Then he goes into the living-room. The coffee-table's overturned, and there's crockery and cutlery all over the floor. He goes through the rooms one by one. There's no one here.

'Harber!' he shouts, going out again into the storm. The only answer is the hollow boom of the sea. He looks round, disorientated. High on the ridge of the dune stands a figure silhouetted against the moon. It's a tall lanky man. Whoever he is, he's looking down at him, and Holger is conscious not only of his own fear, but also that he's just stumbled into something as an intruder. He's suddenly aware of the cold which is stiffening him motionless.

If Harber had been at home, this would have involved nothing more than a textbook package of tearful reproaches and the threat of calling the police. At the moment he's hardly in a fit state to do anyone physical harm. There's no logic to this: in fact the very lack of logic is why he's standing here.

With arms outstretched, the man comes half-sliding down the dune through the snow, keeping nimbly to the narrow pathway between the scrubby rose-bushes. When he gets into the light from the house he recognises him.

'Henry!' he exclaims in astonishment.

Henry regards him with cool contempt. His eyes are black as coal, and he's sweating, so that the snow on his face and in his tousled hair is melting into droplets in his beard. Henry puts his hand in his jacket pocket and fishes out half a photograph.

'You can give her this.'

Holger Strand looks at it.

'Thank you,' he says, confused, and feels a heavy hand on his shoulder.

'Have a safe journey home. Say hello to your wife from me.'

He nods, and makes a muddled attempt to decipher the picture. Then he walks back through the drifts to his car.

43

The wind has backed to the west, and the weather has radically changed with the sudden warmth. A thick mist lies over the town. The houses are dark contours in the whiteness, and bare tree branches seem to be floating over roadways, disconnected from their trunks, like the claws of birds. From every direction comes the sound of flowing water. Drains babble. The yellow lights of a solitary car lie like rods along the road.

Erik had come to collect him yesterday evening. They were having a party, and he was invited. He'd found himself in one of the town's smartest villas, with a view over the heath to the crow-stepped tower of the famous church buried in the sand dunes. He was told that it was here that Soffi came when she felt like company. Most of them were his age. Happy, with loud voices. Tine had stood in the kitchen and smiled as she pushed some wayward hair off her forehead. He'd recognised a couple of musicians from the pub, and Frode and the girls from Linjen.

Dorte had come downstairs in a glittering low-cut dress. From where he stood in the living-room it looked as if it had been made for her. With her blonde wavy hair, and the smile Henry said was the root of every problem, she'd come over to greet him.

'Who's house is this?' he'd asked, deeply impressed.

'My mother's.'

Anne Sofie hadn't come as Erik had promised. He'd been really keen to hear how the meeting with Knud Harber went.

He wriggles half-free of his rucksack, so that it hangs from his right shoulder, opens the gate and goes up to the door. Her father, the Permanent Secretary, must have arrived yesterday evening, so he knocks politely.

In the kitchen is an old man with a rather bent back, whom he doesn't recognise at first. Then his heart gives a jump. It's the gardener. He's standing with a black bag in his hand, in the process of emptying the fridge. The gardener looks at him without surprise.

'Oh, it's you,' he says, carrying on with his task. Mikkel looks round the living-room. Everything has been cleared away. A small sheet of glass and a pot of putty are on the table.

'I came to say goodbye to Anne Sofie.'

'She went back with her father last night.'

Why did they go off last night, he wants to ask – but leaves the question unspoken. The gardener has nothing to do with what he wants to know and what he feels.

'I'll say hello to her from you,' says the gardener crisply from the kitchen.

He makes his way to the dark-room without asking. Everything in here has been tidied away too. On the table is a single black-and-white portrait of a young man. He stands with his arms at his side and his head slightly tilted. Out in the snow, as naked and white as God created him. Mikkel is surprised at the serious expression on his face and the gleam of the moonlight, which makes the snowflakes sticking to his skin shine like diamonds.

On the floor is a black plastic bag. He takes a look inside. It's her pictures. He empties them onto the table. Most of them are damp and every one of them has been torn in half. He gathers them together as best he can. They're lying naked in bed, forehead to forehead, as if asleep. Mother and daughter in the intimacy that had long been denied them.

He hurriedly pieces together the various halves. Tine in the churchyard. The ghost. A close-up of someone's eye, with a drop of water hanging on the temple. This puzzle isn't complicated. He finds one of himself, angry and afraid. And here's one he doesn't recognise. Swirling black water with bright blotches and slush-ice, and hands like the claws of a bird clutching a plastic drum bearing an inscription in Cyrillic letters. That was what she was after. He stares for a long time at the drum and the fingers. Then he stretches over the table for the matching half.

It's a face. Someone who's just got his head out of the ice. Looking up at the camera in bewilderment. What's terrible is the knowledge that she's given herself time to adjust the focus, because technically the picture's perfect.

He gathers the pictures and shoves them with trembling hands back in the bag. He takes the portrait of the young man in the snow and places it carefully in his rucksack where it won't get bent. Then he goes back through the house, out of the door and down the road.

In the mist in front of him he can just see another person. For a moment he's nervous, before he hears a woman's laugh. The outlines of the station loom out of the mist. On the forecourt waits a taxi with its engine idling. He passes it by and goes into the station and on to the platform.

When the twins woke him this morning, there'd been a text from his parents. 'Remember to water the plants as soon as you get back. And don't forget to set the alarm when you leave.'

The train arrives almost soundlessly out of the mist. First two yellow eyes: then it fully materialises and slowly comes to a halt. A little further along the platform he can see Zeppo waiting with two small boys. Some people in high spirits are getting off the train with their suitcases. For a brief moment, they can be heard speaking Norwegian and Swedish. Then silence falls again.

Mikkel stands for a time fingering the ticket in his pocket. A few beings board the train without a word like grey shadows. Then the doors close, and the sound of the engine seems to emphasise the surrounding silence as the train slides along the platform and disappears into the mist.

He picks up his rucksack and sets off on the little path along the railway track, towards the part of town where the tourists never go.

He hadn't managed to say goodbye to Anne Sofie, and there had been a question he'd wanted to ask her. But now there's no need.

She got her picture.

Author's note

This book is a work of fiction, and any resemblance on the part of its characters to individuals in real life is coincidental and unintentional. On the other hand the setting, Skagen (where I was brought up), is described with near accuracy: I have sparingly exercised a writer's privilege in making some adjustments, for example to the opening times of the museum.

I record my thanks to my son Andreas for his help with Mikkel's project, and to my youngest daughter, who readily agreed to allow her name to be given to Anne Sofie.

Eddie Thomas Petersen